# CHEAP THRILLS

# CHEAP THRILLS

*A Novel*

David Kloepfer

$\lfloor N_1 \lfloor O_2 \lfloor N_1$

**CANADA**

**Library and Archives Canada Cataloguing in Publication**

Title: Cheap thrills : a novel / David Kloepfer.

Names: Kloepfer, David, 1979– author.

Identifiers: Canadiana 20190154764 | ISBN 9781988098869 (softcover)

Classification: LCC PS8621.L64 C54 2019 | DDC C813/.6—dc23

Printed and bound in Canada on 100% recycled paper.

**Now Or Never Publishing**
901, 163 Street
Surrey, British Columbia
Canada V4A 9T8

**nonpublishing.com**
*Fighting Words.*

We gratefully acknowledge the support of the Canada Council for the Arts
and the British Columbia Arts Council for our publishing program.

*For Erin*

# I

Strands of telephone and electrical wire crossed overhead like sutures through an open wound of the city. Underfoot, deep puddles pockmarked the asphalt. Beside a rusted shopping cart lean-to stood a heap of wet cardboard boxes crammed full of old magazines and damp paperbacks. He paused and peered into the top box of a knee-high pile at the edge of the heap.

The musty smell of old paper filled his nose. Ethan Blaise pulled a book from the box. The hand-painted cover depicted a woman lying fetal in the light of a street lamp. In the shadows, a figure in a trench coat and fedora stood over her. *Cheap Thrills*, it was called. He flipped through the pages. They were damp but still legible. He tucked the paperback into his coat pocket, took a quick look in each direction, shielded himself between a dented green dumpster and the shopping cart, and unzipped.

As he pissed, something sticking out from another of the boxes caught his eye. A glossy magazine, pebbled with rain. The cover was a photograph of a woman squeezing her breasts together and smiling. Ethan smiled back.

Such magazines were nothing new to Ethan and he'd seen this particular issue before.

When Ethan was a boy, before his parents had divorced, this same magazine had been delivered to his home. On its cover was the model and actress Marley Malone.

He'd been at home reading comic books that day, having skipped school while his parents were at work, when he heard the mailman slide something through the slot in the front door. Ethan took the magazine back to his room and ripped open the package. The centerfold featured Malone, lying naked on her belly on a blue-tiled floor, arcing her back and holding a barely perceptible smile.

In the alley, a drop of rain fell from a fire escape and struck him on the shoulder. He finished, picked up the magazine, and leafed through to the photos of Malone. There she was, just as he remembered her. He recalled the Coke ads with Marley Malone from the early '90s: Malone at a gas station on a lonely stretch of highway, in frayed jean shorts, tossing her hair to the camera, teasing the boys sitting by the pumps, teasing all the boys watching at home.

Sparse drops fell from the sky, a few straggling remains of an earlier heavy rain. Ethan flipped the magazine closed and tucked it under his arm. As he backed away from the pile, his heal caught on something firm and low to the ground. He tripped and fell to the asphalt.

He sat himself up, wiped his hands across his jeans, and looked over to see what had brought him down. A single leg, clad in blue jeans and a white sneaker, stuck out from beneath a mound of garbage bags. Ethan clambered to his feet and kicked away a few wet bags and sodden boxes, to reveal a blank, grey, and wide-mouthed corpse.

## 2

At the mouth of the alley, Phillip Wilford, having just finished a slice of cheese pizza, stood smoking a cigarette in the thin bleak rain. It was the last smoke of his pack.

Blonde haired and blue eyed and built like a farmhand, he grimaced as traffic crawled by in the street. His day was starting poorly: Simon, his dealer, wasn't answering his phone.

Usually Simon could be found walking the street, drinking a coffee from one of the many cafes along Commercial Drive or hanging out in the pizza shop around the corner. He'd been less reliable lately, even for a street dealer.

Phil took the final drag of his cigarette and threw the butt into a puddle at the curb. A rainbow rippled the grease on the surface.

Behind him, his roommate came out of the alley, magazine in hand.

"What's that?" Phil asked.

"It's the Marley Malone *Good Sir* from when I was—"

"Have you heard of the internet? It's got everything. For free."

"Yeah, the—"

"Or you could try getting laid occasionally."

"Okay, Phil. Sim—"

"Simon hasn't showed up," Phil said.

"That's because he's back there," Ethan said.

"What's he doing back there?"

"He's dead."

"What do you mean he's dead?"

"I mean he's dead."

"Are you sure?" Phil said.

Ethan gave Phil a long, blank stare. "There's a hole in his face. Two holes," Ethan said.

Phil turned and entered the mouth of the alley.

"What're you doing?" Ethan said.

"I'm going to look at him."

Phil bent over the corpse. It was Simon without question and without question he was dead. One arm was pinned beneath him, the other stretched out under a pile of black garbage bags. His jeans and hooded black sweatshirt were soaked from last night's rain. His mouth, agape in final sorrow, revealed stained and crooked teeth. Two blank green eyes stared to the heavens. There was a dime-sized hole below his left eye and another above his right. A piece of scalp flapped out onto the asphalt behind his head. The rain had washed away most of the mess.

"We should call the cops," Ethan said.

"We're not calling the cops," Phil said.

"Why not?"

"I don't like cops."

"Neither do I," Ethan said. "Nobody does. Not really the point at the moment."

"I'm not helping the cops with anything."

"You don't have to. I—"

"Let them figure it out for themselves. What're we supposed to tell them? Here's our dealer. He's dead. By the way, got any bud?"

"You make a decent point."

"Just relax," Phil said, shooting Ethan a tenth of a smile. "We still don't have any weed. We'll go to Sam's and get nice and high and somebody else can deal with Simon. All right?"

Ethan shook his head.

## 3

Ethan had never been to Sam's. When Ethan and Phil ran out of weed and couldn't get hold of Simon, it was Phil who made the trip.

Ethan sat quietly in the passenger seat of Phil's rusted Pontiac, trying to convince himself that abandoning the body had been a wise thing to do. His panic had begun to peek through the fog that had settled about his mind after the morning's first joint. Before leaving their apartment in search of Simon, Ethan and Phil had rolled whatever detritus they had left—repurposed roaches, a fine dust of grindings, and a miniscule bit of actual bud—and smoked it.

From the car's cheap stock speakers came the tinny wail of some thrash-metal song. Ethan could make out the occasional curse word, but the rest was a blur of amphetamine-fuelled guitar and relentless industrial drums. The frantic screaming of the presumably big, bald, and bearded lead singer did little to calm Ethan's nerves.

It wasn't long before Phil brought the car to a stop in front of a two-storey apartment building, the middle in a row of similarly depressed complexes just west of a public park. The two men left the car on the street and went inside.

In the building's vestibule a dishevelled man in a dirty bathrobe sat hunched in a white plastic lawn chair. A mostly ashen cigarette hung from his lips. He paid the newcomers no heed as they examined the intercom system to his right.

Half the buttons on the buzzer panel were missing, including the one for Sam's place. Phil jammed his car key into the hole beside number 1708. A moment later a female voice came through the intercom.

"Who is it?" the voice asked.

"It's Phil. I've got somebody with me."

The shouting of a different voice, a male one, the words indiscernible, came from deep inside the apartment.

"Is he cool?" the girl said.

"Of course he's cool," Phil said. "He's with me."

The door buzzed and the two men entered the lobby.

Beneath the mailboxes sat a two-toned shaggy mutt, years past its last bath, sans collar. No owner was in sight. Ethan made to pet the thing, but Phil held him back. The mongrel eyed them warily as they summoned the elevator.

A dull ding signalled arrival at the fourth floor. Stale smoke, frying oil, and body odour loitered in the hall. The two men approached apartment 404, but before Phil could knock, the door swung open and revealed a young woman, slim, dark haired and golden skinned, standing at the threshold. She wore blue sweatpants and a T-shirt, both bearing the crest of the local university. A happy smirk owned her face and the corners of her eyes. She greeted Phil by name, introduced herself to Ethan as Sam, and invited both men into the kitchen.

Dank yellowed wallpaper lined the walls. Faded wood cabinetry held burnt-orange appliances, decades old. A forgotten meal was reincarnating in a pot on the stove. The living room roared with the rattle of gunfire.

Phil helped himself to a seat at the kitchen table and Ethan followed suit. Strewn across the surface was a slew of marijuana-related accoutrements: pipes, papers, lighters, vaporizer, bong, and an ashtray. Sam opened a kitchen drawer by the sink and pulled out two pillowy bags of weed. She held one up in each hand.

"This one is the usual stuff," Sam said, flopping the bag in her right hand down on the table. It was about three-quarters full of intact buds; the rest was stems and leaves.

"This," she said, shaking the slightly darker, brownish-green bag in her left hand, "is better. It's a little more than usual."

"How much?" Phil asked.

"It's seventy a quarter—"

"Seventy-five," a voice said from the next room, over the clamour.

"Better be good for seventy-five," Phil said.

Another disembodied bleat from the living room: "It's the good shit."

The screaming and gunfire went silent. A moment later, a shirtless, slouched, hairy-chested young man slumped his way into the kitchen. He pulled a chair out from the table and settled his scrawny frame into the seat. Crumbs of nachos or chips or some other packaged salty snack were nestled in his chest hair. With arms too long, eyes too far apart, and a bearded, squashed face, he resembled a tree sloth, Ethan thought.

The sloth took the bag of dope from Sam, opened it and pulled out a nugget of weed. He picked up a pair of scissors lying on the table, quickly cut up the bud, and stuffed the choppings into a glass pipe. He held a lighter to the bowl and took a pull for himself before passing the pipe and lighter to Phil.

Phil took a long drag and held the smoke. As he passed the pipe to Ethan, Phil exhaled and nodded approvingly.

Ethan looked at the pipe in his hands. It was shaped like a naked woman lying on her back, her arms stiff at her side, legs together, feet touching to form the mouthpiece. Where her head should have been was the bowl. She had ludicrously large and full round breasts with absurdly pointed nipples.

"It changes colour," the sloth said.

"What?" said Ethan.

"The pipe," the sloth said.

"How?" Ethan asked.

"I don't know. Whatever the fuck kind of glass it is, I guess. The heat does it or something. After awhile you'll be able to see her bush."

Ethan looked at the pipe-woman's bush. It was dark black, as was the rest of her, from her belly button to her toes. The bowl and shoulder area had turned a cloudy purple. How her bush was supposed to get hot enough to change colour, Ethan didn't know. If it could, he didn't want to be holding the pipe when it happened.

"What do you think?" the sloth asked.

"I think somebody sold you some serious bullshit about this pipe," Ethan said.

"No," the sloth said. "About the weed."

Ethan lit the bowl and inhaled. He blew a long plume of smoke from his nose. In his brain, things went funny.

"It's all right, I guess," Ethan said. "Phil?"

"Nothing special," he said, glassy eyed.

"That's the best shit I've had in months," the sloth expounded, nearly rising from his chair. "That's a special strain, man. Limited."

"What's it called?" Phil said.

"Socialized Medicine. You might not see that shit again."

"Maybe not," Phil said, waving the pipe back his way for another hit. "But I'm not sure if it's worth an extra fifteen bucks. Ethan?"

Ethan didn't answer. A cartoon was playing inside his head. It began with a bird's-eye shot of the alley from earlier that day. From above, Ethan could see the mountain of garbage bags and sodden cardboard boxes. As the camera panned slowly into the alley, the top of the mountain drooled a lava of glossy porno mags. They cascaded down the slopes and over Simon's corpse in a rainbow of flesh tones.

As the conversation continued around him at the kitchen table, Ethan watched his own personal horror film. The lava flow stopped, revealing Simon's ghastly form. The open holes in his face were filled with dark blood. Skin and flesh poured off his skull. When Simon was only bones, the process reversed: organs, flesh, and skin crawled back onto the skeleton.

As Simon's carcass oscillated between forms, the fully live and naked Marley Malone climbed from the trash and began to slink across the corpse. Simon took the nude model's head into his hands and pushed it down, tissue and skin peeling from his bones as Malone—

"Ethan," Phil shouted, snapping Ethan from his waking dream.

"Yeah?" Ethan said, blinking hard.

"I say I'll do it for sixty-five. For you guys, you know," the sloth said. "Good customer discount."

The sloth leaned into Ethan, trying to get his attention. The sloth's lined and leathery face—no older than twenty-five, Ethan figured—had the wrinkles and crow's feet of a hard-living forty-year-old.

"Oh," said Ethan. "Sure."

"And you know," the sloth continued, "you always get a free joint when you bring in a new customer."

"Great," said Ethan.

"But clear it with me. Don't just be showing up with people I don't know," the sloth said as he stood up and patted a canister in a small holster on his belt.

"Is that dog spray?" Ethan asked.

"Bear."

"You carry bear spray?"

"Got to."

"Jesus."

"So you'll take the new stuff?" the sloth asked.

"Sure," said Phil. "Yeah. What's it called again?"

"Uh . . . American Dream. It's the best around right now, by far."

"Good," Sam said, concluding the proceedings. She was leaning back in her chair, her hands behind her head, a slight smile signalling her amusement at the negotiations, or more simply her satisfaction with the weed. "Now that that's settled, let's spin one up."

Phil began to chop up weed for another joint. As Sam watched Phil work, Ethan watched Sam.

Ethan had always assumed the Sam that Phil talked about was male. Ethan had never met a female weed dealer, if that's what she was—the arrangement between her and the jungle creature was unclear. To Ethan, Sam was too clean, fresh, and joyful to be associated with the sloth, who for his part seemed genetically languorous, constitutionally dirty.

Phil pulled a rolling paper from the pack lying on the table and cradled it in the fingers of his left hand. His right spread the fine, green choppings evenly from end to end. With his thumbs and middle fingers holding the paper in place, he used his index fingers to compress and level the filling. He licked the glue and twisted it all together. The finished product looked machine made.

Phil lit the finished joint, took a healthy drag, and passed it around. Sam took it first, and Ethan watched her lips as she drew in.

She passed it to the sloth, who leaned forward, puckered, and squinted his eyes into slits. He took a long haul. Ash fell into his chest hair. The end of the joint glowed bright-hot orange. He blew out a cloud, got up, and walked back into the living room.

Soon, the heavy siege of gunfire resumed.

Ethan shouted over the assault.

"What're you playing?" he said.

"What?"

"What're you playing?"

A temporary ceasefire.

"What?"

Ethan got up and walked into the living room.

"What're you playing?"

The sloth was sitting on a taupe sofa. The matching loveseat was occupied by a shirtless young man, asleep, his beer gut dangling over the side. Ethan wondered why everybody was shirtless: it was April, twelve degrees, and raining.

"*Scarface*, dude," the sloth said, then unmuted the TV.

On the flat screen, an expertly rendered Al Pacino sat in the booth of a lounge, enjoying a beverage, bullet shells hailing down around him. Other Cubans fired submachine guns recklessly about the club.

"You seen the movie before?" Ethan asked.

"Yeah, man," the sloth replied, pausing the game. Ethan took a seat on the couch beside him. He ran his hand over what felt like a very new and expensive sofa.

"Is this microfibre?" Ethan asked.

The sloth puffed the joint, nodded.

"I love this movie," he said. "And the game. Tony Montana is the man. True gangster, man. That's how to live."

"Like *Scarface*?"

"Yeah, man."

"Have you seen the end?"

Sam entered the room with Phil following her. She woke the man on the loveseat, swatting him on his beer gut.

The young man, barely more than a teen, awoke looking as if he'd teleported in from another world. He swung his feet from the loveseat, rubbed his eyes, stood and walked out of the room. A moment later the apartment door slammed shut behind him.

Sam took the now empty space on the loveseat. She pulled a book out of a backpack on the ground, then curled up into the cushions and began to leaf through the pages.

Phil sat next to the sloth and picked up a video game controller from the coffee table.

"You down for some *Danger Close*?" Phil asked.

"I'm always down for some *Danger Close*."

There was a brief ceasefire as the sloth changed the game, but soon automatic gunfire resumed from the speakers.

Phil and the sloth chased each other around the big screen with MiGs, hand grenades, rocket launchers. The shudder of ordinance shook the room.

Each gunshot flashed Simon's mangled face across the screen of Ethan's mind. After only a few minutes of the siege, a thin sheen of sweat had formed on his skin.

"I'm outta here, Phil," Ethan said, getting up.

"Just hang on, give me a half and I'll drive back."

"I gotta go," Ethan said.

"It'll take you three times that long on the bus. Sit tight. Smoke a joint or something."

"I'm too stoned."

"Smoke through it."

Gunfire clapped like heavy applause and Ethan suffered another flashback of the alley. Ethan, Simon's corpse, and Malone all stuffed in a long box lined with porno and pulp novels.

"I'm hungry," Ethan said, breaking the spell.

Sam looked up from her book. On the cover was a frog or a toad with a ridge on its head, giving it the appearance of a dragon.

Ethan had licked a frog once. Someone told him it would get him high. It had only tasted bittersweet and made his tongue swell.

"Me too," she said. "Let's go get something."

"Where can I get a something to eat around here?" Ethan asked.

"The gas station," the sloth said. His eyes narrowed, nearly closing, focussing on the happenings on the big screen.

A camo-clad soldier, conducted by the sloth, shot Phil's digital embodiment in the face. His avatar crumpled to the ground, his arm pinwheeling oddly before the whole corpse vanished into the void. Phil blipped back into existence, then took a seven-inch survival knife in the back.

"Fuck," he said.

"The gas station?" Ethan asked. "The Esso or Marly's?"

"Marly's?" the sloth scoffed. "Nobody goes to Marly's. The Esso, man. Get the egg salad."

"The egg salad from the Esso."

"Yeah, man," said the sloth. "The egg salad. Or the Italian hoagie."

"The egg salad or the Italian hoagie," Ethan repeated.

"You going?" Phil asked.

"Yeah."

"Get me something?"

"Sure. Egg salad or Italian hoagie?"

"Hoagie," Phil said.

"Egg salad," the sloth said. "And an orange juice."

"Okay." Ethan mentally discarded both orders. "Sam?"

"I'll come too."

"Yeah?"

"Yup, I'm hungry." She closed her book and slid it into her backpack. "I want a burger."

"The Esso's got good burgers," the sloth said. "But the microwave's broken, so you have to bring it back here."

"Microwave the burger," Ethan said.

"Are you all right, man?" the sloth asked angrily, his black little eyes half closed.

"Sure," Ethan said. "Good. All right." He turned to Sam. "Ready to go?"

Sam nodded. She grabbed her jacket from a rack by the door, and they left.

## 4

On the street, the morning rain lingered. The Esso and Marly's stood guard kitty-corner over the intersection. Two crashed cars formed a crumpled $T$ of steel and plastic, halting traffic in all directions.

Ethan and Sam crossed the street toward the Esso but continued past it. Sam had a better idea: the FreshBurger a few blocks down. Ethan had never heard of it, but he wasn't hungry anyway. Nor was he particularly inclined to ingest a mayonnaise-based sandwich from a gas station. He had just needed to get out of the confines of the apartment and give his worry- and weed-congested brain some breathing room. Even the short walk and somewhat-fresh air had done wonders for his psyche; the horror show had ended, and he was fairly certain he was no longer going to die.

FreshBurger was set in the middle of a small string of stores, sandwiched between a pharmacy and a coffee shop. The giant red-and-white sign, nearly as wide as the storefront, glowed above two glass doors. The red-and-white theme continued into the dining area: red tables and white chairs, a long, red ordering counter and a glowing white menu above it, items and combos all in red lettering.

A bleary-eyed cashier in a white apron and red paper hat stood behind the till.

"There's no beef," Ethan said, reading the menu.

"No," the cashier said.

"Not even chicken."

"No," Sam said.

"What am I supposed to eat?"

"I'm getting the quinoa burger," Sam said.

Ethan surveyed the vegetarian options, perplexed. He had no qualm with mushrooms, he admitted.

"I'll get the mushroom, I guess."

The two took a seat at a molded Formica table, the FreshBurger logo painted on top. They sat quietly, Ethan trying not to linger on Sam's eyes, but failing.

Sam looked up.

"You have eyes like a cat," Ethan said.

"Is that good?"

"I think so."

"Yours are all right, I guess. Brown. Kind of like dirt."

Ethan nodded. "Shit brown, yes. Or like whatever the hell that is." Ethan pointed at a neighbouring diner's plate of ReFried BeanGasm. "Is this place better than the Esso? Because what's his name gave a pretty positive review of the Esso."

"Well, I'm vegetarian, so gas station cheeseburgers aren't really part of my diet," Sam said.

Soon the food arrived, brought out and set between them silently by the wastoid cashier.

Ethan unwrapped his burger and prodded the bun. It was dense as wood. Underneath was a garden of fresh vegetables and sprouts, topped with a dollop of guacamole. The patty was beefish, yes, but Ethan wasn't fooled. He took a bite, chewed, and swallowed.

"How is it?" Sam asked.

"It's okay, I guess," he lied, thinking he'd have been better off with the microwaveable cheeseburger. The patty had the texture of sodden, flaking driftwood.

"Don't you eat vegetables?"

"Yeah, I eat vegetables," Ethan said. "I like vegetables. I don't get this kind of food though."

"You don't get vegetarian?"

"I just don't understand why the food needs to be shaped like meat. It's like you really want to be eating meat, but you need to be righteous, so you can't? Like some sort of repressed desire."

"I've never eaten meat," Sam said. "Or at least not on purpose. So I doubt I have any repressed desire for it."

"How have you never eaten meat?"

"I was raised vegetarian. My sisters too. My parents have been vegetarian since before we were born."

Ethan took another bite of his 'Shroomburger. It tasted suspiciously like refried bean.

"It's not bad, actually," he said.

"Are you a convert?"

"Nope," Ethan said. "Raised vegetarian? You and the sloth sure make an odd couple."

"Sloth?"

"What's his nuts, your dude. The skinny, tree-dwelling furball you live with."

"Hugo? I don't live there. He's not *my dude*. Exclusively or anything."

"Do you get paid or something?"

"What?"

"No, not like a prostitute. I mean, the—"

"Jesus," Sam said. "Smooth."

"No, I mean, you do all the work, seems like. You know? The selling."

She shrugged. "It's no big deal. I'm usually just the first one off the couch."

"And you don't pay for weed?"

"Well, no. I like Hugo. And it keeps me out of my parents' place. He's not what you think he is."

Ethan figured Hugo was pretty much exactly what he thought he was, but decided to keep his opinion to himself.

"Don't get along with the parents?" he asked instead.

"I've got three little sisters. They're my stepsisters. Busy house. I get more studying done at Hugo's, surprisingly."

"I'll say. Even with all the warfare?"

"Even so," Sam said. "Mostly because I hide out in the other room."

Ethan sipped his beverage. It tasted, he thought, like the smell released from his vegetable crisper the last time he remembered he had one.

He looked at the cup. It said "The Rolling Stone Gathers No Mossaccino." Above the caption a wagging tongue hung through a set of big red lips and licked at a mossy stone. Ethan figured it was a trademark infringement suit waiting to happen. But then again, who cared about FreshBurger.

"You know, Hugo's not even a dealer."

"Had me fooled."

"No, I mean, he's like an employee."

"You mean he's not the brains of the operation? I thought the shirtlessness and low rent were just a cover."

"I mean he doesn't make much. He lives there for free, makes a little cash. Smokes on the cheap."

"Not free? Or just the stuff he pinches from our bags? What's the markup on this stuff, anyway?"

"No, the—What are you, a cop?"

"Just interested."

"Anyway, he doesn't tell me about the business. He's paranoid."

"I think that's a qualification for the job."

"Yeah, but things have gotten worse lately. His boss comes around more. Hugo thinks there's something going on and he's worried about it."

"Like what?"

"Like, ah . . ." Sam paused, trying to remember what Hugo had said. "'Jockeying for position,' I think Hugo called it. He's worried."

"Is that what the bear spray's for?"

"He had that already. But I guess, yeah."

"Who the hell bear sprays somebody?"

"Hugo."

"Really?"

"Yeah."

"Who does he bear spray?"

She paused.

"He thought some guy was trying to rip him off the other week," she said.

"And he bear-sprayed him?"

"Yeah." Sam shrugged. "I wasn't there." She paused again. "Some people have gotten killed—"

"That rodent *kills* people?" Ethan said loudly, attracting the attention of a pair of diners to his left. Ethan thought of Simon, lying in the alley. "I'm not buying from this nutbag anymore. Only reason we're over here is because, ah, Simon, this other—"

"Yeah, Simon," Sam said.

"You know him?"

"Yeah, he works for the same guy Hugo does. He was supposed to come by today but he never showed up. Hey, look—I didn't mean Hugo, okay?"

"Didn't mean Hugo what?"

"Would kill anybody. I mean, Hugo hasn't killed anybody. He's in over his head. He's worried. I've been hanging out less. I was thinking of stopping altogether."

"That's good," Ethan said. "You can hang out at our place, if you're looking for somewhere to go."

"Maybe," she said. "Sometime."

"Where are you going now?" Ethan asked.

"Back to Hugo's. I've got more studying to do."

"What're you studying?"

"I'm in biology."

"You want to study animals or something? Keep hanging out with Hugo. He'd make a good lab specimen."

Sam ignored the jab. "I'm going to be a vet," she said.

They finished their meals in near silence, Ethan enjoying the meatless burger a little more with every bite.

When they left, police cars, fire trucks, and ambulances were circling the collision in the intersection. A wide streak of blood smeared an open car door. Ethan rubbernecked as he crossed the street.

## 5

Back at Phil and Ethan's apartment, the first order of business was to get deliriously high. Further orders of business were struck from the agenda.

The two men had settled into a room-sized smoky cloud that complemented the apartment's general colour scheme, an enthusiastic ovation to grey: two charcoal couches, formerly black, inherited from the previous tenant; walls painted a blotchy taupe; a slate-grey and slightly warped coffee table; sporadically stained Gainsborough carpeting; a silver flat screen; the sunless, ashen skin of Ethan and Phil, nicely baked and drooping contentedly into the sofa.

Phil watched TV while Ethan read from the copy of *Cheap Thrills* he'd found in the alley alongside Simon, whose festering corpse continued to occupy more mental real estate than Ethan cared for.

Questions rattled his brain: Was the body still there? Had anybody seen them standing over it? Should the cops have been called? Ethan had again broached the subject of the police with Phil on the way home from Sam's, but it was a nonstarter.

He knew Phil had run ins with the law at least a few times in his life—something to do with an incident on a hockey rink, some DUIs, more than a few fist fights and public intoxications. Phil's size was something the comparatively minor Ethan had no desire to argue with. But if anyone had seen them in that alley . . .

Something had to be done, Ethan figured, but the newly purchased bag of weed on the coffee table had other ideas.

Business carried on into the evening, until Ethan thought it best to venture back out into the world for sustenance, for cigarettes, for something to take his mind off the day's events.

After great deliberation over whether waiting three hours after meeting a girl was long enough to ask her out, and deciding it was, he called Sam, inviting her to a movie. She declined. She had to study for an exam in the morning, remember, idiot?

Instead, Ethan took the SkyTrain to the nearest theatre and sat alone in the back row, half watching another lifeless

Hollywood thriller full of gunfire and false suspense, half replaying the scene in the alley and the lunch with Sam.

After the movie he returned to an apartment empty of Phil, and slept.

# 6

The Portly Jester, just three blocks down the road from his apartment, had become Phil's watering hole for its proximity and reasonably priced drink specials. Populated by pull-tab vending machines and family-less men, The Jester was a place for drinking heavily, watching sports on big screen televisions, and contemplating life as little as possible. This last task Phil was currently struggling with.

Phil occupied a stool at bar's end and was ruminating on the day's occurrences. The big screen replayed sports highlights.

Leaving Simon in the alley wasn't what was bothering Phil. Simon was garbage and had ended up where garbage does: rotting in a back alley where no one, save its collectors, had to see or think about it.

Dealing weed wasn't what made Simon garbage, and Phil suspected that he must have been moving something else now, too, to end up dead in an alley. Simon was of the streets. He occupied the sidewalks, solicited passersby, sold there, had probably lived there, or certainly looked the part, at least until very recently. New baggy jeans and white sneakers, an oversized down-filled black jacket, more frequent shaves. Regardless of his appearance, that Simon did his business in public put him on par with the homeless and addicted beggars of the Downtown Eastside, whose lives, in Phil's mind, were quite obviously worth less than everyone else's.

What was worrying Phil was also why he'd prevented Ethan from doing anything about the body: Phil had no desire to deal with the police again.

Phil's troubles began after being chosen by the Atlanta Thrashers in a late round of the NHL Entry Draft. The summer before what was to be his first professional season, during a game of pickup with high school friends in Belleville, a local goon looking to prove himself and knowing Phil had been drafted as an enforcer, spent the majority of the meaningless game trying to goad Phil into a fight.

Even at twenty, Phil had encountered many men who saw him not as a person but as a challenge. Phil was not one to back down from challenges, but a string of coaches had reminded him there were times more appropriate than others to accept them. It was only when the buzzing gnat that had hacked and speared him for the majority of the game turned its attention to a smaller, nonviolent teammate that he decided that the time was now appropriate.

Gloves were dropped and helmets were removed but Phil had the opportunity to throw only one punch: the gnat fell backward and hit his head on the edge of the boards.

A thirty year old man named Gerry Reinholt was removed from the ice in an ambulance; Reinholt's girlfriend, in the stands, called the police, and Phil Wilford was removed in handcuffs. A few hours later, Reinholt died. Phil was charged, and his hockey career—though no certain thing to begin with—became the second casualty. After serving his sentence he devoted more time to alcohol and driving under its influence. He became increasingly less reluctant to take on new challengers.

Phil drank his beer and watched the big screen above the bar. Two boxers swung at each other in the corner of a ring, the crowd cheering them on.

He replayed the scene on the rink in Belleville for the millionth time, blaming his life on Gerry Reinholt, or at least his life from the point when Reinholt's head had struck the boards until now, sitting on a bar stool hoping the police would not again come calling.

He ordered another beer with a shot of whiskey to accompany it.

# 7

Ethan rose early the next afternoon and joined his returned roommate on the couch. An early-season baseball game was playing on the TV. More joints were rolled, more salty snacks consumed. Ethan brushed Cheeto crumbs from his belly. He noticed another burn hole in his favourite T-shirt. That made four burn holes. It was probably time to retire it anyway: he'd found it in a thrift shop for ninety-nine cents.

On the TV, the pitcher gave up a three-run shot. Phil and Ethan swore in unison, watching the ball sail toward orbit. The season had barely started and it was already apparent the team wouldn't make the playoffs. The rest of the year would play out like a trashy pulp paperback—a predictable plot hopefully made interesting by the details. Same went for life, Ethan thought.

He had more important things to worry about than baseball anyway: Simon's festering corpse continued to strobe Ethan's mind.

Simon was joined in the spotlight by the recently admired Samantha Holley. Ethan hadn't had a girlfriend in three years. He wondered what it would take to get her away from that tree animal Hugo.

Ethan recalled the can of bear spray Hugo had hanging from his hip. A paranoid sloth, Ethan thought. Weird. Although a little paranoia was probably an evolutionary success strategy in that line of work.

Ethan's wobbling train of thought was derailed by a knock at the door.

He swept the paraphernalia on the coffee table into an empty shoebox saved for this purpose. Phil sat silently, hoping whoever it was would go away. Last time there had been an unexpected knock, it had been a homeless woman selling loose cigarettes door to door.

Both men listened as a key turned in the lock. The door swung open.

In walked a young blonde, Phil's ex, Emma. She still had a key to the place and dropped by from time to time to smoke whatever was lying around, drink a few beers, then pocket some weed and leave.

Ethan didn't understand what Phil was thinking. Well, to be fair, Ethan understood perfectly what Phil was thinking. Secondary sex characteristics whittled by natural selection into stupefying utility. Youth is fleeting, Ethan reminded himself.

Emma swung the door shut behind her, turned and started at the two men's presence. She greeted them as casually as an uninvited guest with a key could, then headed to the refrigerator. Ethan's eyes followed her to the kitchen, her white dress shirt only barely buttoned up, her bobbing school kilt threatening to reveal all that evolution gave her. She pulled three beers from the fridge then made her way to the couch and reposed herself between the two stoned roommates.

"Who's winning?" Emma said, popping open a beer.

"The other guys," Phil said.

"What's the score?"

"Seven to three."

"Awesome," she said. Then got to the point. "Want to smoke some weed?"

"Sure," Ethan said. "Got any?"

Emma silent.

Phil dumped the shoebox back onto the coffee table. Pipes, weed, papers, and lighters spilled out.

A couple drags into a neatly rolled, cigarette-sized spliff and Emma was venting about school and parents, girlfriends, boyfriends.

It was old hat to Ethan. Since the breakup, the only thing that had really changed between Emma and Phil was the frequency of sex: Phil's advances were more frequently rejected. Today would have been no different, but Phil opted to save himself some face. He interrupted her complaints.

"I have to go," Phil said.

"Where?" Emma asked.

"To see my foreman about more work," Phil said.

"What?" Emma said.

With that, Phil got up, gathered his keys and wallet, and left.

Ethan went on distractedly watching the end of the ball-game. Emma sat coiled on the couch, her kilt hiked up enough to reveal an area, as far as Ethan could tell, unencumbered by clothing. Ethan tried his best to ignore it, hoping she'd leave on her own, but the strategy had yet to prove successful.

At the game's last pitch, Emma picked up Ethan's laptop off the coffee table, opened it, and began socializing digitally.

Ethan flicked off the television.

On the coffee table, beside the sundry weed paraphernalia, on top of the water-damaged *Good Sir*, sat the copy of *Cheap Thrills* he had pulled from the cardboard box alongside Simon's dead body. What had caught his eye about the book when he saw it in the alley was the author's name, set in bold yellow lettering above the hand-painted cover: Thelonius R. Grave.

Ethan had read some of Grave's forty-plus books in the past. He was passingly familiar with Grave's nutty fan base, but didn't involve himself in the fringe lunacies forwarded by Grave's most obsessed devotees. Ethan had never heard of *Cheap Thrills*, Grave's twenty-sixth novel, published this very year of the Lord 2009, much less read it, but knew it continued the saga of PI Grunt Rutherford, and was set in Fraser, British Columbia, a thinly veiled version of Ethan's own Vancouver.

Rutherford was only one of the ongoing series' released under Grave's name, and there were a number of stand-alone titles. Thelonius R. Grave was a pseudonym, most assumed, but not one that anyone had taken credit for in the forty-plus years of Grave releases. Grave's publisher insisted they received the manuscripts anonymously.

Much debate over Grave's identity existed among the author's small but loyal fan base. Many, citing similarities in theme and style with existing mystery, crime, or literary novelists, claimed Grave was a pseudonym employed by several different writers; others insisted Grave was a sole passionate hobbyist who made his living some other way—how else could a crime novelist survive without ever attending a conference or a signing, and never replying to a single fan letter? Every so often, with little warning, Grave's publisher would quietly release a new novel, and that would be it.

As Emma surfed away, sipping a beer and passing a thin joint back and forth with her couch mate, Ethan opened the paperback and began to read:

I knew from the minute I laid eyes on her she'd be trouble, which isn't always a bad thing. I like a little bit of trouble in a woman, and usually don't have much problem finding one who's got some. But there's good trouble and there's bad. And Darla Carmine was all bad.

It was about noon on a Saturday, and another miserable Fraser afternoon. I hadn't seen the sun in what felt like months and was starting to wonder if it wasn't just a false memory.

I wasn't supposed to be in the office, but my neighbour had her elephantine boyfriend over again. The noise of those two rutting pachyderms had robbed me of the pleasure of enjoying a day off with a good book in my bedbug-infested apartment.

I had picked up lunch from FreshBurger on the way to my office, where I was hoping to find some solitude. I was sitting at my desk, hunkered over a tomato, avocado, and hummus on rye when Darla Carmine walked in, unannounced and uninvited.

She slid across the floor like a model on a runaway, looking the part in a painted-on emerald-green dress with matching heels, her long red hair tucked up in a tight bun. I could have cut my sandwich in half with those high, sharp cheekbones, and rested my Coke on that high, round—

"Mr. Rutherford," she said, and took a seat across from me in the beat-up old kitchen chair that served as a seat for my clients.

Then came the spiel. Without bothering to explain what exactly it was she wanted me to investigate, she leaned on me with all she had. She knew my past and what it could do to me. If I didn't help her, she said, a few ill-tempered men who worked a mean pair of pliers might find out where I was and the new name I'd appropriated.

"Unusual," I said.

"What's that, Mr. Rutherford?"

"Usually people don't threaten me until after I've rejected whatever shitty thing it is they want me to do."

"Do you get threatened often, Mr. Rutherford?"

"Often enough to know what's usual and what isn't, unfortunately. Going all in on your first hand generally isn't a winning strategy."

"I'm not much for games, Mr. Rutherford," she said.

She looked at me like my compliance was inevitable, like the sun rising in the east, or my rent being past due.

"How do you know about Montreal?" I asked, genuinely intrigued. As far as I knew, there were only a handful of angry Italians in Montreal that knew my old self ever existed, and those angry Italians thought I was dead.

"That's none of your concern," she said. "What's of your concern is that I know the nature of your, shall we say, unfulfilled obligations to the Rossetti family, and that I am well aware of how Italians feel about obligations, being half Italian myself. Half Rossetti, actually."

Damn it.

Admittedly, I was a bit interested in hearing the rest of the story, but more interested in quickly finding a new name, occupation, and place to live. I had suddenly realized being a PI wasn't all that it was cracked up to be, and Fraser was a depressing port town stuck in a rainforest, anyway.

I swallowed the piece of sandwich I had in my mouth, took a swig of Coke, then told Carmine, with the courtesy every woman deserves, to get vigorously stuffed. If the mob wanted me that bad, they probably would have found me by now.

"And next time," I said, "make an appointment."

She took a deep breath and settled into her chair. She clearly wasn't about to be dismissed so easily. I noticed a small gold crucifix dangling from the end of a gold chain around her neck.

Ethan looked over at Emma. A small gold crucifix dangled from her neck.

"What're you looking at?" Emma asked, looking up from the laptop. She looked down at her risen skirt. She closed the computer, put it on the coffee table, and slithered across the couch, settling next to Ethan.

"What're you reading?" she asked.

"A book."

"What kind of book?"

"A crime novel."

"For school?"

"No."

"Then why are you reading it?"

"I don't know," Ethan said. "I like reading."

"Why? Reading sucks."

Nothing from Ethan.

"Why would you read, anyway?" she said. "I mean if it's any good they'll make a movie out of it."

"Are you fucking with me?"

Emma screwed her face up at him.

"Why would I waste like a million hours reading when I can watch a movie in two? I've got better shit to do."

"Like smoking our weed?"

Emma nodded, blankly.

"How come you read so much but still talk like an idiot?" she asked.

Emma leaned over, picked a baggie of weed off the table, and dumped a nugget out onto a video game case. She took up a pair of slightly rusted scissors and began to cut up the buds. As Emma leaned over, her white dress shirt opened.

"What're you, like an English major or something?" Emma said, still leaning over the table.

"I was. I didn't finish."

"Oh! Your parents must be so proud!" she said.

"Yeah, well, what're you doing with yourself?"

"I'm going to be a lawyer, like my dad."

"A lawyer?"

"Yup," Emma said.

"You want to be a lawyer?"

"I'm *going* to be a lawyer."

"You know you probably have to read if you want to be a lawyer," Ethan said.

"You don't say?"

Emma turned and put on a wide-eyed, dumbfounded look.

"For real," Ethan assured her.

"I just don't like fiction," she said, returning her attention to the task at hand. "What's the point? There's so much living to do. Why would I waste my time reading somebody else's made-up story?"

Ethan didn't answer.

"No rebuttal?" Emma said.

"None that I care to give."

"Well, you wouldn't make much of a lawyer," she said.

"Real life is stranger than fiction, anyway," Emma continued after a brief pause. "Ever read oral arguments? Or Supreme Court judicial decisions? Or interrogation transcripts?"

Oral, Ethan thought.

"You don't really look like the kind of girl who'd want to be a lawyer," Ethan said instead.

"Oh yeah?" Emma said, looking up from the weed. "What do I look like?"

Ethan had considered this previously. A few months ago, on a night when a drunk and high Emma was sliding around the apartment, and a drugged Phil was slumped into a corner of the couch, Ethan had leered at Emma and thought, What will become of this girl? Never has to get a job. Rich family. Drives a new Range Rover. The best outcome Ethan could think of would be for her to marry some rich doctor, keep that body going until she did, and not develop any serious addiction problems.

He laughed out loud.

"What?" Emma said, finishing up the joint. "Why's it so funny that I'm going to be a lawyer?"

"Because you're rolling a joint and not wearing any underwear."

"Yes I am, actually. And I'm only just finishing high school."

"That's your defence?"

"Of course," she said, lighting up the joint. "High school doesn't matter for shit. I've got good enough grades to get into whatever school I want."

"I've never seen you do homework."

"Why the fuck would I do homework here? This is where I cut loose, man," she said, indicating the room with a pass of the lit joint. "This place is a dump, by the way. Have I ever mentioned that?"

"No."

"Well, there you go," she said, then downed the last third of her beer in one noisy gulp.

"Lawyer," Ethan said.

"Yup. Don't be envious just because you don't have any goals."

"Thanks," Ethan said, feeling envious because he didn't have any goals.

"Oh, cheer up."

Emma slid closer on the couch and passed Ethan the joint. He dropped it on the floor.

"Fuck," he said.

Emma bent over to pick up the joint, revealing the full curve of her behind, which turned out not to be entirely bare, but so close as to make the distinction irrelevant.

"Fuck," Ethan said again.

"Want to?" she said.

"What?"

"Fuck."

"What do you mean?"

"Do you want to have sex, moron?" Emma said.

"With you?"

"I'm the only one here," she said, blowing a stream of smoke out the side of her mouth and grabbing Ethan's crotch. "I mean, you could go hide in your room and jerk off like you usually do, if you want. Either way."

"Well, no . . . no . . . I don't want to . . . ah . . . ," he sputtered, wondering how she knew about that. "But Phil. You know?"

"Yeah, I know him. He knows we're not together or anything."

"I don't think he's too happy about that."

She rolled her eyes. "I'm seventeen, all right? It's not like I'm going to marry the stupid ape."

"Yeah, well, listen, I've had a rough couple days, okay? Phil probably won't be long."

"Do you want him here too?" She worked her hand into Ethan's pants. "You two can shish kebab me," she laughed. "That'd be fun."

"I disagree," he said, after figuring out what she meant.

"Then I guess it'll just be you and me."

## 8

Emma wasn't a headache, she was a migraine: arriving through mysterious causes and debilitating to the effect of needing to lay motionless in the dark. She'd been inflicting herself upon his psyche for . . . how long?

Phil calculated the duration as he took the stairs down from the apartment, leaving the migraine on the couch for Ethan to deal with. Phil and Emma had met . . . when? A year ago? It had been downtown at The Roxy, a top-40 nightclub featuring a live band trudging through inferior versions of songs already in impertinent rotation on the radio, drunken revellers of all ages traversing floors sticky with decades of spilled beer, and a fleet of pituitarily large bouncers trolling the room for potential punching bags to be dragged out back and tenderized.

Phil could no longer recall the song Emma had been dancing to, but the beat somehow remained around her memory, a sleazy aura of stale nightclub air, cigarette breath, and tacky sweat.

Not much had happened that first night: Phil had gotten drunk, broken a guy's orbital bone, gotten Emma's number on the dance floor, stumbled out into the street, fought a cop, escaped in a stranger's open-topped Porsche, puked over the side.

But not long after that night, Emma was parking her mom's or dad's Range Rover in front of the apartment and smoking hell out of Phil's stash.

Somewhere along the way, over countless nights of drunken revelry in the apartment or at house parties or at Venue or Party! or Fortune (but never again at The Roxy), Phil had fallen so far as to envision a future with Emma beyond the next week or month or . . . year?

In the embarrassing glare of hindsight, like the lights flipped on after last call, Phil realized that Emma had always been intent on catch and release, nothing more than a rich girl AWOL from a life of privilege, slumming it with a washed-up hockey player.

Because she is a stupid child, Phil concluded as he crossed the parking garage to his waiting aged Pontiac. As this afternoon had proven, onset of Emma was inexplicable. Phil, already self-medicated to the eyeballs, had decided it was best simply to leave. He'd given Emma the excuse of needing to visit his foreman, which he did, though he'd had no intention of doing it when he'd spoken the words. He could have called or waited to be called, as he usually did, but now, as he set himself behind the steering wheel, Phil realized he didn't have anywhere else to go. Odds were the visit would be futile—as far as receiving some answer as to when he would next work—but at the very least he could remind his foreman of his existence.

Phil pulled out of the building and drove the few kilometres to the worksite he'd spent a month at—a new condo tower in the heart of Vancouver's most drug-addled neighbourhood—but had been vacant from for the last week. Most of the concrete for the foundation had been poured. Phil and his crewmates had been laid off until their services were again required.

Driving downtown in a dejected state, Phil took note of the surroundings he'd come to take for granted. The mountains to the north, a parapet of snowy white, slate grey, and forest green, shielded urban Vancouver from the relentless encroach of the natural. Or perhaps the other way around. In any case, Black Mountain, the twin domes of The Lions, Grouse Mountain, and the rest had come to feel like guardians to Phil, now a Vancouver resident long enough to accept their splendor as background scenery, save on rare occasions when they declared themselves leads. He shook off the thought, but was left with an urge to escape through, around, or over that rampart of mountains to the north.

When he arrived at the site, he parked the Pontiac across the street and approached the white trailer that served as the foreman's site office. Chuck, the foreman, a smirking wide-headed linebacker, could be seen through the window sitting at his small desk, filling out paperwork or—more realistically, Phil presumed—reading the sports section.

Phil climbed the three wooden steps to the door of the trailer and knocked.

"Open," Chuck said.

Phil entered.

"What?" Chuck asked without turning. His back was to the door. A spreadsheet was open on his small laptop.

"Just here to see about more work."

Chuck checked over his shoulder at the voice and rose upon seeing Phil in the trailer. He stood a half head shorter than Phil and was thirty years his senior but retained the stature of a former athlete. He was still thick in the legs, arms, and neck, but his remaining muscle was now covered in a healthy layer of fat supplied by wife-made casseroles and domestic beer.

"When are we back to work?" Phil said.

Chuck's blank face twitched at the eyes, a look of someone who recognized the person standing before them but not in what capacity or with any name to apply.

Phil identified the look for what it was.

"I'm Phil Wilford. I was pouring with Kenny and Mike and Donut's crew."

"Yeah, yeah, Wilford," Chuck said, registering the name, or at least pretending to. "You'll hear from somebody next week, I think."

"Are Donut or Kenny back?"

"Now?"

"Yeah."

"No."

"Out on another job?"

"I don't know."

Chuck went back to his laptop and spreadsheet, which Phil noticed was filled with players and their associated stats.

"Can you give me a date?"

"With Kenny?" Chuck said, still facing his screen.

"For work."

A pause.

"You'll get a call."

Phil grimaced at Chuck's back. At least Chuck knew he existed.

Phil turned to leave, but when he opened the door to the outside world his path was blocked by a familiar face. It was Frankie, a lanky rebar peon, a pairing of body type and occupation not lending itself to longevity. Frankie was also the worksite weed merchant. Phil may have owed him twenty or fifty bucks but wasn't really sure.

Upon sight of Phil, Frankie's sunken eyes lit up.

"Phil, dude," Frankie said.

Phil brushed by him without a word.

# 9

After Emma finished with Ethan and absconded with what was left of the weed, he was left sitting pantless on the sofa, awaiting the impending return of his roommate and, presumably, the impending collision of said roommate's fist with his face.

The episode with Emma had left Ethan confused. That a girl so superficially dimwitted could have such lofty ambitions—and that they were plausibly attainable—left the comparatively inert Ethan cowed and awed. What was also confusing was that he was left thinking not about Emma, whose character he was mostly familiar with, but about Sam, the paranoid, hirsute weed dealer's attractive companion.

Ethan thought it was about time he got off the couch, out of the dank apartment, got himself a half-respectable job and, above all else, found himself a girl like Sam. No, not *like* Sam. *The* Sam.

Ethan's thoughts swung from Emma to Sam and finally to Simon, the overstayed houseguest of his well-baked brain.

Ethan wasn't quite sure why Simon's corpse haunted him. It wasn't simply the sight of a dead body: dead bodies he'd seen before, in plenty. He'd paid his way through an unfinished bachelor's degree at York University by working nights as a security attendant at St. Mary's Hospital, ejecting the homeless for stealing a warm place to sleep, doing the same to more conventional thieves, and escorting the recently deceased to the hospital morgue. It was there, while helping nurses lift the dead onto transfer cots, that he discovered suggillation, the settling of blood into the subcutaneous tissues, forming a deep violet gelatin beneath the skin. This, along with the endless other signatures of death, had dulled for Ethan any element of surprise in the final physical form.

His waking dream of a de- and re-composing Simon had become a recurring one, though, and now included whatever woman he laid eyes on: Emma and movie starlets, Sam and internet girls, Marley Malone staring up at him dead eyed from the prison of her glossy magazine.

Regarding Emma, though, Ethan was worried. Just how cool was Phil, anyway? Ethan tried to convince himself that Phil was the live-and-let-live kind of guy who'd be okay with his roommate stooping the object of his affection, but the less stoned part of Ethan's brain didn't buy it.

Perhaps he'd been too hard on Emma about her ambitions. At least she had some. And now that he thought about it, if she wasn't complaining about school or some other triviality, she was usually going on about a court case she'd read about or heard on the news.

Ethan pulled on his pants and walked into the kitchen. He took a can of beer from the fridge and popped the tab. As he sipped at the foam, a knock came at the door.

Ethan paused mid-sip. If it was Emma back for something else, she had a damn key. If it was Phil, then Ethan might as well finish his beer and hope for the best.

The knocking continued, and then:

"Mr. Ebrahim," the door said. "Mr. Ebrahim, this is the Vancouver Police Department."

"Christ."

"Mr. Ebrahim, we know you're in there. Open up, please."

"Hold on," Ethan said. He looked around the apartment. Drug paraphernalia littered the coffee table. As the knocks continued, Ethan swept the pipes and other instruments back into the shoebox and stuffed the whole thing under the couch. He hustled to the door, opened it as far as the chain would allow, and stuck an eye and nose through the crack.

Two uniforms stood in the hallway, a female and her greying buffalo of a partner.

Ethan didn't recognize these two cops in particular, but the building had enough addicts and low-rent dealers to account for more police and ambulance visits than an emergency ward. Better to stay on the good side of them than the bad, he figured, but on no side at all was even better.

"We have a few questions about an incident that occurred in the building last night, Mr. Ebrahim," the female cop said gently.

"I wasn't home," Ethan said, relieved that this didn't seem to be about Simon's corpse.

"Did you hear anything unusual above you last night?" the male cop asked in monotone. Ethan gathered that was as amiable as the cop was going to get.

"No," Ethan said. "I didn't hear anything. I was at the movies last night."

"See anything good?" the female cop asked.

"I saw *Missing Cargo*."

"Which one is that?"

"Scorsese."

"Based on the Grave novel," the female cop said.

"Yeah," Ethan said.

"A gangster flick?" the male cop said.

"Yeah."

"You like gangster movies?"

"Yeah. Some of them. This one wasn't anything special though."

"That's too bad," the female cop said.

"Notice anything when you got home?"

"Nope."

"Where'd you see the movie?" the male cop asked. His hand pushed the door against the chain. "How about opening this door and letting us in?"

"I'd rather come out there," Ethan said, holding the door with his foot. He released the chain and slid out into the hall, leaving the door slightly ajar.

"Where did you see the movie and what time?" the male cop asked again.

"At MetroVille. Nine forty," Ethan said. It occurred to him that the stub still might be in his pocket. He dug in, found it there, and handed it to the female cop.

The male cop, his face looking like a fingertip after too long in the bath, stood menacingly over Ethan. He could feel the anger radiating off the officer like heat from an overworked engine.

The female cop was tiny compared to the raging withered bison next to her, but still stood a good inch taller than Ethan. With a slender yet strong jawline, and a head of short greying auburn hair, the cop looked fit, strong, and composed, but still managed a serene and welcoming smile. Good cop, bad cop was a real technique, the internet had told him, not just the stuff of a Grave novel.

"Do you live alone, Mr. Ebrahim," the woman cop asked. "It is Massoud Ebrahim, correct?"

"I've got a roommate," Ethan said. "I don't think he was home either. Who am I speaking with, anyway?"

"I'm Detective Woit," the female cop said.

"Smolin," said the male cop. "You are Massoud Ebrahim?"

"Yeah," Ethan lied. Massoud Ebrahim, his old roommate, had moved back to Iran. His name was on the lease and all the bills, some of which were getting paid irregularly.

"You don't look like a Massoud," Smolin said.

"That's a bit racist, isn't it?" Ethan said.

Then Woit said something Ethan didn't understand.

"What?" Ethan said.

"Oh. You don't speak Farsi, Mr. Ebrahim?" Woit said.

"No."

"Unusual."

"Not really. Lots of people don't speak Farsi," Ethan said. He swallowed hard. This was probably one of those purposeless lies that—if not quickly excised—would grow into a malignant tumor.

"Anyway," he continued, "I don't know anything about any incident, other than that it seems like there's an ambulance pulling somebody out of here once a week. Half the time with a sheet pulled over their head. Good work on that, by the way."

"We need to talk to your roommate," Smolin said.

"He's not here," Ethan said.

"Where is he?" Smolin asked.

"You'd have to ask him."

"You don't know where he is?"

"I've got a general idea."

"Then why don't you tell us?"

"If you ask nicely, maybe I will."

"What're you, sensitive?" Smolin said, aggression registering on his face like a bull bound in a flank strap. "I don't need to ask nicely. You just need to answer."

"Is he always like this?" Ethan asked Woit.

"He's had a rough morning," Woit said. "I apologize."

Smolin's stare remained firmly on Ethan.

"The only name on the lease is yours, Mr. Ebrahim," Woit said, emphasizing the name. "The owner of the building would probably like to know who's living in it. Wouldn't they, Mr. Ebrahim?"

"Yeah, and I'd probably like him to fix the sink in the bathroom, repair two of the burners on the stove, and"—he pointed up to a hole the size of a portly handyman—"fill in this hole in the ceiling. There's also some cat shit in the hall that's been there for a week. I hear it has squatter's rights now. I think we can call it even."

Smolin looked to be vibrating, but maybe Ethan was still high.

"Mr. Ebrahim, I believe we got off on the wrong foot," Woit said, remaining calm and focussed. "Can we start over?"

Ethan took a long breath. He reminded himself that the reason for the police visit didn't have anything to do with him—nor Simon, apparently—and that the police had better things to worry about than a little bit of weed in a shitty apartment.

"Yeah, of course," he said. "I honestly wasn't home last night. I didn't hear anything or see anything. I can give you my roommate's phone number, if you want." Phil wouldn't appreciate it, but Ethan had no real reason to continue being difficult.

"Thank you," Woit said. "That would be excellent. We're also warning residents to be extra vigilant about safety. Chain your door—as I see you're already doing—and install a deadbolt. Be dutiful about keeping non-residents out of the building."

Woit handed Ethan her card, took Ethan and Phil's numbers, and asked that Ethan contact her if he noticed anything out of the ordinary.

"Out of the ordinary, or out of the ordinary for this place?" Ethan asked. "There's a difference, as I'm sure you're aware."

"For this place, then," Woit said. "All right?"

Ethan agreed, and the police left down the stained and stinking hall.

## 10

Phil returned toting a sack of cheeseburgers, the brown paper bag nearly translucent with grease. Ethan filled him in on the police visit, excluding the part about giving them his number, even though he had provided an incorrect one. Neither did he mention Emma's visit, figuring one piece of bad news was plenty for the day.

Phil's response was to pick up the foot-tall glass bong shaped like a sitting giraffe that stood on the coffee table before them. The bong's upturned hoof held a small bowl. Its smiling snout provided a mouthpiece for inhaling. Phil stuffed the bong, lit it, partook, then passed the bong across the couch to Ethan.

With lighter held to bowl, Ethan drew thick swirls of smoke into the bong and up its long neck. He inhaled, attempting to blast the past day's events from his brain. He held for a count of five, then tilted his head and released a tall, billowing plume.

The two enjoyed the silence of the hazy room, playing video games and enjoying the slow, purposeless wanderings of their stoned minds.

A knock at the door interrupted the vacation.

"Who is it?" Phil shouted at the door.

Ethan considered Emma, who would not knock, or the police, who would.

"There's a water leak," a male voice said from the hall. "I need to check your suite."

Phil and Ethan both looked up at the ceiling. It looked no worse off than usual. Phil set his partially smoked joint in a tray on the coffee table, then went to the door and opened it.

A muscled man in a black balaclava took up the doorway. A thatch of hair climbed from the neck of a white tank top. Two clenched fists completed arms covered in coarse hair and vaguely tribal tattoos, arms built for curling weights or beheading smaller men with the ease of a twist-off beer cap.

Ethan considered the intruder's resemblance to a gorilla. Then the gorilla punched Phil in the face.

Phil arced backward in free fall. His head struck the corner of the coffee table with a wet thunk then thudded to the carpet.

Ethan stood up, then froze.

The gorilla spoke.

"Where is it?" he said.

"I don't know what you're talking about," Ethan said.

"I know you've got Simon's shit."

"I don't."

"You killed him and left him in the alley."

"I didn't kill anybody," Ethan said. "We were supposed to buy weed from him. Then I found him while I was taking a piss."

The gorilla scoffed.

"What kind of person kills a man and then pisses on him?"

The gorilla swung the apartment door closed behind him, then turned the deadbolt and strung the chain. He stood just inside the apartment, his knuckles hanging nearly down to his knees, his chest swollen. Ethan expected him to climb up onto something, to start waving his arms and grunting.

The gorilla stepped over Phil and climbed onto the coffee table.

Ethan thought his premonition was about to come true. Instead, the gorilla unzipped his fly and began to relieve himself on the motionless body of Phil.

It occurred to Ethan that he should do something, like try to knock the intruder off the table.

He didn't think he could do it: Ethan weighed a hundred and seventy pounds; the gorilla carried at least an extra fifty pounds of steroid-enhanced muscle.

The gorilla finished pissing and stepped down from the table. He stepped over Phil and walked into the kitchen. A bulge protruded from the small of his back: a gun was tucked into the waist of his jeans. He opened drawers and cupboards and dumped them out, looking for the bag or whatever had been in it.

"I don't want to beat you," he said, not even turning to face Ethan. "But I will."

The gorilla walked back into the living room and stopped in front of Ethan. He stood a full head taller, toe to toe. Two blue eyes peered out at Ethan from the holes in the mask. The gorilla put one animal hand in the middle of Ethan's chest; he could almost grip Ethan's torso like a basketball.

The gorilla pushed Ethan back onto the couch. He put one foot up on the seat, laid a paw on top of Ethan's head, and squeezed. Ethan worried his eyes might pop out—like that scene in *Casino* where they put the crooked gambler's head in a vice. He wondered if the gorilla, like Hugo, had a poster of Al Pacino on his wall. Or maybe a bad oil painting of him. Ethan figured he probably did. Ethan laughed.

It was a bad time to laugh.

The gorilla picked the remote up from the couch and whipped Ethan across the face with it. Pieces fell into Ethan's lap.

"This is funny?" the gorilla said.

"No," Ethan said. "I was thinking about something else."

"You think you're tough?"

"Absolutely not," Ethan said.

The gorilla took his foot off the couch and turned to the coffee table. Ethan slumped back into the cushions in momentary relief. A barely audible moan came from Phil.

The gorilla picked up Ethan's laptop from the coffee table, raised it high then smashed it against the top of Ethan's head.

Ethan raised his hands and gently touched his hair. Blood ran across his forehead and into his eyes from a cut in his scalp.

"I'm going to try this again," the gorilla said. "One last time. And I'll keep it simple. Where is the bag you took from Simon?"

"I don't know anything about a bag."

The laptop came back down on Ethan's head.

Blood ran from his nose. He tasted metal.

"Where is it, you shit?" the gorilla shouted.

"I didn't take any bag from Simon," Ethan said as calmly as he could. His voice quavered. "He was dead when I found him. I didn't even buy any weed."

The gorilla picked up a video game controller, held Ethan by the neck and thrust the controller into his forehead. Ethan winced and squinted away the white dots that had appeared before his eyes.

The gorilla threw the controller across the room. He let go of Ethan. He adjusted his shirt—which had risen up with the effort of smashing various pieces of technology against Ethan's head—and Ethan noticed a prominent tattoo on the gorilla's shoulder: Jesus, smiling as if forced to sit for a photo he wanted no part of.

"You burnt out little turd," the gorilla said. "All you can think about is smoking dope. How long have you been buying from Simon, Turd?"

"A while," Ethan said.

The gorilla slapped him.

"What's *a while*, Turd?"

"Like a year, maybe. Probably a year."

"You know what, Turd? Simon, like you, was a worthless shit."

The gorilla seemed scatologically fixated. Ethan pictured a real gorilla flinging its own feces. Ethan laughed a short, uncomfortable laugh.

The gorilla slapped the back of Ethan's head.

"What's so funny now, Turd?"

"I was thinking of what a turd Simon is."

"Was."

"Was," Ethan agreed.

"Because you killed him."

Ethan wiped the blood from his eyes and mouth with the palm of his hand.

"I didn't kill anybody. I don't want to kill anybody. I don't have anything to do with this."

Ethan pointed at Phil on the floor.

"I should get him to a hospital. What if his brain is swelling or something?"

"What the fuck do I care about his brain?"

The gorilla got up. He picked up the bong from the coffee table and threw it into the television. Long cracks spread across the screen.

Finished with breaking electronics, he slapped Ethan across the back of the head once more, then lumbered down the hall toward the bedrooms.

Ethan leaned back on the couch and thought things through as best he could. He didn't remember seeing any bag with Simon. He remembered the piles of trash, the copy of *Cheap Thrills*, the Marley Malone magazine and, of course, Simon's corpse. He remembered being pretty high. But no bag.

His head ached from the physical beating. From an armed and violent intruder in his home. From Phil unconscious on the floor in a stain of his own blood and the gorilla's urine.

Seeing Phil lying there like the newly dead made Ethan angry. He hadn't been angry yet, just scared, paralyzed. Maybe he was in shock, he thought. Whatever that meant.

He listened as the gorilla trashed his bedroom. There wasn't much in there—a stereo and CDs, books, clothes, a small television—but it still angered Ethan that the thick goon was ruining his stuff, no matter how wanting.

Ethan looked at the door. He could make a break for it, but could he get the deadbolt and chain unlocked before the gorilla came running back out with his gun?

But leaning in the corner, beside the television, was Phil's crude home security device: an aluminum baseball bat.

Ethan got off the couch. He picked up the bat and stood out of view of the hallway. He waited there, looking at the wreckage the intruder had caused. Cutlery and broken plates and glasses lay on the linoleum floor.

The clatter stopped. The hall's hardwood floor creaked as the gorilla left the bedroom.

"Where'd you go?" the gorilla said to the empty room.

Ethan hitched the bat over his shoulder and held his breath. From the hall a handgun emerged, held by two heavy paws, followed by those thick arms covered in hair and black-ink tattoos.

Ethan swung the bat down on the gorilla's hands. A bullet tore into the far wall of the apartment. The gun clattered to the floor.

Ethan brought the bat back over his shoulder and stepped out from the corner. The gorilla stood holding his injured wrist.

"Come on," the gorilla said.

The aluminum bat connected with the side of the gorilla's head, sounding a nauseating ping. The bat followed through and punched a hole in the drywall. The gorilla crumpled to the floor.

Ethan stood over the intruder's collapsed body. He considered hitting the thug again, but it didn't seem necessary. The gorilla breathed shallowly and croaked a wet spatter of blood into his mask.

Ethan kicked him in the gut for good measure, then bent over and picked up the gun. He walked to the window and stuck his fingers between two slats of the closed blinds, pried them open and peered down at the street. A black sedan was parked in front of the building. The rear passenger side door hung open.

Ethan took his jacket with his wallet and phone in it from the couch and grabbed Phil's keys from the coffee table. He jammed his feet into a pair of shoes by the door and ran.

He hurried down the hallway to the stairwell and took the steps four at a time down the three flights to the parking garage. He ran to Phil's Pontiac, parked at the far side of the lot, fumbled the keys into the lock, dumped the gun on the passenger seat then started the car and swung it out of the stall.

As he approached the incline of the exit ramp, a pair of blue jeans walked into view against the backdrop of the apartment building across the street. Ethan gunned the gas and put the Pontiac up the ramp, hitting fifty as he exited into daylight.

The pair of blue jeans belonged to a man standing at the top of the ramp with a gun in his hand. Ethan lowered himself behind the steering wheel and pressed the pedal the rest of the way to the floor. Bullets struck the car's headlamp and grill before its bumper kicked the man up and over the hood. He bounced off the windshield frame, cracking the glass with his heel as he spun off onto the pavement.

Ethan came up from behind the wheel in time to stop the car from driving onto the lawn of the building across the street. He jerked the wheel right and the car hopped the curb, careening across the grassy boulevard before he straightened it out and back onto the road.

Wide eyed and sweating, Ethan sped away from the apartment to the urgent wail of approaching emergency sirens, his hands on the wheel as if hanging desperately from a building's ledge.

## II

Wynne Duncan steadied himself against the wall with one hand and held his jaw with the other. He spat a mouthful of frothy blood and two teeth into his palm and picked two more off the carpet.

He looked at the teeth. Three were intact. One was split top to bottom. He stuffed the whole mess into his pocket, wiped his hands on his pants, then pulled his shirt up to clean the blood from his mouth.

He looked around for his gun. The little turd had taken it.

Wynne picked himself up off the floor. He took a final glance at the man he'd knocked unconscious, still lying insensate on the carpet, then left.

An old woman in a nightgown ducked back into her apartment at the sight of him, slamming the door behind her. Wynne stopped and leaned against the wall, halted by a piercing lance of hot pain.

The flash of pain passed. He hurried down the hall and took the stairs down two flights to the front lobby. He opened the front door to the sound of gunshots and the sight of a tan Pontiac tearing out of the parking garage. It swerved across the boulevard then sped away westward.

A black Lexus waited out front. A tall, muscled, red-haired man in jeans and a black T-shirt hustled from the car to the mouth of the parking garage, then came back, helping another man hobble toward the back seat.

"What happened?" the redhead said. "We heard a gunshot."

Wynne left the front steps of the building, passed the two men, and lowered himself into the front seat of the Lexus. The hobbling man eased into the back seat and closed the door. The redhead circled around to the driver's side and got in. He pulled the already running car away from the curb, turned it around and sped away from the building.

The redhead sped along Ash, then onto Burnwood, Birch, and Oak without heed for traffic sign or pedestrian, then pulled onto Broadway and headed east.

The men sat silently. Wynne held his jaw as the car jostled over imperfect road.

A few kilometres later, the redhead merged onto the highway and blended into the thick vein of traffic running eastbound and out of the city. He pulled into the HOV lane, achieved a legal speed, then flicked on the radio, tuning the station to country.

A southern-twanged Alabaman sang about his state and pickup trucks, by make, and women and the land and riding 4x4s across it while drinking Budweiser.

Wynne grimaced.

"How's your jaw?" the driver asked.

Wynne turned and looked at him blankly. He still held his face in one hand.

The redhead pointed to the glove box.

"There's some Oxy in there," he said.

Wynne opened the box and pulled out a prescription bottle. He shook a few pills into his bloody mouth and swallowed.

"Do we need to get you attended to?" the driver asked.

Wynne nodded.

"What happened?" the redhead asked.

Wynne shrugged.

"What'd he hit you with?"

"Fell offa ladder."

"I'm not the emergency room, you idiot. What'd he actually hit you with?"

"Ah bet."

"A bat?"

Wynne nodded.

"Who got shot?" the redhead said.

"Nobody," Wynne said.

"You should have just shot him and saved us all this bull-shit," the redhead said.

"We didn't know if they had it or what," said the man in the back. Then, to Wynne, "Did they have it?"

Wynne shook his head.

"So where is it?" asked the redhead.

Wynne shook his head.

"So what are you gonna tell Jack?"

Wynne shrugged.

"Fuck him," he said, spitting blood onto the dash.

## 12

Ethan flew through the first half-dozen stop signs and traffic lights, nearly flattening a ratty grey Shih Tzu on a long leash two blocks down from his apartment and causing more than one pedestrian to go rigid at the curb with fear. He corrected course and took the car east, checking his mirrors for pursuers until he reached the nearest TransCanada entrance and merged onto the highway.

The highway was busy with cars, but traffic was flowing in an uninterrupted stream.

As the last dregs of adrenaline dissipated from his blood-stream, he calmed himself and slowed the car to a law-abiding speed. Malls, auto dealerships, condo towers, and box stores lined the highway as he abandoned the city. Soon civilization was interrupted by short stretches of forest blurring by on either side.

Ethan drove without purpose or destination for nearly an hour, the violent scene at the apartment replaying over and over in his mind. The wet thunk of Phil's skull on the table. The hulk-ing gorilla pissing on Phil. Phil lying there while warm blood and stinking urine soaked into his clothes and the carpet beneath him. The sickening ping of the aluminum bat. The wounded ape crouching in the hall. The undulating ring in Ethan's ear from the fired gun.

Eventually a highway sign jolted him back into the present: "City of Langley: Where City and Country Meet."

Returned from his reverie, Ethan realized how far out of the city he'd come. He passed highway exits until he saw one that advertised amenities. He flicked his turn signal on and curved down the ramp of exit 463, finding himself among the usual roadside mainstays: gas stations, fast food franchises, mostly vacant motels.

Ethan pulled the car into one of the first parking lots off the highway. He turned off the ignition and relaxed back into the seat, finally releasing his hands from the wheel. He wiped his forehead with the sleeve of his coat and came away with sticky, partially dried blood. As he drove, he'd held a T-shirt Phil had left on the front seat against his head to staunch the bleeding. The cut on his head had stopped bleeding, as had his nose. He turned the rearview mirror to take a better look at his face. His forehead was smeared with dark blood, and his nose was purple and swollen. He touched it, and it hurt, but he didn't think it was broken. Or at least not badly.

He'd left Phil on the floor, alone. Ethan slipped his phone out of his pocket and dialled 9-1-1.

"Police, Fire, or Ambulance?"

"Ambulance."

"Hold the line," the woman said.

The line clicked.

"Ambulance for what city?" asked a new voice, male this time.

"Vancouver," Ethan said.

"What's the address?"

Ethan gave his address and apartment number.

"Tell me what happened," the voice said.

"My friend hit his head on the coffee table," Ethan said.

"Where is he now?" the man asked.

"On the floor," Ethan said.

"Is he alert?"

"No. He's out. He hit his head."

"How did he hit his head?"

"This guy punched him."

"In your home?"

"Yeah, the—"

"Is the assailant still in your home, sir?" the man said.

"No. Look, I don't know, I left." Ethan said. "Just send an ambulance. And police." He hung up.

The phone rang back almost immediately. Ethan turned it off.

He reached to the back seat for something to clean his face with. Some of Phil's CDs were there: The Morbidly Cool's *State 51*; Big Prairie's *The Canadian Dream*; Beats of Jesus's *Bass Lines for Good Times*. An old green sweater. His jacket, the copy of *Cheap Thrills* peeking out of the pocket.

Ethan took the green sweater and wiped his face, to little effect. He needed at least water to remove the tacky blood.

He dumped the sweater on the passenger seat beside him, covering the gun he'd retrieved from the apartment, then took stock of his surroundings. He'd pulled into a Taco Bell parking lot.

Ethan opened the door. The air smelled of rain and ozone and fast food. He swung his feet out onto the wet asphalt and tried to stand up. His legs were shaking. He sat back in the car and took a few deep breaths, clenching and unclenching his fists.

When he was calm and ready, Ethan got out of the car and entered the Taco Bell. He found the bathroom and used a wetted bunch of paper towels to clean his face, ears, and neck. He looked in the mirror. He'd gotten the blood off his forehead and face, but parts of his hair remained matted from the cut in his head. He turned to the side; blood had dried in his ear. He dampened more paper towels and cleaned out the crevasses. Two days worth of stubble was turning to scruff. He looked like some of the downtrodden tenants of his apartment building. Particularly the one he occasionally found sleeping in the front vestibule, too tired or high to make it all the way to his own unit.

Ethan pushed his hair around, attempting to smooth it into something more presentable. He failed. He stood looking in the mirror, not knowing what to do next.

He left the bathroom, went to the counter and stared at the menu, void of expression.

The chubby teenager behind the cash eyed him suspiciously, waiting as Ethan looked over the options.

Ethan thought about the man he'd run over coming out of the garage and wondered how ordering Taco Bell was supposed to improve the situation.

"Sir?" the girl behind the cash said.

"What am I doing?" Ethan said.

"Sir? Are you okay?" the girl said.

She pointed at Ethan's chest. There were streaks of blood across his white T-shirt.

"Oh. Yeah," Ethan said. "I'm fine."

"Can I get you anything?"

"Oh, sure. Yeah. The soft taco deal."

"I meant to clean up. Or an ambulance. But I'll put that through."

Ethan nodded.

"You want a drink with that?"

"No," Ethan said, thinking of alcohol. Then, "Oh, yeah. I'll have a Coke."

"For here?"

"No. To go."

The cashier punched in the order. It came to $7.47. Ethan remembered Taco Bell being a lot cheaper, but such was the way of the world.

He dug into the pocket of his jeans and pulled out a ten dollar bill, some coins, and a business card. It was Detective Woit's. Ethan handed the bill to the cashier, took the change, then stepped away and waited for his food.

He examined Woit's business card. The Vancouver Police Department crest sat in the top left corner. A wreath of maple leaves framed a totem pole. The whole thing was topped with the Queen's Royal Crown. It's only missing a hockey stick and a fucking beaver, Ethan thought.

The center of the card said Margaret T. Woit and provided her contact details.

The cashier brought the order to the counter. Ethan collected the brown paper bag of tacos and the waxed plastic cup of Coke and brought it all back to the car.

He set the Coke into the cup holder below the radio and the bag of food on top of the sweater on the passenger seat, then looked at Woit's card again, thinking of Phil on the floor of the apartment. He pulled his phone out of his pocket, turned it back on, and dialled Woit's number. There was no answer. He left a message:

"I'm from, ah, 423 Maple, the apartment at 423 Maple. Unit 236. You were there the other day."

He left his number and hung up.

He scrolled through the recently called numbers in his phone, trying to decide what to do next.

Phil had no family in town that he knew of, and Ethan definitely had no contact for them. The cops and hospital would have to figure that out for themselves.

Ethan's own father was back east. Ethan hadn't spoken to him in six years and had no intention of breaking the streak. Ethan's mother was in town, occasionally, when she wasn't travelling, but he only saw her a few times a year, at most, over dinner at a restaurant, usually, and without her new husband, some big shot lawyer Ethan had met once but couldn't really remember. This was his mother's fourth husband. He had only been around for a year. Ethan had given up on step-dads after number two. Conversations with his mother were terse; they seemed to be speaking across a vast distance, even when they were sitting at the same small table. It had been this way for years.

Ethan laughed at himself for thinking of his parents. What could they possibly do?

Toward the end of the list of numbers in his phone was Sam's. He had called her the night before, but she had been busy studying. She told him to call back again in a few days.

Ethan thought about their lunch the other day, and what Sam had said about Hugo: that Hugo knew Simon and that they sold together, and that Hugo was worried about recent infighting. He also remembered that Sam said she wasn't comfortable around Hugo's place anymore, regardless of whether Hugo's paranoia was justified or not.

Ethan called Sam. She answered on the third ring.

"Hello?"

"Sam? This is Ethan."

"Hey. What're you up to?"

"Are you at Hugo's?"

"No. I'm at home. Why?"

"Don't go to Hugo's," Ethan said.

"Why? What's the matter?"

"A guy just broke into my place and punched out Phil."

"What?"

"He punched out Phil. He had a gun."

"Where are you now?"

"Langley."

"What're you doing in Langley?"

"I hit the guy with a bat. There were more of them waiting outside. I left Phil. I ran."

"So where are you now?"

"Langley. I just told you."

"You *ran* to Langley?"

"Not literally ran. I drove."

"Where in Langley?"

"At a Taco Bell."

"Why?"

"I didn't know what to do."

"Did you call the police?"

"I called 9-1-1."

"No, I mean after. Did you go to the police?"

"No. Hell no. I called this one cop, but she didn't answer."

"You should go to the police. What're you doing?"

"I said I'm at a Taco Bell. I got some tacos."

"You ordered tacos?"

"Yeah, I ordered tacos," Ethan said. "I didn't know what else to do."

"You get assaulted, and you don't know what to do, so you order tacos?"

"I don't see the concern here," Ethan yelled. "Look, I called to tell you to stay away from Hugo's, is all, okay?"

"Okay, all right. Where are you going now?"

"I don't know. I can't go home. I hadn't thought about it yet."

"So, what'd the guy want?"

"I don't know. He wanted a bag. Presumably with drugs or money in it."

"Oh."

"What?"

"Well, ah, Hugo said—"

"Just hold on," Ethan said. "I don't want to say any more over the phone."

"Why not?"

"I don't know. They're looking for me."

"Who? The police?"

"No. Well maybe," Ethan said. "I don't know. The guy. This gang or whatever, I guess."

"Nobody's tapping your line, you idiot," Sam said, then laughed. "What the hell is wrong with you?"

"I don't know. I'm not thinking straight. Do you know something about this?"

"Maybe, the—"

"Does Hugo know where you live?"

"No."

"Good. Look, I'll talk to you soon. Don't go over there, and don't talk to Hugo."

Ethan hung up without saying goodbye.

## 13

Wynne Duncan had been delivering bags of cash to Jack Struhl for more than three years. During that time, Wynne had developed a sincere hope that the eccentric little weirdo would die. Dumped in the ocean somewhere. Eaten by starved animals. Wynne would've liked to have done it himself—the feeding, not the eating—but he was certain time and fate would have their way and save him the trouble.

Struhl's behaviour was becoming increasingly unpredictable: he was disappearing for a week or more at a time, cutting off old associations, harbouring unexpected new ones, and taking too long to pay his debts.

Usually, Wynne met Struhl in a small but lavish suite high in a tower in downtown Vancouver, overlooking English Bay. On bag day, Wynne would park in the underground garage and ride the elevator skyward to the twenty-third floor, accessible only by key card or appointment. The entire floor was owned and operated by Winston Carmello, Struhl's superior and de facto leader of the loose organization to which Wynne and Jack Struhl both belonged.

After being directed to a room by the receptionist, Wynne would find Struhl, alone, sitting in an armchair and smoking a cigarette. After taking the bag from Wynne, Struhl would call the receptionist, and soon a woman—or sometimes two—would visit the suite and Wynne would leave.

Today, however, Wynne sat on a faded brown sofa in the living room of a dilapidated bungalow. This was the first time Wynne had been to Struhl's most recent abode: Struhl shifted residences at an alarming rate, even for a man of his occupation.

This place was a dump.

Bags of garbage sat around like lazy, overfed children. Flies zigged a little too comfortably, zagged like they owned the place. It smelled faintly of dog shit and fish, and though Wynne didn't actually see any coils or turds, it was safe to say one of the four or five mutts scrambling about the yard had taken a recent dump somewhere inside the house.

Things were different this time. For one thing, there was no bag to bring. Its carrier was dead in an alley with two holes in his face. Instead, Wynne delivered only bad news.

Jack Struhl entered the living room, trailed by two drooling mongrels and a wobbling basset hound. Both mongrels—Rottweilers mixed seemingly with every other breed—sniffed Wynne's legs, hands, and crotch before turning away and coming to rest at the foot of a tattered leather recliner.

The basset hound chased its tail, barked at its own ass, then walked headlong into a leg of the coffee table. Struhl picked the hound up and tucked it under one arm like a senseless flopping football.

Skinny and ill-tempered like a malfunctioning weed whacker—all untimely whips and lashes—Struhl looked like some kind of nightmare stick insect: a long, bony thorax attached to arms and legs that resembled probing antennae. He lowered himself into the chair across from Wynne and set the basset hound in his lap. A tongue too long for even a dog dangled out of the animal's mouth and piled on Struhl's knee.

Wynne gave an up nod, pointed at the hound, raised an inquisitive eyebrow.

The dog sounded the short, whimpering howl of the mentally bereft.

"No teeth, glaucomic, and brain damaged," Struhl said. "You have a dog?"

Wynne shook his head.

"The mark of a good man is if animals like him, and if he likes them," Struhl said. "Dogs in particular. I've got no truck with cats. Anything else, really."

Wynne nodded.

"Mark of a good man's if dogs like him," Struhl repeated. "Same with society. Mark of a good society's how it treats its dogs? You know?"

Wynne nodded.

"This society's no good, is what I'm saying. Understand? This dog? Doesn't know whether to shit or go blind. Somebody beat it. Helpless little dog. What kind of society is that?" Struhl picked up the hound in one bony hand and displayed it to Wynne. Its tongue flopped hopelessly.

Wynne shrugged. He wished Struhl would get on with it so he could go about taking more painkillers and napping in the dark.

"A man can't buy an ounce of weed or cocaine or any other thing legally—which is fine for me and my finances—but can go buy a dog for the same price, hang it by its legs, and beat it with a broom handle. How's that for sense?"

Wynne shook his head.

"You're not saying much," Struhl said, setting the dog back on the floor.

"Meh jaw."

"Your jaw? Where's my money?"

Wynne shrugged.

"The problem is we have the wrong type of guy on the street," Struhl said, petting the hound. "What was his name? This guy who lost the bag?"

"Shymon."

"Shymon? What the fuck kind of name is that?"

"Suh-EYE-mun."

"Simon? Who hired him?"

Wynne shrugged.

"Was it you?"

Wynne nodded reluctantly.

Simon had shown initiative, brought in new business, had never been late or short with cash. As a reward, Wynne had set him up with a car and put him on collection duty, sending him round to receive payment from Struhl's most reliable distributors. More recently, he'd entrusted him with moving more valuable drugs than weed: powders and pills of all variety. Pick up the cash. Stick it in the bag. Put it in the trunk. Drive the speed limit. Put the cash in the safe at Corleone's and wait for Wynne to arrive.

Things don't always go according to plan. Two bullets in the face for Simon, and a bat across the head for Wynne.

Struhl gave Wynne a hard look. Struhl's cheeks were sunken and his eyes were hollow and heavy. He had his usual unkempt scruff on his cheeks and there was a pen tucked behind his ear. Wynne wasn't sure what was wrong with Struhl; as far as Wynne knew, Struhl neither drank nor took hard drugs. It was probably because he was a vegetarian—a worthless affectation, in Wynne's opinion, that achieved little other than a sickly pallor and weak constitution.

"You think Troy or Rowan shot him and took it?" Struhl asked.

Wynne shook his head. "They were wif me."

Rowan, the driver from the incident on Maple Avenue, was dumb, but not quite enough. Plus, he'd been at The Pink Curtain, a Carmello-owned strip club on the East Side, with Wynne the night Simon was shot, as had Troy, who was none too pleased with the fractured ankle he had suffered in the getaway.

"So, the two deadbeats you're looking for have it?" Struhl said.

"Says Omar," Wynne said through a clenched jaw. Earlier, a doctor of questionable ethics but reasonable reliability had told him the jaw wasn't broken. But it sure felt like it. "Saw em walkin through th'alley."

"What're their names?"

"Leash on th'apartment belongs to Mashoud Ebrahim," Wynne muttered. "So shays the buildin manger."

Truth was, Wynne had no idea if the two deadbeats in question had the money or not. But it was his best current guess.

The whole thing had been fucked from the get-go, made worse by two failed attempts to get the cash back from this Massoud Ebrahim and his partner, whom Wynne had KO'd. Now that Wynne thought of it, neither of them had looked particularly like a Massoud Ebrahim. And he still couldn't believe the first man he'd sent had gone into the wrong apartment and knifed a bystander.

As for Simon's body, it had been found behind Corleone's, a dollar-fifty-a-slice pizza place cum laundering facility Struhl owned. Corleone's was also where Wynne brought weed and cocaine to other street scum for distribution, and where he was supposed to have met Simon the morning he was shot. One of Corleone's dough-tossing lackeys, Omar, had recognized the two deadbeats walking out of the alley: the deadbeats also happened to frequent the pizza shop. Omar told Wynne what he saw, and the rest was recent history.

"The cash wasn't in their apartment?" Struhl asked.

Wynne shook his head.

"You know what I'm gonna say next?" Struhl said.

Wynne nodded.

"So?" Struhl said.

"Shymon shouldna hah de money."

"Exactly. So?"

"He fuck up."

"That's right, *he* fucked up," Struhl said. "And the money's gone."

"I'll fine it," Wynne said.

"Could be anywhere."

"I'll fine it."

"If you don't, Carmello's cut comes out of your pocket, not mine."

Wynne nodded.

The hound crooned sorrowfully.

## 14

Having finished his meal, Ethan lamented that Taco Bell was somehow tastier in the States. Maybe it was something to do with beef regulations. Or MSG. Or that they had those Tater Tots there.

He stared blankly out the windshield, smoking a bent cigarette he'd found in the handle of the door, taking long, slow drags and letting the smoke settle about him in a stale fug.

On the sidewalk in front of him an obese couple waddled past a lidless garbage bin and a rotating sign. Man and woman alike wore grey tracksuits with the manufacturer's logo crested boldly on the front, a hefty grey rhinoceros. Both man and woman had obscenely large, hooked noses.

Gluttony knows no borders, Ethan thought.

He contemplated his predicament. He could not return to the apartment. He was certain the muscled gorilla could not have appreciated taking an aluminum bat across the face, neither could his colleague have enjoyed being run over by an aged Pontiac. They would not let the incident pass lightly.

Could the police put him in witness protection? Did that exist in Canada? With all the cop shows, gangster movies, and crime books he'd read, Ethan assumed he'd be able to work his way out of this conundrum all on his own. Maybe not so much.

With no job lined up for the coming week, or any week for that matter, funds were at an all-time low. Eight days ago a temp agency had placed him at a car door assembly plant, but he'd stopped showing up after only the second day—his spirit had crumbled under the weight of a ninety minute commute on public transit, followed by an existentially monotonous workday.

For the time being, all that there was to do was get high.

Ethan popped open the glove box and dug inside, hoping to find a joint, or at least the remnants thereof. Car insurance, three dead lighters, a geologically ancient condom, two ketchup packets, a photo of what was presumably Phil's family (without Phil), and a pen from The Pink Curtain strip club. But no weed.

Ethan continued his search in the compartments of the doors, the cup holders, the coils in the car's built-in lighter, behind the sun visor, under the floor mats, between the cushions of the back seat, and under the . . . pay dirt. A small polyethylene sandwich bag of bone-dry buds stashed and forgotten beneath the passenger seat.

Ethan quickly spun up a thin joint. He lit it, then tilted back into a semi-supine—and fully oblivious—position in the driver's seat.

After a few long, deep inhales, his dilemma dissipated into the thickening cloud swirling about him in the cabin.

On the passenger seat, peaking out of his jacket pocket, was the copy of *Cheap Thrills*, with its female victim and shadowy criminal on the cover. Ethan picked it up and flipped open to the earmarked page at which he'd last stopped reading.

Grunt Rutherford sat in his office with Darla Carmine, who was now explaining the details of the murder she was extorting him to solve. She'd sweetened the extortion pot by offering a reward for Grunt's cooperation:

> "I see you consider me a dog, Mrs. Carmine. Rewarded for performing a trick, punished for bad behaviour."

"Considering men animals has been an effective philosophy for me, Mr. Rutherford. Women, too, for that matter. So, do you accept my offer, or should I get on the phone to Montreal?"

I begrudgingly accepted, and Darla explained the situation at hand.

Darla's husband, Hillcoat Carmine, had gone missing three weeks prior. The small fishing boat Hillcoat used to smuggle drugs into the U.S. had been discovered washed up on shore outside of Port Angeles, Washington, covered in copious amounts of blood. Hillcoat was performing a rare run on his own—a mule had been busted at the last minute—and someone had taken advantage of Hillcoat's vulnerability. My job was to find out who had killed Hillcoat Carmine: his associates on the Canadian side of the border, or his buyers in the States.

Hillcoat had enemies in all corners of God's creation, Darla said calmly, and had most likely died suffering, to the great pleasure of his executioners. Her tone and demeanor led me to wonder aloud why she cared at all to find out who had killed him.

"I've got leverage on this," Darla said plainly.

"From what angle?"

Darla gave the impression that she'd never had a pure motive in her life. If she wanted to know who had murdered her husband, it wasn't just for emotional closure.

"Important people are angry about an effective businessman being dismissed without their consultation. It would be to my benefit, and my children's, if these important people knew we were on their side."

"I thought everybody hated him."

"They did. He was ruthless, rude, and was continually fucking people's wives and daughters. He stole, lied, and had people killed who didn't deserve it. But so what?"

"Good point," I said.

"He made many people a lot of money, Mr. Rutherford—"

"Grunt's fine," I said. No need to be formal, what with the extortion and all.

"Until that recent bust, none of his deals had been intercepted. Unheard of in this business," Darla said.

"All by boat?"

"Not usually, no. By cattle."

"He delivered marijuana by cattle?"

"*In* cattle, to be precise," Darla said.

"How much do people pay for weed that's been up the ass of a cow?"

"The insertion method wasn't so crude. And they pay plenty, in cash or cocaine," Darla said.

She leaned forward. I kept my eyes up as best as I could but wasn't about to win an award for it.

"I don't have to remind you about the sensitivity of this information, do I, Mr. Rutherford?" Darla said.

"Grunt will do. And no. This isn't my first cross-border intra-bovine smuggling operation."

It was.

"Where did the beef go, though?" I asked. "Did they just dump it?"

"No, my husband was too efficient for that. The receiving end of the operation was a slaughterhouse. The beef ended up in someone's takeout combo, I'm sure."

Ethan closed the book and considered the beef tacos he had just scarfed down.

Outside, the pair of obese rhinoceros exited the Taco Bell, each carrying a bulging brown paper sack. The male of the pair was cramming a rolled carpet of Tres Cheezy Beefy Burrito into his mouth, while his female companion made indelicate adjustments to her tarp-sized sweatpants.

The Tres Cheezy Beefy Burrito was Ethan's favourite, and if he had been thinking clearly he would have ordered one himself.

The squawk of a ringtone through cheaply made speakers interrupted his thoughts.

Ethan dug his phone out of his pocket and checked the caller ID. An unknown number. He let it ring four times before deciding to answer.

"Hello?" he said.

"Is this Mr. Blaise? Ethan Blaise?" A female voice.

"Who's this?" Ethan said.

"This is Detective Woit of the Vancouver Police Department. Ethan, where are you?"

Ethan remained silent.

"Last week you introduced yourself as Massoud Ebrahim. You misrepresented yourself to us, Ethan."

"I wasn't thinking straight," Ethan said. "How'd you find me?"

"It's not hard for us to learn who's paying the bills on phone numbers, Ethan. Or in your case, not paying them."

"What happened to Phil?" Ethan asked.

"Phil Wilford is in hospital," Woit said.

"How is he?"

"Your friend is seriously injured. We know there were others involved. Several witnesses saw a man fire a gun into the underground garage, then two cars flee at high speed. We need you to come in and talk to us."

"You'll arrest me," Ethan protested.

"What have you done? What would we arrest you for?"

Ethan paused.

"For anything," he said. "I'm sure you'll find a reason. It's what you do."

"We have no reason to arrest you right now, Ethan. We just want you safe. We have a good idea who you've become involved with here, and believe me, you're in over your head."

More silence on Ethan's part.

"Where are you now, Ethan?" Woit asked again.

"I'm out of town already," Ethan said.

"Where are you staying?"

Ethan hung up.

## 15

Emma pulled her forest-green Range Rover up the Woodgrave household's long, snaking driveway, bordered on each side by a line of tall alders standing guard over the property like soldiers at attention. Between the trees, short faux street lamps lit the driveway in the evening darkness.

The home was a modern West Coast design featuring straight lines and an unassuming façade, its more impressive features—floor-to-ceiling windows, cedar finishings, an infinity pool—saved for the back and the view of the bay. Tonight it was dark save for one light shining above the front door.

The Range Rover crunched over the loose limestone that comprised the driveway, then came to a halt in front of the attached three-car garage. Emma pressed the button opener built into the dash and watched the garage door rise.

As the door opened, the Range Rover's headlamps lit the rear of her father's silver Jag. Strange, Emma thought. Her father wasn't supposed to be home. He had said he was going to some function downtown.

Emma wasn't supposed to be home either. She was supposed to be spending the night at a friend's place. But after leaving Phil and Ethan's, she'd arrived at Jenny Nan's only to find her friend passed out on a dose of Mrs. Nan's Valium. Emma had arranged her unconscious friend on the sofa as demurely as she could, called Jenny's boyfriend, and left.

Emma, however, still needed someone to talk to. Since Jenny had been in no condition for anything save drooling catatonically onto the couch through a slight smile, Emma instead met another friend for sushi. They grazed on a variety of inauthentic rolls and a platter of tempura vegetables while Emma detailed her afternoon: fucking Ethan—described to her friend as "stupid, but like a well-meaning Labrador"—and Phil's unusual and surly departure.

After dinner, while driving across the bridge over the inlet from downtown, Emma had started to appreciate the solitude promised by the evening alone she was now expecting. With her younger sister at a sleepover, her stepmother not returning from

Ontario until tomorrow, and her dad at a function, Emma would have the Woodgrave household to herself for the first time in as long as she could remember.

No such luck. Dad was home early for some reason or other, as evidenced by his car now parked in the garage. Emma backed away from the Jaguar, circled the roundabout driveway that surrounded a grassy island, then parked off to the side, leaving a spot in the garage for her stepmom.

Emma took her gym bag from the passenger seat, then beeped the car locked and walked into the garage, dropping her bag on a shelf with a collection of other sports equipment.

She stopped in her tracks. On the far side of her Dad's Jaguar, gleaming like a rare gem in a jeweller's gift box, sat the newest Q-Series EarthR, in green. She'd asked for the Q-Series for her birthday, but instead, a year ago next Sunday, Emma had woken to find a brand new Range Rover parked in the driveway.

When her father removed his hands from her eyes that birthday morning, Emma's first thought had been, What kind of self-ish, earth-loathing idiot drives a gas-guzzling tank like this? Daddy, as usual, knew best—the Range Rover was a safer vehicle, higher off the ground, a solid build.

Now, as Emma appreciated the curves of the little electric coupe sitting in the garage, she cursed aloud:

"Holy shit. He actually bought me one."

Material bliss pulled the corners of her mouth into a smile, put a hop into her step that sent her bolting into the laundry room—and into a chorus of grunts and slaps as Eric Woodgrave, hunched like a fevered dog in the park, his bald head gleaming with sweat, diligently worked at a long-legged redhead bent over the washing machine.

The redhead yelped. Emma's father grunted.

Emma retreated through the garage, leaving the door open behind her. She stopped in the driveway, disgusted. Thinking she might vomit, she bent over, leaned on her knees and took three deep breaths, her body rigid in expectation of her father running out after her, ready with some worthless explanation, breathless himself from his unspeakable rigors in the laundry room.

When her father didn't appear, Emma ran back to her car and drove off into the night.

## 16

Softwood Lumber's "This Ain't CanCon, This Is For Real" bumped Ethan out of a deep sleep. An imprinted crescent of steering wheel arced across his forehead. The copy of *Cheap Thrills* fell to the floor as Ethan looked around for the source of the tinny bass that reminded him he should really upgrade his phone: Carl Correct, aka The Bidness, sounded like a drive-thru speaker.

Softwood Lumber was low on Ethan's list of favourite hip-hop groups, but there was something about the bass line of "CanCon" that made him want to hear it every time his phone rang, which was about once a week.

Today was a bit busier. Ethan's usual routine had been rudely interrupted by unexpected violence. It was a thing out of a Hollywood movie: spilled blood, gunshots, car chases. Missing money and drugs. Calls from the police. Taco Bell. It was all too much for Ethan, particularly because it really shouldn't have had anything to do with him at all.

Ethan finally found his phone on the floor beside him, inside an empty fast food bag along with a couple of greasy taco wrappers and several squirts of hot sauce. He pulled the phone out, wiped it on his pants, and answered:

"Yeah?"

"Ethan?"

"Yeah?"

"It's Sam. Are you all right?"

"Yeah, I think so."

Ethan looked at his hands and legs, then pulled down the sun visor to check his nose. It was dark out and he couldn't tell for looking. He gave it a poke. A wave of pain pushed through his head.

"Mostly," he said.

"Where are you?" Sam asked.

Outside, an "Open Late" sign lit the hood of his car.

"The Taco Bell parking lot."

"Still?"

"Yeah."

"Don't you have anywhere to go?"

Ethan thought about it.

"No. Not really."

"Come here."

"Yeah?"

"Yeah. I'll text you my address, all right?"

"Okay."

With evening descending, traffic was sparse, and the drive to Sam's was interrupted only by a stop for gas and coffee.

Ethan parked the Pontiac in front of Sam's place, a well-kept '60s-built home, all brick and shine and lush green grass. Under the light of a street lamp he inspected the Pontiac for damage from the getaway. Getaway, he thought. Like straight out of a Grave novel, Grunt Rutherford in over his head, speeding away from angry gangsters and cops on the take.

The mirror on the passenger side of the Pontiac was folded in, something Ethan hadn't noticed on the drive to and from Langley. He flipped it back out. The mirror was broken.

He circled to the front. The thick plastic casing of the driver's side headlamp was cracked, though the light itself had worked on the drive back into town. And part of the cheap plastic grill was smashed out. He'd been lucky. Regardless of how soon he went to the cops, he didn't need the attention of a shot-out windshield in a car that wasn't his.

Finished with his inspection, Ethan approached the short iron fence and gate protecting the front of Sam's house. A lamp by the door lit the front of the house and its small veranda. A swinging bench hung from the ceiling. Lovely, Ethan thought. His childhood had included no idyllic swinging benches. The last home his family had shared as a nuclear unit was a two-bedroom apartment in Etobicoke, the second bedroom shared by Ethan and his sister, Carolyn. Looking at Sam's place brought him back to that worn little apartment: Ethan and Carolyn on twin beds in the second bedroom, Carolyn designing dresses in Crayon on scrap their father brought home from the paper packaging plant, Ethan reading comics from the library then drawing his own on scrap too.

The heavy wooden door was painted bright baby blue to match the faux shutters of the windows on the front porch. A weighty brass knocker hung from the middle of the door. Ethan pounded it twice, and the slightly ajar door swung open. Ethan leaned in and called Sam's name, to no answer, then stepped inside.

In the front hall a carpeted staircase with a white wooden handrail led to the second floor. Hanging on the wall of the entrance and continuing up the stairs were a series of framed photos displaying Sam and, unmistakeably, her siblings, together and individually at various times in their lives. In the middle of the bunch was a photo framed in black and laid on white matte, a recent portrait of the whole family dressed in white and sitting along the white rail of a veranda. The background, judging from the rugged shoreline and chopped water, was some untamed portion of the BC coast. The whole family wore beatific smiles and were resting their hands on each other lovingly.

At first glance Ethan thought they had forgotten to switch out the stock photo that came with the frame. As he examined the portrait for signs of PhotoShop, Sam appeared on the landing of the staircase, dressed in her usual varsity athletic garb.

"Looks like we're waiting for the flying saucer, huh?" Sam said.

"I was going to say cult leader. But same difference, really."

"Spot on, actually. My dad's friend is a photographer. The whole thing was his idea. We're all smiling because we were laughing about how ridiculous we looked," Sam said.

"Well, there you go. I was wondering how a whole family could be so happy at the same time," Ethan said.

"By accident," Sam said.

"Or misinformation."

Before Ethan even had his shoes off, Sam pulled the day's story out of him: the gorilla, the car chase, the cops, the unknown condition of Phil, the Taco Bell. The body of Simon. That last one registered something on Sam's face.

"You know that guy, don't you?" Ethan said. "You made on the phone like you'd heard of him. And at lunch yesterday."

Sam nodded. She invited Ethan into the kitchen and they each took a stool at the granite island. An open textbook, a rolled joint, and a ball of fur the size and colour of a championship pumpkin sat on the counter. The pumpkin uncurled itself and meowed.

Sam picked up a joint and lit it. She took a drag, passed the joint to Ethan, then hoisted the globular feline to the ground. It trundled away, sweeping the blue tiles of the kitchen floor with its dangling gut.

"What's the deal with that thing?" Ethan asked.

"That's Darwin."

"I've never seen a cat that big in my life."

"She's got a weight problem."

"I'll say."

"She's actually lost a few pounds since I adopted her," Sam said.

Ethan contemplated the physics of a larger Darwin.

"I don't see this as being possible," he said.

"Her last people fed her nothing but cereal." Sam blew a thick smoke ring that hovered over the island. Ethan attempted to blow his own. A glop of spit broke his ring and wet the table.

"Like cat cereal?" Ethan said.

"No, like fucking Fruit Loops."

"You can live off Fruit Loops?"

"Barely. She's diabetic."

"I didn't know a cat could be diabetic," Ethan said.

"She gets insulin every day."

"With like a needle?"

"Yeah, with a needle. How else is she supposed to get it?"

"I don't know. Who knew a cat could get diabetes?"

"Anybody would get diabetes if all they ate was Fruit Loops!"

"I suppose this is true," Ethan admitted.

Ethan watched Darwin settle down over a heating vent. Her paws barely reached the floor. Food crumbs or some other detritus clung to her fur. Ethan was reminded of Hugo, the sloth.

"So, Sloth—" Ethan said, getting to the point.

"Hugo."

"Sure. Hugo knew Simon?"

"Yeah," Sam said. "I've met Simon. He works for the same guy as Hugo. He used to come by just to hang out or whatever. Smoke weed. But recently, it was different. He'd be the guy bringing Hugo the supply."

"How much?" Ethan asked.

"Maybe just like a week's worth? He'd collect the money, too."

"A lot?"

Sam shook her head. "I don't know. But if I ever sold any, you know, while I was hanging out, I just handed the cash straight to Hugo and never saw it again."

"Simon was collecting the money?" Ethan asked.

"Recently, yeah."

"For who?"

"Hugo's boss."

"Who's he?"

"I don't know," Sam said. "This big guy."

"Like a gorilla? Bald, big-ass muscles, tattoos?"

"Yeah, that sounds like him. Well, I don't know about the gorilla part, but otherwise."

"Tattoo of Jesus on his shoulder?" Ethan tried to remember which shoulder the goofy smiling Jesus was on but figured it didn't really matter. If she'd seen it, she would know.

She had.

"Do you know his name?"

Sam thought about it.

"Yeah, it was Wynne," she said. "Hugo talks about him now and again."

"Have you talked to Hugo lately?"

"No. Well, he's called me, but I haven't gone over there. I'm not—he's been talking like something's up, and now you're saying all this. I don't want anything to do with this anymore," she said, shaking her head.

"For whatever reason, this Wynne thinks Phil and I have that bag. Simon's bag. I don't want anything to do with it either."

"Simon was supposed to come by with more weed the day you and Phil were over, but he never showed up. He'd picked up cash from Hugo the night before. More than usual. And he was supposed to come back, but he never did."

"What'd Hugo say?"

"Nothing. I was surprised he wasn't pissed off about it."

Sam stubbed the joint out in a coffee cup.

"Your parents don't mind you smoking weed in the house?" Ethan asked.

"No," Sam said. "Well, not with my sisters around. But the family's gone for the week. Visiting my grandma up the coast."

"Where about?"

"Up Haida Gwaii, actually."

"Aren't you Chinese?" Ethan said.

"Are you autistic?" Sam said.

"What?"

"Nothing. I'm Haida. My grandmother's Haida. She does community work on the islands now."

"So nobody's home?"

"Just me," Sam said.

Ethan tried to think of something witty to say.

"Want to have sex?" he said.

Sam stared at him blankly for a moment.

"No," she said.

"Oh," Ethan said. "Should I leave?"

"You have somewhere to go?"

"Not really."

"Then you can crash here."

Ethan entered Sam's room and completely forgot about sex. A nightmare of fauna covered the walls: a wingless and frightened anorexic bat; a long-clawed groundhog with a nose like a gunshot wound; an albino lobster wearing a furry winter coat. Ethan looked closer at the posters for evidence of computer manipulation. All were horribly real. More animals lined the other walls: a slimy phallic tuber and a loose-tongued, mentally deranged bear.

For the first time in his life, Ethan would've been happy to see photos of pets dressed like humans, playing poker.

Ethan puffed his chest. "'I have reached the mountains of madness,'" he said, waving his hand across the room, "'and looking out over the accursed ultimate abyss, I cannot help feeling these are evil things.'" He finished, arm held high, staring at her through his best expression of gravity.

"What?"

"H. P. Lovecraft."

"Who?"

"These things are seriously ugly."

"They're beautiful."

"You're beautiful."

"Don't be corny."

"Why would such a splendid creature as you choose to surround herself with evolution's failed experiments? Creatures left in the garage to gather dust? Stuffed under boxes of old newspapers and sports equipment?"

"They're here just the same as we are. I don't see how they've failed," Sam said.

"Who's running this show?" Ethan asked, then pointed at the horrible lobster thing. "That freak? Or *Homo sapiens*? How many of those things can there be?"

"There are more beetles and rats than people, you know. Maybe they're running this show."

"Not likely."

"If you go back far enough, we're all the same, anyway," Sam said, clearing her bed of textbooks and clothes.

"I refuse to believe I'm related to that thing in any way. My family is of blue blood."

Sam pulled the twisted sheet and blanket from her single bed, shook them out, laid them down again.

"You can sleep here," she said, pointing at the bed. "I'll sleep in my sister's room."

"I could just sleep on the couch. Or in your sister's room. Or with—"

"No, that's fine. I don't think my sister would appreciate a stranger in her bed. But then again, you aren't much more than a stranger to me either, I guess."

"Well, I'm insulted," Ethan said, feigning offence.

"We met yesterday," Sam said.

"Bah, our souls know no calendar."

As Ethan took his jacket off, the copy of *Cheap Thrills* fell from his inside pocket and onto the floor. Sam picked it up.

"Thelonious Grave," she said, reading the cover. "Hugo's got a pile of this guy's books."

"Hugo can read?"

Sam tossed the book at Ethan.

"I read one of these once, when I had nothing to do at Hugo's place. *Prisoner's Dilemma*, I think. Not exactly Shakespeare. And every woman has huge boobs stuffed into a tight dress. I've never read so many descriptions of a woman's ass in my life. Male fantasy stuff, basically, right?"

"Uh, sure," Ethan said. He hadn't really thought about it that way.

## 17

While Ethan lay in her bed, Sam went downstairs and tidied the kitchen. She washed a few pots and pans and loaded the dishwasher, then gathered the marijuana, papers, and ends of joints from the table.

Sam had been around weed most of her life. Her father told stories of growing and selling in his youth, and still smoked the occasional joint on the deck with old friends. But the situation with Ethan and Hugo was of another order entirely.

Sam had assumed Hugo's tough act was just that, but with the recent stories Hugo had mentioned, she was starting to believe violence was encroaching far too closely on her own life. Simon wasn't selling only weed any more, and he had been carrying a lot more cash. They wanted Hugo to start selling cocaine, opioids, meth. So far Hugo had been able to refuse.

Finished with the cleaning, Sam gathered Darwin's insulin syringe from a drawer by the sink. She scooped up the orange ball of fur and settled into an armchair to inject the feline with her nightly shot.

Sam didn't really think anymore about how fat Darwin was; she only loved her. As frequently as she reminded herself that, though intelligent and uniquely conscious, animals were not humans, she still looked at them as equals.

Holding the blubbery heft of Darwin reminded Sam of her goal: her own veterinary practice. At twenty-one, she was well on her way. She had achieved excellent grades in high school and through her first two years of university. She volunteered extensively at local animal hospitals, the SPCA, and other animal welfare organizations. Once this year was finished, she would continue to take courses specific to animal biology and medicine, and focus significantly on preparing for the MCAT, a prerequisite for veterinary school. She knew her grades weren't quite Cornell material, but California-Davis or Colorado State would keep her closer to home, anyway.

Beyond that, she envisioned a home with acreage outside the city. Two horses and numerous dogs and cats. This image of herself at, say, thirty—after school and internships—included a man to live and travel with, husband or not, but no children. The happy vision of life she had created for herself simply did not include them.

She finished with the shot and let Darwin off her lap. The cat scampered across the floor, investigated her empty food dish, then lay down in her usual spot over a heating vent in the living room.

After tonight, no more Hugo, Sam decided. And no more Ethan either.

## 18

This was not how he had envisioned things.

Even as a young man, Eric Woodgrave's interminably smiling mind had assured him that he would be successful. That he would be vastly wealthy and own many expensive cars. That he would own a large house and have enough money to allow his family the best in vacations, hobbies, and private schooling options.

Beyond money, he envisioned a version of power and prestige. He would be a leader and men—somehow it had never occurred to him that he would work with and employ women, or that if he did mixing business with pleasure would be inadvisable.

This lack of foresight was responsible for significant fallout. Eric Woodgrave was now on his fourth marriage.

Having just watched his daughter speed away from his infidelity, Eric stood in his driveway, as forlornly as he was capable, a chemically ensured erection pointing south over his property, a mostly open women's bathrobe baring his hairless chest to the cool night air.

When his daughter had burst into the laundry room, Eric's lust-swamped mind had blocked her out. It was Jennifer Arensberg's second scream that had alerted him to the catastrophe. By the time he had found something to cover himself with his daughter was peeling down the driveway and Jennifer Arensberg was retrieving her clothes from the floor and cursing up a hurricane.

I've married four times, Eric thought as he scrambled out of the garage in pursuit of his fleeing daughter. I can't do it again.

Eric's first wife, Ula Wilhem, having tired of his wandering eye and other organs, left him in 1983, taking their firstborn son back to her mother's in Holland. The son was now some sort of conceptual artist who, according to his website, created "installations to counter the capital-industrial simulacrum." Eric hadn't spoken to his son in eleven years.

Eric's second wife, Isabella Caliez, a Honduran accountant he'd met in 1985, was the one he was certain he would spend his life with. Except he hadn't. Eric's indefatigable upbeat demeanor could be a bit much to handle for some people, particularly when its object was you, and you had just caught your husband sodomizing—well, anyone, really and anywhere you could possibly fit two consenting sodomy participants.

So that was the end of Isabella.

Luckily for Eric, it wasn't until after the divorce from Isabella that his income really started to explode. He started his own firm, and it grew to be the largest real estate law firm in the province.

Things went well for Eric over the next ten years, halfway through which he met his third wife, Katelyn Wiebber, a marketer for an exponentially growing Seattle-based coffee chain. They had two children together: Samantha Emma, and Charlotte Sally. Eric and Katelyn had maintained a relatively healthy marriage until the day Katelyn fully realized she had married a man more than twice her age. The progeny of Texan oil wealth, Katelyn didn't have to worry about money. She left of her own accord and with little ugliness.

Eric wasn't surprised: the marriage had always felt a bit too good to be true.

He retained a relationship with his children and their mother; and then, eight years later, at age fourteen, Samantha Emma moved back to Vancouver to live with her father and attend a private Catholic high school, just like her older brother had.

She adjusted to life in Vancouver well, aside from a few typical teenaged rebellions, including a new insistence that she be called by her middle name—there were too many Sams in her class, she argued.

Life was again righting itself.

Samantha Emma's nominal Catholicism provided Eric with his fourth wife, Linda Kennedy, a divorced lawyer from Toronto on fragile terms with her two adult children, and with three failed marriages of her own. Eric and Linda met in church on a rainy Sunday in November barely more than a year ago.

As he stood in the drive, lamenting the errors of his life and formulating an explanation for Linda, a few lonely drops of rain struck Eric on the shoulder. A quick gust rustled the leaves of the alders behind him and blew the skirt of his robe around his knees.

Linda deserves better, Eric thought. He'd slipped. But only once! he reminded himself. Only once. He'd been a saint, so far. And he'd been relatively faithful with Katelyn as well, as far as he could remember. Only once, he told himself. Maybe he could explain that to his daughter and she would keep quiet. I drank too much at the function, Sammy, and I screwed up. And maybe that doesn't make it much better, but it was only the once. Okay?

Maybe that'd work.

Well, it was twice, really. Three times depending on how you defined it. But this was only the second woman, so . . .

Behind him a car door opened and closed.

Jennifer Arensberg's Q-Series backed out of the garage, paused just long enough for its driver to flip Eric a severe and fluttering bird, then purred off down the driveway.

As if protecting himself from the gesture, Eric pulled his wife's lotus-print silk bathrobe closed across his chest. He watched the tail lights of Jennifer's car disappear into the distance. It's a nice car, Eric thought. He should've bought one for Emma on her seventeenth birthday. She'd been weird about the Range Rover from the get-go. He already had a birthday present upstairs for next week's party—a family trip to Disneyland and a Murbury watch—but another gift certainly couldn't make the situation any worse.

Eric Woodgrave decided it would be best to go inside and start pricing BMWs on the internet.

## 19

Emma's first thought was to call Linda and tell her what, or more accurately who, she had just found her father doing. But as she sat in her Range Rover outside Phil and Ethan's building, mentally drafting obscenity-laced tirades to be hurled at her father, she let the idea pass.

Emma considered her stepmother a wilful and confident woman who would be packed and out the door before her father got halfway through his explanation. It was entirely possible she wouldn't even return from her trip to Ontario at all.

Emma admitted to herself that she hadn't called Linda yet because she was so sure of what her stepmother would do. She knew this was selfish, but didn't want to lose Linda from her life. Instead, Emma called Phil, of all people, who wasn't bothering to answer his phone. Emma turned her car off, pulled the key from the ignition, and went to disturb Phil and Ethan in person.

She looked up at the apartment building, its need of a paint job apparent even in the dim evening streetlight. A plastic tricycle lay toppled in the center of the lawn, as if its rider had run off in search of a better neighbourhood to play in. Jeans and a jacket hung from a third-floor balcony like reconsidering suicides. On the front step, a man sat folded over his own legs, occasionally lifting a cigarette to his hidden mouth, his arm otherwise dangling morosely.

Emma made her way upstairs to the apartment. She fully expected to find one or both roommates chronically reposed on the sofa, engaged in video games or sports or insulting each other, their own tandem stand-up routine.

Instead, police tape crossed the doorframe.

Confused and surprised, Emma knocked on the door anyway, then tried her key. It no longer worked. Emma's first thought was that Phil, having learned about her afternoon with Ethan, had wigged out and done violence to Ethan's head. Which, now that she thought about it, had some really weird, like, indentations to begin with. Malformations? A definite oblong-ness.

On the way out of the building, as she passed the stoop man, now fully asleep, the cigarette burnt to its filter but still tucked between two fingers, her phone rang. She slipped it out of her pocket and checked the caller ID. Ethan, again. She dismissed the call. Boning him had really been a mistake.

When Emma had first met Phil, she'd assumed he would possess a maturity not found in men nearer her own age. She was wrong. Doubly wrong with Oblong Head Guy.

Emma climbed into her Range Rover. If Phil wouldn't answer, then maybe she could get some info out of Ethan. She pushed his missed call, tucked her cell phone between her ear and shoulder, then dug into her purse for a weed grinder and some rolling papers. A joint would settle her nerves, she reasoned, help her forget about Dad and some fire-patched, condo-pushing whore in the laundry room.

It rang. Ethan answered.

"Hey," he said, "I've been trying to get a hold of you."

"I've been busy," Emma said.

"With what?"

"Stuff."

"What kind of stuff?" Ethan said.

"What is this? A cross-examination? I'm the one who's going to be a lawyer, remember? You're the hopeless loser."

"Great," Ethan said. "That's just wonderful. Where are you?"

"I'm outside your place. Where are you guys? Should I go in? What's with the police tape across the door?"

"Why would you go in if nobody's there and there's police tape across the door?"

"I don't know. How should I know what you two doofuses get up to for kicks?"

"Fuck," Ethan said. "Listen, some big, thick gorilla came by looking for me and Phil—"

"A gorilla?"

"Not literally a gorilla. A big meathead dude. Came looking for a bag he thought we had. Anyway, we don't. Or I don't. Pretty sure Phil didn't, but the guy fucked him up—"

"What do you mean 'fucked him up'?"

"Punched him out. Phil hit his head. He's in the hospital."

"What?" Emma said. "Which one?"

"I'm not sure. VGH, I think. I don't know."

"Where are you?" Emma asked.

"I'm at a friend's place."

"Where?"

"What does it matter?"

"I guess it doesn't," Emma said.

"Yeah. Look, I have to go. I just wanted to tell you to stay away from our place, even if Phil comes back. If you talk to him, tell him to stay out of there too. The apartment is in somebody else's name, anyway. That guy will be back for us. Can you handle that?" Ethan said.

"All right, but—"

Emma was left with a dial tone.

Poor Phil. For all his bad habits, Emma knew he was a good soul. She really did care for him, but when he had started to get all boyfriendy she'd had no choice but to cut off the relationship. Or whatever it was.

Emma gave up on the joint she'd been attempting to roll. She slipped her phone into her purse and took out a slightly crushed pack of cigarettes along with the Zippo she'd lifted from her friend's place earlier that night.

She thought about Phil, and her father, and pulled a cigarette from the pack.

As she flicked the nearly dead lighter, the door opened and a set of rough hands dragged her from the car.

## 20

Having returned home from Struhl's, with a brief visit paid to a dealer downtown on the way, and now too agitated to sleep, Wynne sat curling dumbbells on the end of a bench in his garage.

The weights, bench, barbells, and universal machine in the corner had come from a gym Wynne had been a member of until its recent bankruptcy. When he first offered to purchase the equipment, the gym's owners, knowing his affiliations, didn't want his money. They were concerned about the banking repercussions, they had said. So Wynne's father, Hami, purchased the equipment for him, without protest, but with what Wynne knew was considerable internal distress.

After this latest surrogate purchase—two recent others being the vintage Dodge Charger parked in the driveway, and the down payment on Wynne's townhome—Wynne assured his father that he would soon retire, and with enough cash to start his own legitimate business. Problem was, every time Wynne mulled the logistics of this proposed business—he envisioned a gym of his own—it included some sort of cash-funnelling scheme.

As the halogen tube lights hummed above him, and a small set of speakers sang in the corner, Wynne pushed out another set of curls. Each curl sent a blossom of pain through his jaw, but an array of pharmaceuticals had withered the aching blooms sufficiently to allow Wynne to lift. He felt a little better than earlier, the swelling had subsided, and he was beginning to be able to speak clearly.

A few hopeless punks had ruined his week. Letting Struhl believe the two guys from the apartment on Maple Avenue were the particular punks in question, despite Wynne's uncertainty on the matter, hadn't made things any better for him, either. He had fuelled a bizarre mind with an idea that would not be easily extinguished.

Wynne finished his last few curls, then lay back on the bench and began a set of crunches, aiming for three hundred.

A hard-driving metal song started up from the speakers, featuring buzzing guitars, multiple bass drums, and throaty, bellowing vocals. The song had been his favourite until his girlfriend had shown him the music video earlier that morning: three skinny, awkward, fey kids standing in front of a blank white wall, neurotically bopping their heads and darting their eyes around as if on the lookout for predators.

Pussies, Wynne thought. Homos, probably. The singer looked like the kid who had hit him with the bat: skinny, unshaven, ill-fitting thrift-shop clothes. It made Wynne hate the song even more.

He had started to track down the guys from Maple Avenue with help from friends in the ambulance service. The source hadn't gotten a name, but a man had been taken from the apartment and driven to Vancouver General earlier that afternoon, comatose. The small one that looked like the singer from Wildlife Gone Wild—an unkempt, ferret-like creature—was whereabouts unknown. Wynne had sent Rowan Durgham to stake out 423 Maple Avenue to see if the little weasel would come back.

Wynne powered through his first one hundred fifty crunches without breaking a sweat. He spent ninety minutes a day in the garage or the gym, a practice long ago routinized, as firmly scheduled as the start of a work shift or the brushing of teeth.

The door leading into the house from the garage opened, and Wynne put his set of crunches on hold. His girlfriend, Josie, in formfitting yoga pants and a tight yellow top, her blonde hair ponytailed, leaned into the garage.

"Wanna go for breakfast in the morning?" she asked.

Wynne stared at her. His jaw ached too much for anything that required chewing.

"Oh yeah," Josie said, realizing her error. "You can watch me eat, I guess?"

"Fun," Wynne mumbled.

"Want me to make you a post-workout shake?"

Wynne nodded.

"And I have to go by my parents after breakfast," she said, then went back into the house and closed the door behind her.

Wynne had been dating Josie Werber for five years, off and on. After the first three, avoiding her parents had become awkward, even for him.

The Werbers were welcoming and courteous hosts, but they knew how Wynne earned his income, or got as close to knowing as they could. They wanted their daughter to stop seeing him, Wynne knew, even though they treated him graciously, inviting him to dinners, accepting him like a welcome guest when he came, even buying him tickets to a hockey game for Christmas last year. Wynne figured it for a Sun Tzu tactic, *The Art of War* still sitting on his nightstand: keep your enemies close, Sun Tzu said.

Wynne didn't think he was doing anything wrong—illegal, yes, but immoral, no—and figured, at least at first, that any parent should be happy to have a motivated man like himself care for their daughter. He bought her whatever she wanted, she spent most of her time at his place, rent free, and he'd even paid her tuition the last three semesters. Josie had wanted to be a nurse since childhood, and he was helping her fulfil her dream.

Wynne completed his crunches, a full and satisfying three hundred, then hauled two heavy dumbbells from the floor and set them back in the rack with a loud, solid clink.

The problem at hand—the missing money—was now his problem, and his alone. Fifty thousand dollars. Gone.

The morning Simon's body was found, Simon was supposed to have been dropping off product to various dealers around the city. Simon had collected money from four people the night before: Frankie, Wynne's cousin; Marcus, a student and dealer at the Emily Carr Institute; Brock, a union man at the theatre downtown, whom Wynne had just visited on the way home from Struhl's place; and Hugo, an apartment-bound peddler on the East Side.

Wynne had already called each of them, and they had all said Simon had come by to pick up the cash but hadn't shown the next day with the new supply of weed.

There wasn't a chance it was Frankie, Wynne thought, because Frankie was his cousin. Frankie had been doing whatever Wynne told him to since he was a little kid and had never shown enough initiative to cut his hair, shave regularly, or hold a steady job, let alone plot a drug heist.

Marcus was some sort of artist, of what variety Wynne had yet to discover. Marcus had told him once, but Wynne hadn't really understood the explanation. Marcus primarily trafficked Emily Carr, the art school. Artists, actors, photographers, journalists—all untrustworthy freaks, as far as Wynne was concerned. But also stupid and weak. It wouldn't take much pressure for Marcus to release any information he was holding.

Brock was union labour at the QE Theatre downtown and was the preferred hookup for musicians and other acts that came through the venue, particularly if they were in from the States and without a local dealer of their own. Brock was an old connection of Struhl's, and the only guy Wynne hadn't brought on himself.

Wynne and his aching jaw had had no intention of visiting anyone this evening, but Brock had called asking for more product, so Wynne figured it appropriate to kill two birds with one stone: drop some more product off with Brock, and dig into him to see if he knew anything about Simon.

According to the recollection-impaired minds of low-level weed dealers, Brock included, Hugo had been Simon's last pick-up for the night. Via a brief phone call, Hugo had confirmed Simon's visit, which, at least in theory, eliminated the rest of the workforce save for Omar, the kid at Corleone's. But phone calls only revealed so much. Wynne prided himself on extracting valuable information in person.

The blender whirred in the kitchen. Wynne towelled sweat from his forehead and considered his next course of action. He would skip breakfast with Josie. He had some visiting to do.

Wynne walked to the corner of his garage and pulled his cell phone from the small set of speakers in the corner. As he did so, the phone rang.

It was Struhl.

Wynne answered.

"What?"

"There's been a new development," Struhl said. "You have to come back."

"What is it?"

The line went dead.

## 21

Margaret Woit stood outside Phillip Wilford's room on the third floor of Vancouver General Hospital. The attending doctor was explaining Wilford's condition. The doctor, a thin, balding man of about forty, looked past Woit as he spoke, focussing on whatever next emergency lurked down the hall.

Woit didn't take it personally. She had long ago accepted that most doctors were insufferable assholes. This particular sphincter was explaining that the basilar skull fracture Wilford sustained when striking the table in his apartment had caused epidural bleeding, leading to severe swelling in his brain. Ventriculostomy vents had been inserted to drain the blood. Phillip Wilford lay comatose, his swollen purple eyes framed by a thick white head brace.

The doctor's disinterested tone provided no clue as to Wilford's chances, but Woit predicted that he would soon become the second homicide victim at 423 Maple Avenue in three days, and the Lower Mainland's twenty-sixth of the year.

Without offering any closure to his explanation, or the conversation in general, the doctor marched away nearly midsentence, leaving Woit standing in the hall with her notebook. She sat in a blue plastic chair outside Wilford's room and began to add to the notes on which she'd spent the previous evening working. Copies of the medical reports would be forwarded to the office, but Woit's method was old-fashioned; she liked to work things out on paper first.

Just last night, a man had been stabbed to death in unit 336 of the apartment complex at 423 Maple Avenue. Wilford and his roommate lived in 236, directly below. A witness, an under-occupied retiree who spent a full shift on the balcony every day watching over the building like an ancient grumpy owl, had stated he'd seen the same black sedan speed away from the building after both incidents.

The first stabbing was almost certainly a case of mistaken identity, Woit reckoned. The murdered occupant of 336 was a forty-three-year-old male on long-term disability who possessed a legitimate prescription for medical marijuana. He'd been using the prescription legally and in full compliance with its rules and regulations for over six years. That he had marijuana in his apartment, even though it was legal, was in part why he was dead.

According to the description provided by the witness, as well as the building manager and a neighbour to unit 236, the victim had the same hair colour and was about the same height and build as the currently unaccounted-for Ethan Blaise. When the intruder found the victim stuffing his pipe from a full bag of weed, he'd probably assumed he was in the right apartment.

The ballistics report on the round recovered from Wilford's apartment wouldn't come back anytime soon, but Woit surmised that it had been fired from a small handgun, almost certainly a Glock. All these guys used Glocks. Their relative affordability, lightness, high-capacity magazine, and ease of availability had made them the common choice for criminals for more than twenty years.

It was obvious to Woit what had happened at 423 Maple Avenue: Phillip Wilford or his roommate had owed money to someone they shouldn't have, and the Shouldn't Haves had come to collect.

Wilford's name had rung a bell with Woit, but his swollen nose and eyes prevented her from connecting the face to the name. During her first brief glance into Wilford's history, Woit discovered that she'd been his arresting constable in a case in Belleville, Ontario, years earlier. It had been an odd situation, even for her. She remembered the scene if not the details: It had been the only time she'd arrested someone in a hockey arena who wasn't an intoxicated fan. Wilford, at the time a boy in a man's body, had come along peacefully. Now, with his puffed face against the stiff white hospital linen, Wilford looked older than he should.

In the hall, a nurse leaned out of a door a few rooms down from where Woit was sitting and shouted something about missing paperwork. Interrupted, Woit finished her notes and tucked the pad back into her jacket. She needed to be at the office in forty-five minutes, anyway.

Woit enjoyed her career and never complained about the long hours, not even to herself. She never saw the point in choosing a job where you counted the minutes, ticking them off like a prisoner does days of a sentence. Her father, a retired policeman, had helped start her career, and helped her make the move to a new department out west.

Woit's life was happily her work, but on the side, when she could spare the time, she wrote fiction. Crime stories. At home, the final chapters of what would become her second novel had sat untouched for weeks.

Her protagonist was a female police sergeant working in a coastal Canadian metropolis. Though Woit and her detective shared occupations, the stories were purposefully distant from the procedural and bureaucratic reality of Woit's daily real life. The stories were pure fantasy. She'd followed in her father's footsteps in that regard, too. In the '80s he'd published a series of crime noir novels under a *nom de plume* that still held a small but rabid cult following. As an homage to her father, and in coordination with the publisher, Margaret Woit used the same pseudonym.

But Woit still had serious work to do before she could return to her project of pleasure. Though she did enjoy policework, at times it felt like an exercise in futility. She hadn't been involved long enough to participate in a full cycle, but it was inevitable that should a kingpin fall, or smuggling channel close, or production operation shut down, another one would quickly pop up in its place.

It was solving murders like the one of the innocent victim from unit 336 that made the effort worthwhile. The occupant had been stabbed to death due to the simple misfortune of living in an apartment with a particular number hanging from the door, a number some selfish and arrogant criminal had imprudently mistaken for another.

As for the apartment the criminals had actually been looking for, a small fragment of tooth had been recovered from the carpet in the hall. If Woit were lucky, the analysis of that tooth would soon reveal a match and a lead. But it would take time. The attacker could already have fled the city, if not the province.

At the moment, the only other thing Woit had to work with was Wilford's car. It was missing from the underground parking garage. Woit assumed the roommate had it, somewhere, but he was no longer answering Woit's calls. That he was avoiding the police led Woit to believe he was somehow involved criminally, but it could be that he was only stupid and scared.

Woit left her seat and walked down the hall past shuffling nurses and attendants. She hated hospitals. The smell. The steady morbid beeps of monitoring equipment. The slow roll of wheelchairs carrying slumped and withered patients. She wondered why hospitals bothered her so much when crime, violence, and death were part of her daily existence. Maybe, she thought, it was because she knew most of the people she dealt with in her job deserved what they got.

Woit summoned an elevator to take her to the ground floor. A moment later, a beep signalling the elevator's arrival joined the chorus of tones from the hallway, sung inharmoniously by ventilators, monitors, scanners, and medical equipment of all possible kinds.

The elevator doors opened to reveal a young woman in a wheelchair, hooked to an IV tree, her head resting on the elevator wall, a hand dangling limply by the chair's wheel.

Woit held the door open with a foot and called for a doctor, but it wasn't necessary: her loud shout woke the woman from her sleep. Nevertheless, a nurse popped out of a nearby room and ran into the elevator. She crouched beside the woman, who groggily insisted she was fine.

Woit wondered what was wrong with the woman, and if she, too, deserved it.

## 22

The room appeared like a stage behind a raising curtain. A single lightbulb dangled from a wire, illuminating a cracked concrete floor, the pink insulation of an unfinished ceiling, and a battered washer/dryer set beneath a wood staircase. The room smelled of mold and something else . . . dog shit, maybe.

Emma wrinkled her nose at the stink. She sat in a white plastic lawn chair, bound at the wrists and ankles with duct tape, working her way through fits of nervous shaking.

Two men stood in front of her: a thick ape wearing a paper bag with two eye holes cut out, and a thin man in a surplus army jacket with green pantyhose pulled over his head. The thick ape, Emma thought, must be the thug Ethan had told her about. His description of the gorilla was spot on, even with his face obscured: long and hairy tattooed arms and a broad, muscled chest. Next to him, the thin gangly one with the stocking on his head ticked awkwardly. He scratched at one arm with the other, like an insect rubbing its wings together.

Like a phasmid, Emma thought, the word popping into her mind. She'd had a biology test the week before. Class Insecta in the kingdom Animalia. There was a short answer section on the order Phasmatodea: stick, ghost, and leaf insects. The skinny little man's thin arms and legs and long neck contributed to the similarity.

A second muscular primate in an ill-fitting goalie mask, red hair pushing out the holes and creases, appeared from behind her with a pillowcase in his hand. A scar escaped from beneath the mask, running down his neck and under his grey T-shirt. Emma recognized him as the man who'd taken her from her car: When he'd first grabbed her, she had shaken loose and bit into his left hand. He'd quickly doubled her over with a short punch to the ribs. In the scuffle, his mask had come loose; the scar on his face was unmistakeable. Emma was glad to see the hand she'd bitten was now wrapped in a bandage.

The phasmid approached Emma. He stood in front of the chair with his work boots against her bare feet. She'd kicked off her slip-ons during the struggle in the car, but only now noticed they were missing as she looked down at her yellow-painted toenails next to the mud-flecked boots of her captor.

The phasmid placed a long finger in the center of Emma's forehead and pressed.

"Who is she, and why is she in my basement?" the phasmid said, turning to face the orangutan.

"It's the big guy's girlfriend," the orangutan asserted. "Or the little guy's."

"Which, exactly?"

"The little one's," the orangutan said, without much confidence.

"What are their names?"

The orangutan and the gorilla said nothing.

The phasmid turned back to Emma.

"What are their names?" he asked.

Emma took in his face. A few days' growth of coarse facial hair was visible through the stocking. His eyes were dark. He was white.

"Which one of those guys is your boyfriend? Big guy or little guy?" he asked.

"I'm not anybody's girlfriend," Emma said.

"She says she's not anybody's girlfriend," the phasmid said, looking back over his shoulder.

The orangutan shrugged. "She's lying."

"He says you're lying," the phasmid said, facing Emma again.

"Neither of them is my boyfriend," she said. She leaned away from the insect and his extended finger. Her chair tilted onto its back legs.

"Well, I don't believe you." He poked her again. "It's one or the other."

"It's neither."

"So why were you there?"

"Just to hang out. To smoke some weed," she said, her voice cracking.

"To buy some weed?"

"They don't sell weed. I was just going over to hang out."

"You giving it away for free?" the phasmid asked.

"What?" Emma said.

"Nailing both of them?"

"Excuse me?"

"I don't want to talk semantics here, kid," he said, poking her in the forehead again. "Those guys have my cash, all right? They shot a guy in the face and they took it, you understand?"

"Phil didn't shoot anybody!"

"Phil it is!" the phasmid said. "What's his last name?"

"He didn't shoot anybody!"

The phasmid leaned over and took Emma's left nipple between his thumb and finger. He twisted. Emma yelped. He twisted harder.

"Last name!" he barked.

"Wilford!" Emma said, struggling away from his grip and into the back of her chair.

"Wilford!" the phasmid said. He released her nipple and shot a victorious finger in the air. The chair rocked forward and resumed its normal position. "How about the little guy?"

"Will you let me go?" Emma said.

The phasmid grabbed both nipples and began to twist. Emma leaned away.

"Ethan!" she yelled. "I don't know his last name! I swear!"

The phasmid let go and the chair toppled backward. He grabbed for Emma's shirt and caught a sleeve, slowing her fall, but her head still thunked on the concrete. Her eyes closed halfway, and she was motionless.

"Wonderful," the phasmid said. He leaned over Emma. Only the whites of her eyes were visible. Her eyelids fluttered.

The phasmid slapped her lightly. Emma moved her head and muttered something unintelligible. Her eyes opened, a flash of confusion wrinkling them at the corners.

"Rowan, get over here and pick her up," the phasmid said.

The name floated through the fog enveloping Emma's brain. The orangutan stepped over and hoisted Emma upright in the chair.

"You couldn't get their names? I have to twist her nipples like that?" the phasmid said.

"You probably enjoyed it," the orangutan said. "And I pushed the building manager for names, but she wouldn't tell me."

"Mustn't have pushed too hard, then," the phasmid said.

"You want me to rough up a sixty-year-old woman, Jack? She insisted she didn't know," the orangutan continued. "All she said is the guy whose name is on the lease doesn't live there anymore. Or at least she hasn't seen him in a long time. Months. A Massoud Ebrahim."

"Neither of those guys was a Massoud Ebrahim," the gorilla said. "We already knew that."

"So what's the deal with the blonde here?" the phasmid said.

"Watched her go into the building," the orangutan said. "She has a key, but the cops put a new bolt on the door already. And the door's taped up."

"You went in the building?"

"No, I put her in my car. Jimmy Chan went in. Risky going back there so soon, anyway. Beyond risky. Plain stupid. I don't think these guys had the bag to begin with. It could be anybody."

"Right now, the best lead we have is Princess here," the phasmid said. "What I understand is that those two losers have my cash."

Emma listened through a shaken and aching brain. A roiling wave of nausea washed through her body.

"Her licence says she's Samantha Emma Woodgrave," the orangutan said.

"Find out who she is," the phasmid said.

"I say just let her go," the gorilla said.

"Not yet," the orangutan said. "She drives a Hummer."

"So?" the gorilla said.

"Maybe she's got money," the orangutan said.

"Find out who she is first," the phasmid said. "Then we'll decide."

The phasmid backed away from Emma, then walked passed the two large men and up the stairs and into the house.

Emma blinked the ache out of her head.

"It's a Range Rover," she said.

The two men looked at her.

"What?" the gorilla said.

"It's a Ranger Rover, not a Hummer," Emma said.

"Is it?" the gorilla asked.

Emma nodded. "I wouldn't drive a Hummer," she said.

"How do you not know the difference between a Range Rover and a Hummer?" the gorilla asked the orangutan.

"It was dark," the orangutan said.

Emma squirmed in her chair.

The orangutan put a paw on her head. "Sit still," he said. "Samantha Emma Woodgrave, did your daddy buy you that Range Rover?"

Emma said nothing.

"You got a rich daddy, Samantha?"

## 23

After watching Jennifer Arensberg's tail lights shrink to tiny points then blip off into the starless night, Eric turned and went back inside, his wife's thin silk bathrobe flapping in the breeze behind him.

As he passed through the kitchen he pulled a bottle of wine from the rack on the counter and carried it upstairs to his home office. To help himself think things through, he poured himself a glass, then four more.

A few hours later, after selecting the BMW he thought would best suit his daughter, he sat blurrily reviewing work documents in a distinguished but painfully uncomfortable straight-backed leather chair he wished he'd never bought.

The work was intended as a distraction from cursing himself, first for his bad behaviour, and then for his bad luck. Now he found he wasn't accomplishing either task with much efficiency. It was by all accounts a complete disaster of an evening. Sam, as Eric continued to call her—having given up on the requested name change years ago—wasn't answering her phone. Linda had called to say she'd extended her visit to Ontario a few days. She hadn't sounded angry, but Eric still wondered if Sam had already divulged the night's transgressions. And not twenty minutes ago, Jennifer Arensberg had called to remind Eric that he was an ass-hole. Eric wasn't sure what that made Jennifer Arensberg, but he could say little to refute the label.

But there had been no call from Sam.

Eric hoped that she'd gone back to the girlfriend's where she was supposed to have been spending the night, and not vulnera-bly into the groping arms of some baggy-panted deadbeat.

She'd only ever brought one boy home, and that was in ninth grade. Some grinning blonde fool with a head like a mailbox, Eric remembered. The boy's parents had driven the kids to the junior prom; Sam had been valedictorian. Why the hell did you need a valedictorian and prom in ninth grade, Eric had wondered? He couldn't keep up. It seemed like there was a ceremony or event every other week. For things like this, time had passed him by.

Linda kept far better track of Sam's full and lively schedule. The two had formed a real bond. Eric knew it was something his wife worked at earnestly, in part as penance for her own failed family: in the city she had one son she rarely talked to—some hopeless loser Eric had met once and wouldn't recognize if he shook his hand—and a daughter in Ottawa with whom Linda was only now beginning to repair their relationship.

He knew his behaviour was pathetic. But occasionally his drive still got the best of him—not like before he'd met Linda, when he couldn't go a week without visiting a certain high-end brothel, but nonetheless unacceptable for a man who'd promised himself he'd turned a new leaf.

That had been his mistake, he concluded, tilting his glass and catching the last burgundy drop on his tongue: not just going to a whore.

Eric turned away from the computer screen and gazed out the window into the night. The roofs of multimillion-dollar homes cascaded down the sloped shore to the edge of the bay. Across the water, a thousand acres of inlet park obscured the small but dense copse of skyscrapers and tall condo towers that comprised downtown Vancouver. One of those buildings held the high-end whorehouse he had made a fast habit of visiting, or had until he met his latest wife. He wondered if one particular girl he used to see still worked there.

To avoid thinking about his angry daughter and soon-to-be angry wife, Eric worked, reviewing the contracts for what would soon become the tallest tower in downtown Vancouver, rising from the former footprint of six Downtown Eastside assisted-living hotels, home for decades to drug addicts, the mentally ill, and other marginalized citizens. The sharp edge of the first shovel had only recently pierced the ground but activists were already protesting.

Eric didn't get it. The fuel that kept the world turning, that drove the cars to bring the addicts and welfare recipients their meals, that kept the lights on in their Assisted Living Residences, that even bought them their drugs, was money. This project, marketed as "Nirvana," would inject a healthy dose of cash into a neighbourhood that had spent the last thirty years rolling penniless in its own filth.

Nirvana would bring customers into restaurants and shops, increase tax revenues, and provide desperately needed dollars for charity work, safe houses, and shelters. The planning committee had partnered with local charities and advocacy groups, and a percentage of proceeds from the massive development project would be returned to the community to build green spaces, erect learning centres, and fund recovery groups.

The penthouse would list for nineteen million dollars. There was already interest from a Japanese technology magnate, a Chinese production mogul, and a Yemeni sheik. High above Vancouver on the seventy-seventh floor, it would feature its own private elevator, parking garage, nanny quarters, personal gym, screening room, and infinity pool.

Eric again turned to look out the window. Across the bay, standing in a cluster of condo towers in Coal Harbour, stood the Gould Building. Eric hadn't been to the twenty-third floor in years.

He thought about Darla, whom he used to visit there; about Jennifer Arensberg, whom he never should have started up with; and about his wife, who could be plotting a divorce—or his demise—from some four thousand kilometres away.

Eric picked up his phone and called his daughter one more time.

## 24

After hanging up with Emma, and finding himself too agitated to sleep, Ethan lay in Sam's bed, examining the posters of bizarre animals on the bedroom walls. A gallery of eyes stared out at him like captives from thin glossed cages.

Ethan took in the rest of the room. A pile of clothes lay on the floor next to a pressboard Ikea desk. A snowboard and boots leaned against the wall. Left of the desk was a tightly packed bookshelf, holding volumes by Gould, Dawkins, Wilson, and Darwin; zoology and biology texts by Griffiths, Alberts, and Campbell; *Nature* magazines; and notebooks. No fiction. A little poetry: Neruda, Williams, Cummings, and Ondaatje.

He reached into his jacket on the floor, pulled out *Cheap Thrills*, and flipped to the earmarked page nearly halfway through the narrow book. He began to read, hoping that moving his eyes over the printed words would relax him into sleep.

Originality wasn't a strong suit in the Rutherford novels, but *Cheap Thrills* seemed especially like a retread. He recalled Grave using the same plot device in another of his books: mob wife seeks vengeance for her husband's murder, employs PI with inseverable ties to the criminal underworld. Nine of Grave's novels were narrated by Rutherford. Ethan hadn't read any of the one's that weren't.

In the chapter Ethan now opened to, Rutherford, whose criminal past included a confluence of Montreal biker gang and Italian mafia affiliations, was recounting the convoluted mystery Darla had hired him to solve:

> Darla had me by the beets, that was for certain. But having my hand forced wasn't my style, so I'd taken the initiative to do a little investigating of my own before heading down to the States. And so, as much as running for South America had a strong appeal, the fee increase I'd negotiated with Darla had something to do with my continued involvement, I'll admit. If she was going to

blackmail me, the least I could do was return the favour: I'd quickly found enough dirt on Darla to bury her, if need be, a particularly interesting clod being that she'd been ploughing Premier Stephenson, that fat, smiling moron, among other people, while her husband Hillcoat was still alive and well. That information going public would surely do the Premier more harm than it would her, but criminals prefer to keep a low profile, and that little tidbit hitting the papers would make doing so a bit difficult, to say the least.

We agreed on a higher sum for my services, guaranteed by the assurance that if I wasn't paid in full, the sensitive information she'd given me about Hillcoat's operation, and that I'd discovered myself about her, would go in one ear and out the other, meeting the conveniently located police and media on the other side.

Hillcoat Carmine, it turned out, was crazier than a cat in a tub. Smuggling marijuana in living cows was an obvious first indication, but it only got weirder from there. The slaughterhouse on the other side of the border was no ordinary abattoir. My old friend Carter Woebeck helped me out with that one, and I'll forever begrudge him for it. I've been called just about everything but naïve in my life, and for good reason. With regards to The Smiling Bovine and the man who ran it, Jeffrey Jerome, I wished the insult still applied.

If not for Carter's cousin Wendell being a reformed Heritage Nation lowlife himself, I never would've found out that the receiving end of Hillcoat's doped-up cattle train was operated by a white supremacist, anti-government survivalist group—not that I have anything against anti-government survivalists, preferring as little interaction with society and particularly the government as possible myself, but the racists I've just never understood. There's only so much hate to go around, and mine's all spent on deserving individuals. Wait for a good reason, I figure, then give it all you got.

The Heritage Nation bit connected nicely with the bikers angle on the north side of the border, the Brokers being a conspicuously white outfit itself. Hillcoat Carmine had been running with the bikers, apparently, and the bikers, if not outright racists themselves, certainly had no problem doing business with the proprietors of The Smiling Bovine, helping to move product via underground tunnels, helicopter drops, cars and vans with contraband stuffed into every conceivable space, and, of course, Prime Alberta cattle filled to the ribs with similarly fine Canadian bud. Coming back our way via the Mexican cartels was South American cocaine.

The bikers were where I was directing my attention until I'd talked to Carter: Darla was certain the local Brokers chapter president Hillcoat had been dealing with, a man named Gainsborough, had ordered the hit. My job, I was quickly learning, wasn't to investigate the murder, but to resolve it: that is, confirm Darla's suspicions and take out Gainsborough. Darla had passed along surveillance photos and some evidence that Gainsborough was looking to cut the Carmines out of the picture, but she wasn't quite sure why. That's where Carter and Wendell came in. Without them I never would have learned that a species other than cattle was being butchered in The Smiling Bovine. The Brokers were using the slaughterhouse to dispose of bodies, and Hillcoat didn't like it. With Hillcoat eliminated, they could continue their cleanup operation and take over his portion of the business entirely.

When Carter told me the story, I should've let it go in one ear and out the other. I didn't want to work in the States, the Brokers angle could be investigated on this side of the border, and Darla was as certain as she could be that it was Gainsborough I should be looking at. But Carter and his whack-job cousin had gotten the ball rolling, and once these things start to pick up speed they usually end up collecting a whole dump's worth of other garbage along the way.

Darla knew Jerome. That is, she knew about the beef operation, and about the slaughterhouse, but had never met the man himself. She didn't figure him for a suspect. But she herself had said Hillcoat was a bastard and the suspect list was a long one, so I wasn't going to rule it out that quickly.

Darla was running the business until things got settled, and she still had a contact with the Heritage Nation. She insisted Gainsborough and the Brokers was where I should be focussing my attention, but if I wasn't going to listen and wanted to take a look at Jerome in person, I could do so on the 23rd: he'd be there to meet the bikers about some deal that had nothing to do with the Carmines. The 23rd wasn't for a week, and I certainly wasn't going to wait that long to investigate a lead. I set to staking out the slaughterhouse the next day.

And that's when things really got interesting. I wasn't the only one interested in what sort of processing was going on inside that slaughterhouse. A set of what appeared to be FBI agents were surveilling The Bovine at the same time I was. A blonde woman and a Clark Kent-looking tight ass had been sitting in a cable company van for two days. If they were cable company employees, they wouldn't be for long because they hadn't laid an inch of cable in the whole time I'd been watching.

Things had gotten very complicated, very quickly, which wasn't my style either. And though Darla knew enough about my past to cause me a lethal dose of trouble, trouble seemed to come my way regardless, so what the hell? Why fight fate? You end up in the same spot, only with a bigger headache. Cognitive dissonance, I think psychologists call it. Go with what God or whoever's running this sloppy operation provides, even if it's a group of murderous beef-smuggling white supremacists, and you'll sleep soundly on your pillow, if you make it there alive.

## 25

Rowan Durgham brushed the scar on his cheek with the back of his hand, a habit formed when his face still held the ninety-seven stitches he'd received as result of a job gone wrong nearly four years earlier.

Rowan had been just nineteen at the time, and slimmer for not yet having discovered steroids. Rowan had accompanied Harry Blydon, one of Struhl's former strongmen, to Richmond, and in particular to Craig's, a mid-scale chain restaurant trying to pass itself off as something more sophisticated, paying more attention to furniture, design, and fresh-faced waitresses than to its cuisine.

At Craig's, Rowan and Harry had met two Indo-Canadian men whom Struhl believed to be selling product for higher prices than agreed upon and pocketing the difference—a small sin, but one that needed to be acknowledged and penance paid upon.

The two skimmers hadn't much interest in negotiating, however, and the discussion had turned violent before the main course had even been served. The bearded, more brutishly built of the two skimmers slashed Rowan across his face and chest with a steak knife. The discussion moved to the parking lot, and Harry Blydon shot the second skimmer dead.

Rowan never saw Blydon again, nor heard his name.

Three weeks later, while sitting at a FreshBurger drive-thru, the surviving skimmer's car was filled with over seventy bullets, more than enough to eliminate the target within.

Alas, Rowan wasn't the one who'd fired the gun; he hadn't gotten his revenge.

Now Rowan was sitting across from Jack Struhl, and beside Wynne, in Struhl's living room.

Struhl looked back and forth between the two men, seemingly scanning their faces for an answer he already knew they didn't have. The conversation regarding what to do with the girl had stalled; she remained bound in the basement.

Rowan had spent the night watching *Magnum PI* reruns on the sofa and periodically checking on the girl, keeping himself awake with reasonably sized—he thought—lines of cocaine. He'd been stuck with watch duty by Struhl, who decided that since Rowan had brought the problem home, it was his to babysit.

Light streamed in through a gap in the drawn living room curtains, sending pounding pulses of withdrawal pains through Rowan's skull. He'd curtailed the coke and had started on Oxys to take the edge off, but they hadn't quite done their job.

A phone began to dance in Struhl's lap. Rowan recognized the ringtone as a Softwood Lumber tune. He hated Softwood Lumber and hip-hop in general, being a country man, but he'd done lines at The Pink Curtain with one of the band members—HardSawz or The Bidness, he could never remember which one—and he'd seemed like a good enough guy.

The phone continued to ring.

A bulky Rottweiler mutt trotted out of the kitchen toward the sound. The Rottweiler sniffed the phone, deemed it inedible, then departed.

The chorus repeated:

> Hendrix sang *Crosstown*
> Naw, this shit cross-border
> Bought with war and murder
> So step aside, gov'nent
> Let the professionals handle it
> Mejico to Cali-forn-eye-eh,
> Best listen close to what we say:
> One cartel to anutha, 'nutha
> One clipped crop to anutha, 'nutha
> BC, where dat shit grow thick!
> Singin: CROSS-BORDER TRAF-FICK!

Rowan screwed up his face. The song still sucked.

"Are you going to answer that or what?" he asked.

Struhl picked it up but the phone had stopped ringing. He looked at the screen. "Missed Call: Dad," it said.

"Speak of the devil," Struhl said. He tossed the phone across the coffee table to Wynne.

"Not in the kidnapping business, Jack," Wynne said, dumping the phone on Rowan's lap. "Nobody asked this meathead to grab that girl—"

"You said watch the building," Rowan said. "So I watched the building."

"Never said kidnap nobody," Wynne said. He turned to Jack, pointing, "We're not ransoming her."

"I didn't take her to ransom her," Rowan said. He spoke to Wynne without turning to face him, instead watching the hound on the floor blink and pant. "But when opportunity presents itself, one must capitalize. Plus, you said find out who those two guys are. So I did. We got their names, right?"

"We don't have the money yet," Wynne said.

"She'll tell us," Rowan said. "Or point us in the right direction."

"She don't know shit," Wynne said.

"But these two guys do?" Struhl asked.

"Maybe," Wynne said.

"So find these two guys and tell them we'll bust her up if they don't give us the money," Rowan said.

"I have a few other people I need to check out," Wynne said. "Rowan can look for these two."

"What other people?" Struhl said.

"Other guys," Wynne said. "Leads."

Struhl leaned back in his chair, stroking the scruff on his cheek. The three men sat in silence as Struhl considered the options. One of the snoozing Rottweilers sighed. Outside the house, cars rolled by on the narrow street. A child screamed in play from a neighbouring yard.

Struhl spoke. "You don't need to look for anyone else. Start with finding these two guys and leveraging the girl against them," he said. "Maybe the money will pop out. If not, we can consider going to the father."

Wynne started to protest:

"Jack, the—"

"Shut up," Struhl said. "And do it."

Struhl stood up.

"Where are you going?" Rowan asked.

"To the place on Danwood, to start another grow. Anything interesting happens, call me."

## 26

The next morning, Ethan awoke to the sound of a blender whirring in the kitchen. A clock on Sam's wall told him it was much earlier than he'd risen in a very long time. Maybe ever.

Sam's collection of eccentric animals was the last thing Ethan had seen before drifting off to sleep, the copy of *Cheap Thrills* tumbling from his hands to the floor. The amount of marijuana he smoked usually robbed him of dreams, or at least prevented him from remembering them, but this past week his sleeping self had walked through a grotesque carnival of images and sensations.

Last night he had again slept erratically, interrupted by images of Simon's body, of the gorilla assailant pissing on Phil, and of Sun Bear, Aye-Aye, Star-nosed Mole and the other curiously adapted creatures climbing down from the posters on Sam's walls and into his aching head. Along with violent criminals and deformed animals, Ethan had dreamed of Grunt Rutherford solving mysteries with the barrel of his gun.

Ethan rubbed his eyes, then winced as a ripple of pain waved through his face and skull. The previous day's events had left him exhausted, and his head throbbed from the rigorous beating it had taken.

He looked at himself in the mirror on the back of Sam's bedroom door. What resembled the imprint of a video game controller was branded into his forehead. His nose was swollen, and though Sam had assured him the cut on the top of his head didn't require stitches, he touched it and winced at the sting.

He pulled on his pants and the clean UBC T-shirt Sam had loaned him, then left the bedroom.

Darwin sat curled in a pool of light leaking in through a bent slat of blinds in the hall window. The cat tilted her head at Ethan, then stretched and purred contentedly. Ethan approached, knelt, and extended a hand. The cat retreated.

Ethan's last girlfriend had had a cat that hated him fiercely. In fact, it hated all men. She'd adopted it from a shelter; the volunteers told her the animal had been abused. At the time of adoption, it had been missing patches of hair from what appeared to be burns and was recovering from a broken leg. That it was still alive was some small miracle, they told her. They also said that abusers were most frequently men, and that consequently many sheltered animals had an instinctive distrust of males. Some get over it, some don't.

Knowing this, Ethan gave Darwin her space. The cat reclaimed its patch on the carpet and settled back into the growing pool of morning light.

Ethan descended the stairs to the kitchen.

Sam, dressed in jeans and a T-shirt, her hair tied back in a ponytail, stood at the kitchen counter pouring deep green sludge from a blender into a glass.

"Want one of these?" she said.

Ethan eyed her drink.

"What is it?"

"Kale, spinach, strawberries—lots of good stuff."

Ethan looked cockeyed at the beverage, then up at Sam. He shrugged. "You only live once," he said.

Sam pulled a second glass from the cupboard and poured a serving of the viscous beverage for Ethan. "How are you feeling?"

"Face is still sore, but I'm all right."

Sam put the full glass in front of him.

"You should call that cop back."

"They'll arrest me."

"Why would they arrest you for?"

"I lied to them about who I was. I left Phil bleeding and unconscious. There was no forced entry. We let that guy in all on our own. For all the police know, there was no intruder at all. I must be their prime suspect. Cops will take the path of least resistance, every time."

"You're crazy. That cop told you there were witnesses. They're not after you. Wynne is."

"So they say. Life lesson number one, Sam: never trust the police."

"What'd they ever do to you?"

Ethan thought about it.

"Nothing yet, because I haven't given them the chance. I prefer not to have their crooked arm all bent up in my business."

Sam shook her head. "You're as crazy as Hugo, you know that? Too many movies and video games or something. Or those crime books."

"Hugo doesn't care for the police either? I'm starting to like this guy."

Sam took a long drink from her glass and eyed Ethan with pity. She set her glass down on the granite countertop.

"You know what the police did to Hugo?"

"What?"

"Same as to you: nothing."

"It's only a matter of time before they bust him," Ethan said. "Or at least arrest somebody more important than him, with the result of Hugo being out of a job."

"Yeah. Because that's their job. What do you want them to do?"

"Legalize the shit?"

"Yes, I'm sure it's within Constable Joe Blow's power to change a centuries' worth of law in the time it takes to bust a small-time dealer like Hugo."

"Hey," Ethan said, "whose side are you on here, anyway?"

"I'm not on anybody's side."

"Have you talked to Hugo?" Ethan asked.

"No. And I'm not going to, either."

"Do you know where I can find him?"

"His house, maybe?"

"Other than his apartment. I'm not going by that animal farm. Last thing I need is to run into Wynne or one of his trained apes. And by the way, what's with all the shirtlessness over there?"

"Hugo doesn't go many other places, actually—"

"The Esso for hoagies?"

"Do you want me to tell you or not? He's locked up in that place six days a week, from eleven in the morning to eleven at night, selling. Sunday is his day off, and he didn't usually spend it with me. But he does go to church."

"Church?"

"Yes," Sam gave an exaggerated nod. "Church."

"My weed dealer goes to church?" Ethan said. He laughed, wide eyed and broadly. "I don't know anybody who goes to church, and my goddamn weed dealer goes to church!"

"I used to go to church," Sam said. "Do they have to be mutually exclusive?"

"I don't know about have to be. But in my experience they tend to. I take it you're religious?"

"Not really. I used to be."

"What kind?"

"Catholic."

"You've been cured of that malady?"

"See," Sam said, rolling her eyes, "that's what pisses me off."

"What?"

"I don't agree with most of what the Catholic Church—or any religion—stands for; that's why I'm not Catholic anymore," Sam said. "But I don't think it's right—that you have the right—to ridicule another person's faith or beliefs."

"I don't see the difference."

"Between what?"

"Religion and faith."

"I do," Sam said. "Faith is the internal belief. Religion is the external expression."

"Inseparable," Ethan said.

"I disagree," Sam said.

"You're wrong," Ethan said.

"You're an ass," Sam said. "This is what I'm talking about. Why do you get to decide what I believe?"

"I don't even know what you believe. Is this a hypothetical conversation?"

"Sure."

Ethan paused to compose his rebuttal.

"Look, if you believed the sun went around the earth, I'd tell you that you were wrong, and I'd be right. If you believed cell phones work because of magic, that little invisible pixies carry your voice from phone to phone, I'd say you were wrong again. If someone tells me they believe that a God handcrafted the universe from absolutely nothing, and that a God is responsible for everything from fourth-quarter touchdowns to surviving car crashes, I'll say the same thing, and for the same reason: we've got better, simpler ways to explain things that make a hell of a lot more sense."

"Faith isn't for finding an explanation or evidence. It's not for the how. It's for the why."

"The why is the how, if there is a why at all," Ethan countered.

"You have no humility, is what I say. If it's for anything, it's humility."

"You're afraid of there being no why. Don't you study evolution in biology?"

"It's the how."

Ethan had no reply. He felt tired, and said so.

"Can you just tell me which church Hugo goes to?" he said.

"No," Sam said, finally. She finished the rest of her drink, then got up from her stool, rinsed her glass and loaded it into the dishwasher. Ethan's glass was only half empty.

"Sorry," Ethan said. "I went too far, I guess."

"Not 'no' because I'm offended, 'no' because I don't have any idea where he goes. I never went with him. So what are you going to do now?"

"I'm going to talk to Hugo," Ethan said. "Maybe he knows something about all this. If Wynne or one of his goons comes looking for me again, I want to be able to give him a good answer about what happened to that money, if not the money itself."

"And you think Hugo knows where the money is?"

"He might. He knew Simon, that much is for sure. Plus, he's the only lead I've got at the moment."

"Lead?" Sam scoffed. "This problem isn't yours to solve. Go to the police and be done with it."

"What if it's not done with me?"

"You didn't have anything to do with it in the first place."

"I do now."

"Only in your head."

Ethan pointed to his purple swollen nose.

"On my head too."

Darwin strolled over to Sam. She rubbed against her leg and purred. Sam hoisted the big cat up in her arms.

"My parents are coming home tonight," Sam said. "It's not the end of the world if you're here when they get back. In fact, it doesn't really matter to them one way or the other."

"But to you?"

"To me? I think you have the opportunity to save yourself a lot of trouble by going to the police. I think I believe Hugo about what's been going on. That's why I'm not going over there anymore. I feel bad that you have nowhere to go—"

"I got it," Ethan said. "I'll go. Thanks for putting me up."

Sam smiled. "No problem."

Ethan stood up.

"See you when I see you," Ethan said.

"Sure," Sam said. "After you talk to the police?"

Ethan agreed, or at least said he did, then gathered his things and left.

## 27

Frankie Duncan hauled another load of rebar onto his shoulder and walked it across the construction site.

Before signing on for this job, he hadn't been to the Downtown Eastside in years. As an eighteen-year-old he'd started to buy heroine in the area's alleys and parks—until his cousin Wynne found out.

It was another overcast day, for which Frankie was grateful. The thick pad protecting his shoulder from the metal made him sweat, even on a mostly cloudy, fifteen-degree morning. The Nirvana project was a few weeks in and he wasn't looking forward to working in the approaching summer heat.

Frankie had just received a text message: Wynne was on his way to the site for a visit. Now not only was Frankie stuck working overtime on a Sunday, he also had to deal with his ill-tempered cousin.

Though he'd never admit it, Frankie was scared of his cousin. As a teen, Frankie had once watched Wynne beat another kid unconscious for insulting him. Another time, he'd broken a guy's ribs for mistreating a girl.

Frankie lugged the rebar past a group of four concrete pourers sitting on a ledge and eating sandwiches. The shortest, fattest one called out to him.

"Frankie. Over here, man," he said.

Frankie set the rebar down and approached the workers.

"Johnny," Frankie said. "You got that thirty-five or what?"

"No, man," the short fat one said, his yellow hard hat tipped back on his head. The sandwich he held was flattened to the height of a stepped-on cow turd. Frankie knew him as Johnny, and the one next to him with the weird forehead lump was Jorge, but he didn't recognize the other two.

Johnny swallowed his bite of sandwich, then spoke.

"Frankie," he said, "give me another eighth today, man. We'll smoke it together." He made a circle in the air with his finger to indicate the proposed group of smokers, which included the other breaking workers and Frankie himself.

"No way, Johnny," Frankie said. "Come on, man. I know you got the cash. Why do you have to fuck me around?"

"I wouldn't fuck you around, Frankie, man," Johnny said, holding his hands up in protest, the flattened, half-eaten sandwich in one of them. "Man, I got four kids back home, you know?"

Frankie knew all about Johnny's three-to-six kids back home, kids seemingly born between one conversation and the next.

"Their mother calls me and says 'send money, send money,' you know?" Johnny said. "What am I supposed to do?"

Not consume a gram of weed and a six pack of beer every night, to start with, Frankie thought. But who was he to judge?

"Johnny, man," Frankie said, "we all got problems."

"Man, you don't have no kids," Johnny said. "Come on."

"That's because I wear a condom," Frankie said. The workers all laughed, including Johnny.

"Pull out don't work, Johnny," one of the other guys said, miming the appropriate gesture. "Don't listen to that priest no more." The men all laughed again.

"Look, Johnny," Frankie said, "we get paid again at the end of the week. You pay me, we start fresh, all right? Plus, I'm out."

"You don't sell no more?" Jorge said.

"No, I will. I just don't have any left right now," Frankie said.

"Okay, Frankie, okay," Johnny said. "I got kids to feed, right?"

"All right," Frankie said, and walked away, cursing Johnny under his breath. Another thirty-five dollars short.

Luckily, most of the guys on the site were more reliable than Johnny; they came to buy with cash in hand and rarely asked for spots. Frankie had been working jobs about six months now and had already learned a few things about how to get along on a construction site, and how not to get ripped off selling weed.

He shouldered the load of rebar and carried it toward his crew. Workers poured and lifted, or otherwise stood considering which of those to do next, attempting to delay the inevitable. The foundation for one of the site's peripheral buildings was going up quickly. The build was on schedule, and overtime had only been called to move a crew onto a project that was lagging.

On the other side of the safety fence sat the foreman's white office trailer. Parked beside it was a jet-black, vintage Dodge Charger. The foreman, a friend of Wynne's who had gotten Frankie the job, was standing along with Wynne beside the car. Even from forty feet away, Frankie could tell Wynne's characteristic grimace was more pronounced than usual. And was that another garden hose of a vein bulging out of his shiny bald head?

It occurred to Frankie that his cousin was about to kill him and dump his body in the foundation of Nirvana.

When Frankie had paid Simon a few days before, he'd been a hundred dollars short. Simon had put on his best tough-guy act, but it hadn't been very convincing. He was kind of a weird dude, too.

They'd shared a joint that night. The news had been playing on Frankie's television. There had been a shooting at a mall in Kentucky. An American senator was calling for tougher gun regulations. As the talking heads debated the issue, Simon explained to Frankie that this latest shooting was a "fake flag." The gist of it, as Frankie remembered, was that it was staged, an excuse the government came up with to take people's guns away. Frankie thought that it did sound like something the government would do.

At the office trailer the foreman handed Wynne a hard hat, then both men entered the construction site. The foreman waved at Frankie. Frankie waved back.

Wynne and the foreman approached, Wynne's jaw held tightly closed, the foreman wearing his usual slight smile.

"Frankie," the foreman said. His smile disappeared and his broad, clean-shaven face hardened. "Your cousin here needs to ask you something important."

"All right," Frankie said.

"He wants to know which one of those Mexicans has the biggest dick. Don't you, Wynne?" the foreman said. He slapped Wynne on the back and laughed. Wynne remained stone faced.

The foreman shouted to the Mexicans, still sitting on a lip of concrete and eating their lunches.

"Hey, Johnny," the foreman shouted. "Johnny!"

Johnny looked over.

"My friend here wants to see your big brown dick," the foreman said. "Get over here and show it to him."

Johnny shook his head and shouted something back in Spanish.

"Then get back to fucking work, Johnny!" the foreman yelled. He returned his attention back to Wynne and Frankie. "Go talk in the office," he said. "But make it quick. Frankie has more bitch work to do."

"Thanks, Chuck," Frankie said.

"Hey, get yourself a trade and you won't have to take shit from immigrants anymore. How's that sound?"

Frankie followed Wynne into the mostly empty trailer. At one end of the room a microwave and coffee maker sat on a table next to a small fridge; filing cabinets, a short couch, and a desk covered in papers and holding a dirty black laptop occupied the other. Wynne gestured to the armless black office chair beside the desk.

Frankie sat and looked at his cousin. Dressed in a baggy hoodie and expensive jeans, Wynne looked his usual self, save for that tensely held jaw.

"Look, Wynne," Frankie said, "I know I was short. These fucking guys around here, you know? They're scumbags. You used to work sites, man. You know, right?"

"It should come out of your pocket, then," Wynne said.

"What?"

"The short comes out of your pocket."

"What the fuck is wrong with your face?" Frankie asked, noticing the swelling and that Wynne wasn't opening his mouth when he spoke.

"Nothing."

"Are you missing teeth?"

"A couple," Wynne said. "Rough day."

"Does that shit hurt?"

"Oxy helps. If I move my lips and cheeks around my teeth without trying to open my jaw when I talk, like this"—Wynne exaggerated the procedure to demonstrate—"it's not that bad."

"Who did it?" Frankie asked

Wynne shook his head.

"Simon—" he said.

"Dude, Simon fucked you up? I knew that guy was a piece of shit! He's always saying the weirdest shit—did you know they brought down the World Trade Center with, like, explosives?"

"What? No, Simon didn't fuck me up. I'm trying to ask you—"

"You know, 9/11, man. There's no way those huge build-ings go down like that just from two planes."

"They were jumbo jets."

"Man, did you—"

"Frankie. Whatever. Simon was a moron. Don't listen to morons. He's dead, anyway."

"You shot him?" Frankie yelled and sprang up out of his chair. He'd always known his cousin had it in him. Wynne always insisted he'd never shot anyone; Frankie never believed him. Who has all those guns but doesn't use them?

"He fucked you up and you fucking shot him!" Frankie said.

"I never shot him. Somebody else did. Did he pick up the money from you the other day?"

"Dead?"

Wynne nodded. "He pick up the money?"

"Yeah. Listen, Wynne, I won't be short again—"

"Did he drop off more?"

"Weed?"

"Yeah."

"No. He never showed up. I thought you were cutting me out or something. I just straightened a couple guys out around here, so the hundred—"

"Would you shut up about the fucking hundred? Simon never came by with the weed?"

"No."

"You call him?"

"Yeah, no answer. I called you, too. No answer."

"What time did he pick up the money the night before?"

Frankie paused. He looked up at the ceiling, trying to remember.

"Nine o'clock, maybe?" he said.

"Did he say anything?"

"About what?"

"Anything," Wynne said.

"Not much. He was going on about the U.S. government. That they're trying to change the First Amendment so people can't have, like, assault rifles."

"What?"

"The First Amendment, man. The right to own guns or whatever. Says he was gonna buy a FAL before it was too late."

"A FAL?"

"Yeah, man. They're tight."

Wynne shook his head.

"He was saying we won't be able to get them much longer," Frankie continued. "Because of the new laws or whatever."

"You know we live in Canada, right, dumbfuck?"

"So?"

"What else did he say?" Wynne said.

"Not much. Was saying something about a quinzhee, whatever that is."

"Did he say anything I might actually care about?"

"Not really," Frankie said. "I figure I should get a gun, Wynne. Why don't you hook me up with one, you know? Just a nice Glock 37 or something. Never know in this line of business, right?"

"You're not in any line of business, idiot. You're a construction worker."

"Man," Frankie said, sitting back down in the chair, "I don't want to be no labour monkey. I'm gonna be like you, Wynne."

"You're going to get your ticket and be a plumber or an electrician or something."

"Man, I don't want a bullshit job, lugging stuff around."

"Then drive heavy machine. Grow a little on the side for extra cash."

"Fifty hours a week is for common losers, Wynne. That's why you don't do it."

"No," Wynne said finally, and rubbed his head. "The last thing you're getting is a gun. The over/under on shooting yourself is about a week."

"Wynne—"

"Shut up. Simon say anything else?"

"No," Frankie said. He looked up at the ceiling. "Ah, wait. He was talking about this girl he was trying to bang. Samantha something. Met her at Hugo's place."

"You know Hugo?"

"Yeah, I just met him the other week," Frankie said. "Simon brought me over."

"Woodgrave?"

"What?" Frankie said.

"The girl. Was her last name Woodgrave?" Wynne asked.

"How the hell should I know," Frankie said. "Yeah, Woodgrave. Sounds right."

"What'd she look like?"

"Don't know. Never met her. Probably blonde. Everybody likes blondes, right Wynne?"

Wynne wasn't listening.

"We cool?" Frankie said.

"Yeah," Wynne said, tuning back in. "But next time the short comes out of your pocket."


## 28

It was too early to follow Hugo to church. Deciding he needed breakfast, Ethan drove to a Thick Burger drive-thru, ordered a combo with an extra-large black coffee, and parked at the rear of the lot.

In the back seat of the Pontiac, he fluffed his jacket up against the door as a pillow and settled in to kill a little time. With the Thick Burger logo, a smiling hippo, now winking up at him from the waxy wrapper resting on his chest, Ethan opened *Cheap Thrills,* picking up where he'd left off the previous evening.

The novel had taken another twist: Darla had passed along the new information that Hillcoat had last been seen with one of Jerome's men, not Gainsborough's, as she had originally thought. Rutherford was on the right track after all. Darla upped the ante:

Take out Jerome on the 23rd, Darla said, and I wouldn't have to hang out in my shoebox of an office anymore, working shit jobs for shit money to provide for a shit life. My reward would increase again, from "significant lifestyle improvement" to "retirement plan," and the debt to the Rossetti's would be forgotten.

It was a line of reasoning I found difficult to argue with. And there was no arguing that a world without Jeffrey Jerome wouldn't be a better place either.

It turned out Jerome had been looking to take out Hillcoat Carmine for a while. Carmine was the man with the weed, but he needed the biker's connections to trade it for cocaine. Jerome had been dealing with Carmine for years, when it was strictly a weed-for-cash trade. But now that the Brokers and the Sinaloa were involved, maybe it was time to seize Carmine's chunk of the action. Despite the shift in attention, I was starting to think the Gainsborough and Jerome leads were the same one: they had colluded to cut out the Carmines.

There was something bigger going on, too, but I wasn't quite sure what it was yet. Weed going one way and cocaine the other with some beef to lubricate the transaction didn't bother me one way or the other. People wanted all those things, and why shouldn't they have them. But everything was getting across the 49th a little too easily, a little too often.

So there I was early on a Sunday morning, huddled in the back of a rented moving van across the street from The Smiling Bovine, casing the joint through a rusted-out hole above the van's wheel well.

The FBI van had disappeared the day before. I was starting to think they had the right idea. I'd been staking The Bovine out for days without having caught a stinking whiff of Jerome. Maybe I would have to wait until the 23rd to see him after all. Darla didn't know I was down there yet; I didn't want her to know where I was at any time. It was still more than reasonable to believe she'd simply have me killed once I was done doing her dirty work.

I was a bit on edge, and the encounter that was soon to follow might've gone a bit smoother on a good night's sleep and a full stomach. But maybe that's just me trying to make excuses for myself, because bad sleeps have outnumbered good ones for as long as I can remember.

It was just after six in the morning when a small grey Toyota pickup pulled into The Smiling Bovine's back lot. A scrawny male of about fifty, bald on top but with greasy shoulder-length hair down the back and sides, stepped out of the truck, shut the door behind him, and walked over to the steel backdoor of the slaughterhouse.

A security light illuminated a pale-yellow circle of the lot and the door itself, which sat a good foot and a half above the ground—no one had bothered to build a step.

The man unlocked the door and entered.

About five minutes later, a gold Cadillac pulled in. Two men climbed out of the car. Waddling out of the passenger side was Jerome, a bald slob with a gut of Saturday-morning-cartoon proportions, dressed oddly in track pants and a sports jacket. From the driver's seat came an impossibly large orc, presumably with some glandular issue, dressed in black jeans and a black wife-beater and wearing a beard you could nest a family of osprey in.

The two moved to the back of the car, Jerome lifted the lid of the trunk, and the hulking goon heaved out what was either a quarter cow in an oversized duffel bag or something decidedly more criminal.

The goon lugged the twitching bag over his shoulder, then he and Jerome approached The Bovine's rear door. Jerome knocked on the door.

Mid-knock, the door opened to reveal the man who'd come in the pickup, now dressed in a heavy green butcher's apron and smiling like a hungry jackal.

Jerome went in, followed by his goon, who had to duck to fit beneath the doorframe.

I rolled over in the van, sat up, and sighed. Expecting the worst was congenital for a Rutherford, and for good reason: I've been shot seven times in my life, but with considerable luck—or misfortune, depending on whom you ask—none of the bullets had found a lethal target. I knew, though, that it was only a matter of time.

Nevertheless, there was business to conduct. I pulled out my pistol, checked the clip, fitted the silencer to the muzzle, then slid the gun back into my shoulder holster. I crept out of the passenger side of the van and circled around to Jerome's Cadillac. It was worth seventy grand if it was worth a penny. Fitted with 22-inch rims and painted with a shimmering gold-powder finish, the car proved that Jerome, if nothing else, had horrible taste.

I crouched behind the wheel on the side farthest from the building and waited. If I was going to do this, darkness would be to my advantage. The Smiling Bovine was in an industrial area, and soon enough people would be pulling into the surrounding factories and warehouses for work.

Time, it turned out, was not on my side. I'd been hunched behind the Cadillac only ten minutes when the sun began to peek its waking head above the horizon. If some passerby saw me crouched behind the Cadillac with a gun in my hand, I wouldn't get a crack at Jerome.

As light began to creep across the asphalt, I scrambled to the door and crouched behind it. If I could get out of this one alive, and then make Darla Carmine live up to her word, I would relocate to the least populated island I could find and be eating mangos, feeding bananas to monkeys, and drinking lagers on the beach by the end of the month. Even the mafia would have a hard time finding me where I was planning to go, assuming

Darla sent them after me as soon as she was finished writing my cheque, which I figured was as safe a bet as came along in a lifetime.

Things of course couldn't be that simple. To my further rotten luck, a car turned onto the road and headed toward me, a plain white SUV with opaquely tinted windows.

I scampered back across the lot to a dumpster and crouched out of sight. A tall stack of empty crates further protected me. I watched from behind my blind as the SUV pulled into the lot, then as its engine rumbled to silence like a dog who'd found a good place to sleep.

A set of black boots stepped out of the passenger side and set foot on the ground. It took me a second to realize it, since they make these guys to spec at the factory, but it was the square-headed FBI drone that had been casing the joint the last few days. These guys didn't work alone, so I was expecting his partner to come around from the other side of the van. But expectations are terrible things to have, and this time was no different. Instead, what came around the other side of the van was our very own Premier, dressed for a cabinet meeting and smiling widely.

My job was to deal with Jerome, not assassinate a political figure. But let me tell you, I was tempted. That son of a bitch hadn't done a thing for anybody that didn't have an offshore bank account in the six years he'd been in office. I'm not political, but I know a criminal when I see one, be him wearing prison tattoos or a five thousand dollar suit.

I watched the FBI goon and Stephenson knock on the back door of the slaughterhouse and be let inside.

Considering Darla had been ploughing him, it would be a mighty big coincidence for Stephenson to be on visiting terms with her husband's white supremacist drug smuggling murderer.

> I began to wonder who really had it coming in this story. Maybe it was everybody.

Ethan closed the book. He turned to the back cover, hoping to find a little more biographical information about the author. The bio was short to the point of curt and not at all informative: "Thelonius Grave is the author of over fifty novels, including The Rutherford Motive, House Calls, and Detective Murphy series'. He is a Canadian citizen."

Many rumours about Thelonius Grave's identity existed— that he was involved in organized crime, or was a police officer, lawyer, or some other official figure with insight into the composition of criminal enterprises. A few novels were set in Mexico, a few more in Montreal and Ontario, the half-dozen most recent books taking place in the Pacific Northwest and California. Some of the novels were first person, some third, and a few had a metafictional bent Sometimes, more than one title would be released in the same year.

The novels occasionally and eerily echoed real-world events. In fact, Grave's novel, *La Guerra Perdida*, so accurately described the hellish drug war in Mexico that Grave had been dragged in for questioning. Or so the internet claimed.

The other rumour around *La Guerra Perdida* was that Grave hadn't received a penny for the movie rights; his disdain for contracts of any kind had resulted in him signing a very lopsided and poor one.

Maybe it was all a publicity stunt. Ethan hadn't read *La Guerra Perdida*, but he'd seen the movie and hadn't been particularly impressed. The conspiracy theories surrounding the real-life events were far more interesting: That the CIA were opening the doors so wide for the cartels that the Agency may as well have stationed greeters in welcome smocks at Customs, smiling and handing out flyers on the week's best deals. Disillusionment with the war on drugs among the Agency's highest bureaucrats had run so deep, the story went, that their best exit strategy had become to let the cartels win, of course making a few bucks along the way.

Ethan assumed it to be nonsense, but it sure made for good entertainment on the big screen. The story was typical Grave fodder, even though it didn't feature Rutherford: smuggling rings, murders, treachery, grand conspiracy, kidnappings and gunfire. *Cheap Thrills* was no different.

The last chapter Ethan had read of *Cheap Thrills*, in addition to Rutherford tracking Jerome to the slaughterhouse, recounted more of what Rutherford new about the affair between Darla and Premier Stephenson. Unsurprisingly, sex wasn't the only currency being exchanged in the relationship.

Ethan had read enough for one day. The murder, drugs, and mystery weren't helping to take his mind off his own predicament.

He stuffed the last of the Thick Burger into his mouth, then pulled a cigarette from the pack on the floor beside him. He lit it, drew deeply, and exhaled, the smoke forming a thin stratus against the ceiling.

As his mind wandered between the events of *Cheap Thrills* and his own circumstances, Ethan recalled the gun tucked beneath the passenger seat. He sat up, reached around to the front, and retrieved the gun.

It was heavier than he expected. He toyed with it a bit, figuring out how the safety worked, and how to eject the magazine, which felt and looked full. The gorilla had only squeezed the one shot off in the apartment.

Ethan considered the gun. He got a feel for the weight of the trigger while the magazine was out and the chamber was empty, then put the gun back under the seat.

The pocket of his jeans began to rattle and sing. He dug in and pulled out his phone: Unknown Number. He answered.

"Hello?"

"Who's this?" a voice asked.

"Who's this?"

"I asked first. Who the fuck is this?"

"It's my phone," Ethan said. "Shouldn't you know who you're calling?"

"Is this Ethan?"

"Maybe."

"Enough bullshit," the voice barked. "This is Ethan? We know you've got our money."

Ashes fell from the cigarette onto Ethan's neck. Smoke crawled across his cheek and into his eyes. He blinked it out.

"I don't have anybody's money," Ethan said. "No money. Nothing."

"You shot Simon in the face in that alley, then you took the money. The big guy—your roommate?—he found out about the fifty grand from Hugo, you found Simon, you shot him, and you took it."

Fifty thousand. This whole mess is Hugo's fault.

"I didn—" he said.

"I wasn't asking, I was telling. Reminding you that you have the money, that it's not yours, and that you're going to give it back. You know why?"

"I didn't take—"

"Shut up. We've established that you have it, you understand? That much is clear. We've got your girl, you understand?"

Sam, Ethan thought. He sat up in the back seat.

"Samantha. You understand? We've got her," the voice said again.

"Yes, I understand," Ethan said.

"You understand what this is about and how to fix it?"

"Yeah," Ethan said.

"This misunderstanding here is about the money. That solves everything. Understand?"

"Yes," Ethan said.

"We'll call you back and tell you where to take it. Understand?"

"Got it," Ethan said.

"Good. That was easy."

The man hung up.

## 29

After leaving the Nirvana site, Wynne called his student deal-er, Marcus, and told him he was coming by for a visit. He'd clearly woken Marcus up; Wynne was surprised he'd even answered the phone.

Wynne hadn't wanted to be out of bed this early, either. Eight AM was the purview of cubicle drones, farmers, and Starbucks baristas. But this Simon problem needed resolving, and quickly.

Simon Hough had been a mistake. When Wynne had first met him, Simon had been bartending at The Pink Curtain. At the time, he was a skinny cokehead in the process of partying himself out of a job. He was also the dancers' source for marijua-na until Winston Carmello found out the weed being sold in his club wasn't his. In Simon's defense, at the time he hadn't known who owned the club. When his newfound unemployment coin-cided with Wynne's need for a street guy on the East Side, a part-nership was made. Simon would now sell Wynne's weed, which was better and, more importantly, also came from Carmello.

Simon quickly proved himself an inveterate partier, gullible fool, and all-around innately disagreeable personality. But as far as low-rent dealers went, he was reliable, good at bringing in new business, and was never short or late with the cash. And for that all was forgiven.

Regardless of who had the bag now, Wynne was starting to believe Simon had been involved in its disappearance. The con-spiracy theories Simon had been spewing to Frankie were odd enough, but it wasn't the first time Wynne had heard them. Struhl had been espousing similar thoughts since Wynne had first met him. He'd always thought Struhl was one wig-out away from going full Unabomber and moving into some shack in the northern backcountry.

Wynne's deranged boss was shaving less often and his hair was getting longer. He had the telltale creeping neck hair of the unkempt man and had begun to cultivate an unpleasant body odour. Sure signs to Wynne of mental instability—personal hygiene and cleanliness being windows into the state of a man's mind.

The last time Wynne had visited Struhl, before this whole mess had started, the conversation had turned to his improving survivalist skills: hunting, shelter building, the will to survive in a lawless society. Wynne was all for self-sufficiency and limited contact with governmental bodies, particularly the Canada Revenue Agency and the law, but Struhl took it to a whole new level.

There was also the question of what Simon had been doing in the alley the night he was shot.

Wynne was supposed to have met him at the pizza place the following morning, so why, Wynne wondered, was Simon there, presumably with the cash, the night before?

Omar, the lackey from Corleone's, had told Wynne that Simon, despite his promotion, still sold in the neighbourhood. The two deadbeats Wynne was trying to find were customers of Simon and, coincidentally or not, Corleone's as well. Omar also claimed to have seen Ethan and Phil leave the alley the morning Simon was found.

Wynne would have to pay another visit to Omar, too. If he'd been stupid enough to shoot Simon and dump his body in with the trash from the pizza place, then it wouldn't take much to crack him. If he knew anything else about these two losers, or Simon, then Wynne could beat that out of Omar, too, if it came to it. Or maybe even if it didn't.

The drive from the Nirvana site to Marcus's place was only a few kilometers, but Wynne hated driving his Charger downtown, no matter how brief the distance. It was inevitable that some fuckwit would hit his prized possession. He probably should have driven his BMW, he thought, but he was agitated from the inconveniences and injuries he'd recently suffered and had hoped driving the Dodge would make him feel better.

The Charger had been a nauseating green and unfit for the road when he'd bought it two years earlier, but now it was a work of art. A jet-black paint job, tan Italian-leather interior, wide whitewall tires, an engine overhaul, and a new transmission had set Wynne back nearly twenty-five grand. The car consumed money at a rate to rival only that of his last part-time girlfriend, a stripper named Charlotte from The Pink Curtain who, with mixed emotions from Wynne and a single, unadulterated one from Josie, had disappeared to Albertan oil money a few months back. But he loved the car like a child, unconditionally, despite how much it cost.

Wynne slowed to a stop in front of Marcus's building, one of many obelisks standing resolutely in the wealthiest part of downtown Vancouver. Wynne couldn't even afford to buy a place in Yaletown. Not that he'd want one, even if he could. Far too yuppie for him. But he was impressed that an Emily Carr Pottery major, or whatever the hell Marcus was, had acquired himself such a swank address. Or, more likely, that his parents had acquired it for him.

Wynne approached the front door of the building and scrolled through the names in the directory on the buzzer panel, stopping on the third page. He dialled the number for "Fields, Marcus," but received no answer. He dialled again.

A groggy acknowledgement came through the speaker. The panel buzzed, and the door unlocked with a click.

Wynne entered the building and crossed the lobby to the bank of elevators. A few mammoth abstract paintings adorned the broad cement walls. Tall ferns littered the lobby. Taller concrete pillars supported the high ceiling.

Wynne summoned the elevator and the doors opened. He stepped in and pushed the button for the fourteenth floor. The doors closed, and the car began to rise.

The wall of the elevator held a small TV, set to a sports channel. Two suited broadcasters smiled broadly and nodded. The channel's logo flashed across the screen, then the show cut to commercial.

The commercial announced an upcoming rock concert at the Queen Elizabeth Theatre, just a few blocks away.

Wynne had been at the QE the night before to question Brock, Struhl's union man at the theatre. Brock's story about the missing money had been nearly the same as Frankie's: Brock had met Simon at The Pink Curtain with the cash, then grudgingly sat through one of Simon's apocalyptic rants.

Brock, a wide-set and surly fifty-year-old with a fireman's moustache and permanent sneer, had told Wynne he didn't want to deal with "the little puke" Simon anymore, and that, from now on, Wynne could do the pickups and deliveries himself. Brock went on to tongue-lash Wynne for entrusting such a brainless, paranoid, burned-out jackass with anything other than not swallowing his own tongue.

Wynne took the abuse without retort. Brock was a loud-mouthed prick, Wynne knew, but had earned Struhl's—and Carmello's, Wynne had heard—respect. Putting him in his place wouldn't make Wynne's life any easier. Plus, Brock was right.

After talking to Brock, Wynne read the events schedule for the theatre and questioned the other members of the QE crew. There'd been a Softwood Lumber show the night Simon had been shot. Brock had worked it, and the cleanup had run until the early hours of the morning. Wynne was satisfied that Brock had nothing to do with the murder.

The short commercial for the theatre ended as the elevator car arrived at the fourteenth floor. The doors opened and Wynne stepped out. Marcus's apartment was the third one left of the elevators.

Wynne knocked on the door. Moments later, it opened.

It was Wynne's first visit to Marcus's place. Why anyone would want to live in a cell-sized concrete box was beyond him. It reminded him of the mausoleum in which his aunt, Frankie's mother, was interred. And, conversely, when he visited her tomb, he was reminded of buildings like these.

A drafting table covered with large sheets of paper and drawing implements took up most of the living room. A stained loveseat, its stuffing creeping out of tears in the cushions and armrests, sat next to the table. Two plastic milk crates and a yield sign served as a coffee table, on top of which sat the elements of a session—lighter, ashtray, bag of weed, scissors, and a white ceramic bong in the shape of a laughing elephant, its trunk raised and holding the bowl.

The bare concrete floor—one of those geothermal heated deals, Wynne assumed—was in severe need of a sweeping, littered with bottle caps, cigarette butts, and tumbleweeds of dust and hair. The room smelled like stale smoke and recent sex and, less disgustingly, freshly brewed coffee.

An original painting hung above the sofa, an oil colour of two men in black suits, white shirts, and skinny black ties in a standoff. The man on the left had his back turned to Wynne and the living room, his right arm and hand extended and holding a small silver sidearm; the man on the right mirrored him, chest to Wynne, right arm extended and holding a similar weapon.

"That yours?" Wynne asked, pointing at the painting.

Marcus, dishevelled and dressed in a oversized T-shirt and baggy sweatpants, the waist of which dipped below his boxer-clad ass, turned and looked at the painting. He had one of those purposefully lopsided haircuts that looked, to Wynne, unfinished, and justified an unexpected haymaker to the temple.

"Uh, yeah," Marcus said, blearily. "That's mine." At this hour of the morning, it was impossible to tell whether he was still up and high from the night before, or recently awakened but yet to visit the bong and coffee maker.

"It's pretty good. Is it for sale?" Wynne asked.

"For sale?" Marcus said, taken aback.

"Marcus?"

A female voice in the bedroom interrupted the negotiations, followed by a short bark. The door beside Wynne opened a crack and a small, mixed-breed dog scampered out. It pulled at Wynne's pant leg, growling.

"What the fuck is this?" Wynne said.

"It's a dog," Marcus said.

"I know it's a dog. What is it? And why is it trying to eat my leg?"

"It's a bulldog cross. He's a little stir-crazy." Marcus squinted at Wynne's jaw. "What happened to your face?"

"Car accident," Wynne said. "Crossed with what?"

"Not sure."

"Looks half weasel," Wynne said. "Or kielbasa." The dog was tubular; its torso was a long cylinder of brown flesh, capped with the blunted head of a bulldog, complete with sullen, dangling jowls. It chortled and slavered and shuffled around Wynne's feet. It looked like it got all the exercise it needed simply trying to breath.

"It might be part dachshund," Marcus offered.

Wynne looked around the apartment, remembering they were on the fourteenth floor.

"Where the fuck does it shit?" he asked.

"PeePad," Marcus said, pointing to the balcony.

Wynne walked the four steps across the living room and looked outside. A box, two feet by four feet, like a child's sandbox, took up most of the balcony. The box was topped with a swath of fake grass. A coil of turd sat next to a tiny red fire hydrant in the middle.

"That's disgusting," Wynne said.

"Gotta go somewhere," Marcus shrugged.

"How about in a yard?"

"I'm on the fourteenth floor."

Wynne nodded slowly. No place for animal of any kind, he thought.

"I've got your money," Marcus said, walking past Wynne and into the bedroom. As the door opened, Wynne caught a glimpse of a nude girl with jet black hair and butterscotch skin lying on the bed, watching or reading something on a laptop. Marcus knelt beside her then reached underneath the bed. He pulled out a small metal case, which he opened with a key he'd taken from the nightstand. He pulled out a neatly bundled and elastic bound stack of bills, closed the lid of the box, slipped it back under the bed, and brought the money out to Wynne.

"Thirty-two hundred," Marcus said, handing over the money.

"Why do you still have this?" Wynne asked, making a brief show of counting the bills.

"I told Simon I'd give it to you directly."

"When was this?"

"He came the night he was supposed to. I told him I'd be dealing with you directly from now on."

"You're supposed to give the money to Simon."

"Well I didn't. And I'm not going to, nor will I be letting him in my house anymore."

Can't argue with that, Wynne thought, Simon being dead and all.

"First: I decide who you give the money to, not you. Second: why?"

"When he came by the other night, he was talking a lot of nonsense. He was either high or coming down off a chemical."

"What was he saying?"

"He started off with his usual gibberish, asking how business was—which is none of his concern, as a delivery man—and if I was seeing any new girls."

"He asked you about girls?"

Marcus looked up.

"He always does. He's either gay for me or hasn't gotten laid in so long he's reduced to living vicariously through others. I don't know which, but he's creepy as hell. He's weirded out more than a few girls that have been here when he comes by."

"You're not supposed to have anybody here when he comes by," Wynne said, nodding toward the bedroom. "Or when I come by for that matter."

"Didn't know when you were coming by, did I?" Marcus said. "Simon is never on time, so I don't know when he's coming, either. And I'm not going to plan my life around that degenerate, that's for sure."

"How late was he here?" Wynne asked.

"Not very. Maybe ten o'clock? I had a good excuse to get him out of here, thankfully. I was only home for a few hours after an exhibit opening."

"Exhibit?"

"At GallerEast. Then I went to the after party. You know Knut Comely?"

"What?" Wynne said.

"You might like his work," Marcus said.

Wynne doubted it.

"Where was the party?"

"The Mint," Marcus said. "On Hughley, just off Pender. HardSawz from Softwood Lumber showed up, freestyled a bit."

Wynne didn't care to hear about any rap group, but the party was something he could follow up on. Wynne knew the owner of The Mint; they used to go to the same gym. He'd swing by later and review the security tape to see what time Marcus was there. It wouldn't be hard: they scanned IDs at the door.

"Heard the new album?" Marcus asked.

"What?"

"*Apocalypse Philosophy*. HardSawz's side project. It's an adeptly tuned, socially conscious album. He's really evolved as an artist," Marcus said.

"Fuck no," Wynne said. From what Wynne heard, HardSawz—real name Kenneth Lowemeyer—was for the most part socially conscious only of young Eastern European prostitutes, in threes, as much blow as Wynne or anyone else could sell him, and combining the two hobbies concurrently. "So, you haven't heard from Simon since?"

"No, and I hope not to," Marcus said, picking up the elephant bong. He held a lighter to the trunk, bubbled up a hit, and sucked back a lung full. He spoke as he exhaled.

"I don't want to deal with Simon because he's untrustworthy, stupid, and crazy. That night he was here last week, he started going off about all this conspiracy theory garbage. That the Taco Bell shooting a few months back was actually a CIA operation—"

"Taco Bell shooting?"

Marcus nodded. He offered Wynne a hit off the bong. Wynne declined.

"Yeah," Marcus said. "In Idaho a few months ago. Sandpoint, I think. Guy walks into a Taco Bell and shoots the place up with a Tech 9. Kills fourteen. Mostly Canadian diners."

"Why would the CIA shoot up a Taco Bell full of tourists?"

"They wouldn't. But for nutjobs like Simon, they say it's an excuse for the government to take away more civil liberties. Deny people their guns."

"Why's he give a fuck?" Wynne asked. He didn't remember Simon being an American, but he probably hadn't asked either.

"Because he's a moron."

"You seem to know a lot about Simon."

"A lot more than I'd care to," Marcus said, replacing the bong on the coffee table, then rising from the sofa and walking into the kitchen. "Trust me. It doesn't take much to get him going."

"So, what does this place Sandpoint have to do with Simon?"

"He said he needed to stock up on guns before the government tries to take them all. Said he was trying to make some extra cash to that end. He kept going on about the Second Amendment. I tried to tell him this is Canada and there isn't one, but he wouldn't have any of it."

"Lots of people have crazy ideas, doesn't mean you don't do business with them," Wynne said, thinking of Jack Struhl and some of his similar theories.

"The guy's a paranoid," Marcus said from the kitchen. "The 9/11 stuff, the false flag stuff—it's all paranoid delusional nonsense. People like that are unpredictable and untrustworthy, particularly when they carry a gun and dabble in meth."

Great, Wynne thought. Simon had been on meth. The money could be anywhere.

"Look," Marcus said, "the guy's a loser. If he's who you're going to keep sending around, then don't bother. Make that"—he leaned out of the kitchen and gestured to the stack of bills in Wynne's hand—"the last of my business with you."

Wynne respected a man with principles. He also respected a man who faced all his bills the same way and bound them in a tight little bundle, the edges uniform like a new paperback fresh off the grocery stand. Marcus, probably not more than twenty-two and appearing even younger, seemed like someone Wynne could trust. Wynne also appreciated the extra effort put into using heavy pink elastics, probably taken from broccoli bunches, to bundle the cash. It was a nice touch. Maybe he could use Eric more in the future.

"Simon won't be coming by anymore," Wynne said.

Marcus came out of the kitchen with a steaming mug of coffee in his hand.

"No?"

"Yeah."

"That was easier than I thought it would be," Marcus said.

"I'm a reasonable guy," Wynne said. "You won't see Simon again."

"Great. So, I'll deal directly with you?"

"For now."

"You got any more bud on you? Simon didn't bring me any after I refused to give him the money."

"No, nothing right now. How'd he take that?"

"What?"

"Refusing to give him the money."

"I just told him I didn't have it. So he put his gun down on the table like a big tough guy, made a little speech."

"What'd you do?"

"Rolled a joint and smoked it. Then he calmed down long enough to forget about being mad." Marcus smiled.

Wynne stuffed the pile of bills into the inside pocket of his jacket, then turned and made for the door.

"When can I get more bud?" Marcus asked.

"Soon," Wynne said, and left.

## 30

The ferry arrived at the terminal on Barnette Island just after lunch.

Sam rode the shuttle to the north tip of the island, where a clutch of homes occupied a hill populated by spruce and Douglas fir trees, the hillside running down to the rocky shore of the Pacific Ocean.

Barnette, sandwiched between the mainland of British Columbia and the long, shielding mass of Vancouver Island, housed nearly six thousand permanent residents. Barnette's inhabitants were a glaringly heterogeneous group: farmers who produced craft goods, both for the residents of the island and for the tourists who nearly tripled its population in the summer; musicians, potters, painters, and other craftspeople who used the solitude offered by the island to focus on their art; and finally, the people who had been born on Barnette but never found a good enough reason to leave.

This last group, no more eccentric than the occupants of any other small town, and intoxicated with equal frequency, accounted for all the other occupations necessary to run a small community and thriving vacation destination: public servants, small-business owners, retail staff, and the like.

Sam had been born on Barnette, but the whole family had moved to the mainland when she was thirteen, when her father had landed a job as principal of a private elementary school in Vancouver. The Holley's retained their three-bedroom home as a summer vacation retreat, the house set among a gathering of Douglas firs at the water's edge.

When she'd gotten the call from Ethan, sitting in the Taco Bell parking lot in Langley, Sam had just finished her last exam. She was done for the term and wasn't taking any classes in the summer: none of her required courses were being offered, and none of the available electives caught her eye. Excited that she was through for another semester, she had called friends and made plans. Her best friend, Beth, was on Barnette living with her latest boyfriend, Sven, some Swede she'd found grooming horses on an inland farm.

Escaping the city for the relative solitude of the island, and for the familiar comforts of a long-held friendship, felt to Sam an appropriate way to conclude her busy academic and unusual personal life of the past few months.

When Sam got to the house she dropped her bag on a bare single bed in her preferred bedroom, then opened the windows, turned on the water, plugged in the appliances, and went about the rest of the opening tasks, being the first Holley to visit Barnette this summer.

When she was done, she made the short hike up the road to Beth's place.

A kilometre up the coast, Beth and Sven had rented a utilitarian faux-log cabin, existing like a forgotten satellite off the boastful main residence, once featured in the pages of *West Coast Living*.

Immaculately manicured gardens of colourful hibiscus, bird of paradise, agapanthus, and elevated ponds surrounded by lush green fernery, led down to a private dock for the homeowner's 50' *Calliope*. The main house, with its five bedrooms, three baths, and a sprawling, multi-tiered veranda, made the cabin, hunkered in the main home's shadow, seem to exist solely for the purpose of mockery, an accoutrement providing evidence of progress by wealth.

The plain cabin consisted of a bedroom, kitchen, and main living space, all heated by a woodstove. Cords of spruce and fir were stacked outside beneath an overhang of the roof. Behind the cabin, a faux outhouse and shower, both plumbed to the main house, added to the cabin's manufactured charm. The cabin also benefitted from electricity, but both it and the fully modernized main residence experienced occasional outages during Barnette's winters of high winds and heavy rainfall. Beth had been able to rent the otherwise vacant cabin—built essentially as a playhouse for the owner's now grown children—as a result of befriending the owner, a mainland real estate tycoon and patron of the cafe Beth operated at the ferry terminal.

Sam had known Beth since they were both children, when Sam and her family had lived on Barnette full time. The two girls had ridden horses at a youth camp on the far side of the island. While Sam's family had left for the mainland when she was young, Beth's had remained. In fact, Beth had never lived anywhere else.

Sam joined Beth and Sven in the cabin's main room. They drank and smoked and listened to music while Sam explained her current situation—Hugo and his concerns, Ethan and his even bigger ones.

"Dude's a fucking loser, Sammy," Beth said. Petite and elfish with wispy blonde hair, Beth sat cross-legged on a couch cushion on the floor, fiddling with her cell phone.

"He doesn't have his shit even remotely together," Beth continued.

"Which one?" Sam said.

"Either. Both. An ambitionless burnout and a low-life dime-bag slinger. Leeeuuuuuzerrrrrs."

"Um." Sam gestured toward the coffee table. A plethora of weed-related ordinance and armaments occupied the surface. Though Beth and Sven grew all their own dope, they sold little of it, Sam knew.

"Oh, come on, Sam," Beth said. "This is a far cry from organized crime."

"I'd hardly call Hugo organized."

Beth finished rolling a thin joint and lit it. She inhaled, then offered it to Sam.

On the table, next to a terracotta bowl serving as an ashtray, a palm-sized wad of hash, resembling a dark hunk of dried chocolate fudge, rested conspicuously. Sven had become a passable hash presser in order to supplement his income as stable hand, Sam had learned, but usually ended up smoking most of it himself.

"How much could you get for that?" Sam asked.

"The weed?" Beth said. "Not much here. There's too much of it."

"No, the hash."

"This is ten dollars," Sven said in sing-song Swenglish. He smiled a wide white smile at Sam.

A slim blonde in a Swedish National Football jacket, its blue matching his eyes, Sven was a young man so stereotypically Swede as to appear drafted into Beth's life by some hack sitcom writer.

Sam wondered how he had ended up on Barnette. She had yet to get the full story, but knowing the island to be a closed social ecosystem, and the resultant dating scene essentially a cage match for fresh meat, she assumed that Sven had simply been the choicest cut available. Leading her to again question Beth's qualifications as relationship councillor. Not that Sam was particularly interested in a relationship with Hugo or Ethan.

"Probably get fifteen on the mainland," Beth said. "It's different, here, Sammy. You know that. It's not traded for coke here. People don't get shot here."

"They don't get shot for weed there either, Beth."

"No, but they get shot for money. You just said so yourself! Direct evidence! This Harvey—"

"Hugo."

"Whatever. And what's the dead guy's name?"

"Simon. But I didn't know him, really."

"Well, you sure never will now. Stay over here for the summer. Just because you smoke weed doesn't mean you have to hang out with shitheads."

"Marijuana, it should be legal," Sven said melodically. He smiled again.

Sam sparked a thin joint she had rolled herself, took a drag, and tapped the ash into the pot.

Beth was right, Sam admitted to herself. And Sam hadn't even told her that about the pills they were trying to get Hugo to move now.

"What the hell am I supposed to do here all summer?"

"Hang out with me, maybe?" Beth said. She curled up on the couch cushion and let her head rest in Sam's lap. "Get a job at the resort again?"

Sam had worked at The Overlook a few summers earlier, at the front desk. That same summer she'd volunteered with one of the local animal conservation and care groups.

"It's an option," Sam admitted.

Beth clapped excitedly.

Sam took another drag on the joint. The last time she'd spent the whole summer on the island she'd sworn she would never do it again, for fear of death by boredom.

But attitudes change when they need to. Spending a relaxed summer on Barnette might be a good idea. And getting away from Hugo, and now Ethan, was probably an even better one.

## 31

There'd been a close call. A woman down the street—an old blue hair with an obnoxious little Shar-Pei that Struhl had been tempted to punt on numerous occasions—had called the police about a chemical smell. Turned out the smell was a neighbour half-assing a meth operation. Struhl had seen the guy. He looked like he could barely operate the lock on the door, let alone a chemistry set. He was probably just a meth head trying to brew up a personal batch. Not a big deal, in the greater scheme of things, but with police and hazmat spacemen swarming the place next door, Struhl had held off starting another cycle until the area was clear.

The grow room beneath the aging split-level on Danwood had sat unused for months. During the downtime, upgrades and repairs had been made. Two new generators had been installed. An electrician had been in the day before to rewire the board for the lights and fans. A new vent had been installed just this morning.

The gap in production would cost Struhl vital income. Winston Carmello wasn't happy about downtime, and an unhappy Winston Carmello usually resulted in a smaller cut for Struhl. When this new grow turned over, Struhl wouldn't cash out like he normally would. Carmello would be even less happy when he heard about this whole Simon issue, of which, because Carmello had been out of the country these past few weeks, he was still unaware.

And Struhl needed more money. Even with this one time desperately acquired windfall, he was behind on payments for the work on his place up north, work that wouldn't continue until the money started flowing again. The threat on his life by the disgruntled contractor was one Struhl took seriously. Selecting that crew had been a misstep. But the build needed to be done discretely, and with some far-from-code modifications.

Now, as he watched two illegal Thai immigrants seed rows of pots in the center of the room, Struhl worried he would be trapped in the Lower Mainland another full year. At this rate he wasn't sure he would still be alive that long. It was all a disappointment. Struhl was tired of the city and its people, tired of keeping his eyes and ears open for police or for some rival criminal—or perhaps affiliated underling—who decided whatever grievance they had with Struhl was severe enough to resolve with a bullet.

He was tired of laundering money, tired of then moving it through a banking system he despised, and tired of dodging a government he didn't believe in. Hence, his nearly finished, almost entirely self-sustainable bunker in the woods, built on land bought for a song two decades earlier, where he would retreat with his dogs and his guns and his mind, alone, save for perhaps monthly supply trips into the nearest dump trying to pass itself off as a quaint northern town.

But due to a few recent errors, he might never get there. The contractors were angry and, more importantly, connected. They needed to be taken seriously. Struhl had recently appeased them to the tune of fifty grand, but appeasement only lasted so long. Perhaps, Struhl admitted to himself, he had made his one big mistake.

His phone vibrated in his pocket. He pulled it out and checked the caller ID. Rowan.

Struhl answered.

"I'm coming down the street," Rowan said.

Struhl hung up.

He climbed the stairs out of the basement, pushed open the door and entered the living room.

The curtains were drawn. An old tube television, sitting on a second-hand coffee table, flickered in the corner. Save for those things and some supplies the Thai workers had yet to lug down to the basement, the room was barren.

Struhl crossed the living room to the front door and opened it, looking for Rowan.

A burgundy Corolla, licensed and registered, sat in the driveway. Struhl paid a man to take it away in the morning and bring it back in the afternoon, alternating pulling it in headfirst or in reverse, or sometimes leaving it on the street overnight and parking his own car in the driveway. The same man dealt with garbage and junk mail, maintained the yard, made sure the timer for the lights was working, kept the generators running, and checked the security cameras. He did the same for another operation across town. He hadn't come yet today, apparently, because the community newspaper still sat on the welcome mat.

A black Lexus sedan approached and slowed to a stop in front of the house. The door opened and Rowan climbed out. He crossed the lawn and walked up the steps of the house and onto the welcome mat, ignoring the newspaper beneath his feet. Struhl opened the door and let him in.

"What've you got?" Struhl said.

"I got a hold of the girl's boyfriend, or whoever he is. The little one," Rowan said.

"How?" Struhl asked.

"His number was in the girl's phone. He answered," he said.

"You called from her phone?"

"No. A disposable."

"So, what did he say?" Struhl asked.

Rowan looked past Struhl. The Thai workers, a man and a woman, had come up the basement stairs and were collecting more fertilizer from a pile of bags in the living room.

"They're fine," Struhl said. "They don't speak English."

"You speak Vietnamese?" Rowan asked.

"They're Thai. I speak enough," Struhl said. "So, what'd the guy say?"

"He said he'd give us the money," Rowan said.

Struhl looked surprised, and Rowan said so.

"What's the problem?"

Struhl's eyes went wide.

"Where's he going to get the money?" he asked.

"What do you mean 'Where's he going to get the money?'" Rowan said. "He took it."

"Wynne said he wasn't sure."

"Well, we're sure now."

"What'd you tell the guy?"

"All I said is, 'We've got the girl.'"

Struhl raised an eyebrow.

"That's it?" he said.

"That's it."

Struhl, though perplexed, wasn't about to argue with an influx of unexpected cash.

"Good, then. Let's get the money. What'd you tell him?"

"Told him we'd call him and tell him where to take the money."

"Who's watching the girl?"

"Nobody. I'm going back now. I didn't want to say much over the phone."

"Let's make sure this guy shows up with the cash, then we can let her go."

"Why don't we see what we can get out—"

"Just do what I tell you," Struhl said. "Call him and get the cash."

Rowan nodded.

"I like this," Struhl said, not entirely sure if he did.

## 32

Samantha Emma Woodgrave was going to die.

She'd spent the night tied upright to her chair, incapable of sleep. Instead, her tiredness manifested as nervous, dry-eyed dread, her brain vacillating between screaming the realities of the situation at hand and negotiating, with herself, the conditions of her release: pledges to settle down, focus on school, give up her recreational activities.

She prayed. She hadn't prayed or been to church more than a half-dozen times since moving to Vancouver, only attending when she went to Texas, or in turn when her mother came to visit her, but even then on a schedule barely exceeding the anniversaries of major events in the life and death of Christ.

The only prayer she could remember in full was the Hail Mary, which she whispered a few dozen times before deciding that prayer wouldn't help her situation any more now than it had when she was eleven, when endless recitations hadn't brought her grandfather back.

After abandoning God, again, she passed the first few hours of hopelessness with bouts of tears and rage, before her brain finally undertook the more productive task of looking for a way out.

In front of her, an aged yellow washer/dryer set squatted beneath a wooden staircase. A single light bulb hung by its wire from the ceiling. A small pile of boxes, filled with what looked like magazines and books, sat against the wall to her left. To her right, two small windows met the ceiling at the top of the wall. Through the tall grass growing in the window well outside the house, thin strands of light wound their way into the basement. On the floor below the windows sat some paint trays, cans, and rollers.

Emma craned her neck behind her. She made out the shape of a large red mechanic's toolbox, on wheels, in the shadows at the back of the room. Beside the tool box, two workhorses held a bench saw set into a plywood board.

She returned her gaze to the front of the room. A patch of dusty floor was lit. Particles of dust were suspended in the light beaming in through the window. Emma watched the dust flutter and dance. She shook her head, and something—maybe the tranquil beam of light, maybe a final sense of hopelessness—washed away some of her nervousness and dread. Emma breathed, and sighed.

She took in the room again, now, if not exactly calm, at least not overcome by fear. The washer and dryer combo, the rickety wooden stairs, the small, high windows. She turned over her shoulder to re-examine the tool box.

It reminded her of a scene she'd watched just the night before in an episode of *House Call*, her favourite HBO show, loosely based on a series of novels from the 1970s by Thelonius R. Grave.

In the episode, Dale Goodman, mafia strongman and undercover RCMP agent, was doing what he did best in a basement that looked nearly identical to the one in which Emma was now trapped. A female CSIS informant sat tied to a chair in the middle of a dank basement. Behind her, a table stained unmistakeably with blood.

Emma put the pictures from that scene out of her mind and reasoned with herself. These men were no serial killers. They didn't intend to torture her, she told herself—though her head and breasts were still sore—they just wanted their money. If she could get a hold of her dad, he'd pay. No matter how much it was, he'd pay.

She struggled against the back of the chair, trying to wriggle her hands free of the duct tape. It was wrapped tightly around her wrists, but it didn't feel as if there were many layers. She curled her middle finger between her palms and began to cut at the top of the tape with her nail. If she could start even a very small cut in the tape, she might be able to tear it.

After what felt like an hour, the tape began to slice. She alternated between twisting her wrists and picking at the tape with her nail. Eventually the tape split, and with some further wriggling she pulled it apart, then reached down and tore the binding from her feet. She rose from the chair and carried it to the wall. She stood on the seat and tested one of the small windows. It was painted or sealed shut. She moved the chair to the other window. Again, painted or sealed shut.

Emma got down from the chair and leaned against the wall, fighting back tears. Now they'll kill me for trying to escape, she thought.

She moved the chair back to the middle of the room, sat down in it, then attempted to wrap the torn duct tape back around her ankles. She managed to seal it at the back, thinking she'd done a decent job. Her wrists were another story. With her arms behind the chair, she struggled vainly to replace the tape.

She quickly abandoned the futile effort, sunk her chin into her chest, and let herself cry.

## 33

About half an hour earlier, Woit had received a call from Vancouver General Hospital. A tired and distracted administrator, seemingly robbed of even the capacity for emotion, had informed her that Phillip Howard Wilford had succumbed to his injuries.

Woit hung up the phone, then added another name to the list of homicide victims that occupied an increasingly larger portion of her brain.

When the phone rang, Woit had been sitting at her desk, going over Wilford's history in search of a motive for his assault. A critical mass of tabs and documents were fanned open on the large screen in front of her. Around the monitor, stacks of paper rose like monoliths gathered in tribute to bureaucracy, all in dire need of data entry by some soon-to-be-burdened underling.

Since being arrested years earlier on a Belleville ice rink, Wilford had accumulated convictions for impaired driving, public intoxication, and resisting arrest. The incident in Belleville was so long ago that, to Woit, it felt as if a different person had tucked the young man's head into the cruiser. Aside from a predilection for drunken stupidity, however, Woit found nothing in Wilford's record connecting him to drugs or trafficking, neither did he have any association with organized crime. His police record certified him only as a common bar drunk who liked to fight—an abundant, unremarkable subspecies of humanity of which Woit had long ago had her fill.

After the call from the hospital, Woit put aside the Wilford case for the day and set to compiling notes and files on a homicide investigation from a few days prior. A low-level street dealer, Simon Hough, had been found in an East Vancouver alley, shot twice in the head.

It didn't take long to uncover Hough's connection to organized crime. A decade earlier, then in his early twenties, he'd spent two years in an Alberta prison for cocaine trafficking. Upon his release he'd moved to BC, where police soon stopped him for driving erratically, swerving across the yellow line of a barren

Korra Road at three AM in Kilgore, BC. The police found a small amount of methamphetamine tucked into an empty Coke can in the cup holder of Hough's car. Hough was also under the influence of alcohol. The offences cost him his licence and rights as a free man for another eighteen months.

Hough made friends in prison and, after serving his time, came to Vancouver and found employment at The Pink Curtain, slinging drinks for gang members and general female-genitalia enthusiasts who preferred to keep to Vancouver's East Side. The Pink Curtain, Woit and anyone else who mattered knew, was owned by one of the province's more notorious figures, Winston Carmello.

The notes in front of Woit detailed the interviews she'd conducted on the day Hough's body had been discovered. Woit and her partner, the aged and ornery Edgar Smolin—who, as he neared retirement, had become as much an impediment to good police work as a facilitator of it—had questioned the owners and operators of the string of shops which lined both sides of the alley where Hough's body was found: cafes and clothing stores, a shoe repair shop, art supply store, comic emporium, bakery, and various Japanese, Chinese, Thai, and Vietnamese restaurants.

Although the rain had washed away much of the evidence, one bullet had exited his head and was found among the piles of trash. The Forensic Identification Unit was confident the murder had occurred where the body was found. They told Woit that preliminary tests suggested Hough had met his end at just after one in the morning. Tomorrow, the bullet would be entered into the Canadian Integrated Ballistics Identification Network in the hope it could be matched to a previously used weapon.

Woit and Smolin had started their interviews with Rennie Duric, the man who had called in the body. Duric was the overnight baker for Ortuna Breads and Pastries, a small, Serbian bakery whose backdoor lent the odour of freshly baked bread to the otherwise putrid alley.

Duric related that he'd discovered the corpse while taking out the trash at the end of his shift. Duric had also said the kid from the pizza shop next door had come into the alley at about the same time, though Duric confessed that he hadn't noticed the boy until after he'd discovered the body.

The baker, who started at three AM, reported hearing no gunfire. Had there been any he wouldn't have heard it anyway, he told Woit and Smolin, due to the volume at which he played music while he worked.

"You know what makes the bread rise perfectly?" Duric told Woit, holding up a braided circle of a Simit loaf. "Metallica. This bread is full of love. And metal."

Woit hoped not literally.

She and Smolin moved on.

By early afternoon they'd found themselves standing on the red- and white-tiled floor of Corleone's. Before questioning the young man responsible for tossing, slicing, and serving the pizzas, Smolin retrieved a slice from the countertop display. When the interview began, he had yet to pay for his lunch.

Omar, a long, lanky, languorous kid covered in flour and spatters of tomato sauce, answered Smolin's introductory questions brusquely, revealing a general and in all likelihood groundless beef with police. Woit was all too familiar with this confrontational disposition. The boy's attitude was not improved by watching Smolin help himself to a can of root beer from the fridge.

Omar sat at one of the two wooden stools to the left of the checkout counter. A glass display case held five or six partially sold pizzas, kept warm under heat lamps. An ancient cash register sat a few feet over on the counter. The operation appeared to Woit to be a cash-only enterprise.

Smolin leaned on the counter and crammed a mouthful of pizza past his moustache.

"What time do you close up at night, Omar?" Smolin said, slopping strings of cheese around in his mouth as he spoke.

"About midnight."

"Last night?"

"Yeah, about midnight."

"Bullshit," Smolin said, pointing a half-eaten slice at Omar. "You're open until three on Fridays."

"How the fuck would you know?" Omar snapped.

"Language, young man," Smolin said, walking around the counter and helping himself to another slice, Hawaiian this time, or what passed for it in a place like Corleone's.

"Omar," Smolin said, examining the slice, "there's only three cubes of pineapple on this thing. Do you not take pride in your work?"

"You're going to complain about the fucking pizza you stole?"

Smolin came back around the counter and approached Omar, a gargoyle on his stool. Smolin poked him in the chest with his index finger, the rest of his hand still wrapped around the can of root beer.

"Again, language. There's no need for talk like that in front of a lady," Smolin said. It was a line he frequently spat at foul-mouthed youths. It invariably garnered the same response.

"In front of a lady? What're you, seventy?"

"No, but I wish I was," Smolin said. "Because then I'd be retired and not talking to you. And to answer your question, I know how late you're usually open because, if you hadn't already noticed, I'm a cop."

"Do you watch '80s movies in cop school to learn to talk like that?" Omar said.

"Omar," Woit said, attempting to get the interview back on track, "this doesn't have to be difficult. This death presumably has nothing to do with you or your business, so if you would just answer the questions. And politely would also be appreciated."

Smolin stared at Omar, as wide eyed and as intimidatingly as he could, his head cocked slightly forward, a thread of cheese hanging from the corner of his moustache.

Omar looked past Smolin to Woit.

"Can this guy try that too?" Omar said.

"Sure, Omar. Or I can ask the questions," she said. "So, to continue, if you answer the questions directly, we can be out of here quickly and you can carry on with your day. Okay?"

Omar nodded.

"So, do you regularly close at midnight?" she asked.

"No," Smolin said, before Omar had a chance to respond. "The place is open until three. We drive by it all the time. Plus, it says so right on the door. Can't say I've ever had a slice from here before, but despite the lack of pineapple, it's actually not all that bad. Want a slice?" Smolin asked Woit.

"No."

"It's good for the price," Omar said. "We use the best flour and ingredients available."

"The best might be a bit of a stretch," Smolin said.

"For the price," Omar clarified. He got off the stool, grabbed a paper plate from a stack beside the cash register, then reached into the display case. He retrieved a slice of pesto with cheese for Woit and put it on the counter beside her.

"Great. Thanks," Woit said.

"The pesto's pretty good," Smolin said.

"Wonderful," Woit said, her patience nearly exhausted. "Listen, Omar, lying about how late this place is open doesn't make a lot of sense, does it?"

"I'm not lying," Omar said.

"He's lying," Smolin said from behind the display case.

"He says you're lying," Woit said.

"Look," Omar said, "I closed at midnight last night. I wasn't supposed to, but I did. I had somewhere I had to be."

"Where was that?" Woit said.

Omar paused.

"The Softwood Lumber show downtown," he said. "I wasn't even supposed to be here last night, for Christ's sake. I was pulling a double because another guy couldn't make his shift. I didn't hear any gunshots, all right?"

"Who said anything about gunshots?" Woit said.

"You guys did," Omar said.

"Didn't," Smolin said, now poking around in the small preparation area behind the counter. Woit remembered Smolin mentioning gunshots in one of his preliminary questions; confusion was a technique he frequently employed. It hadn't worked in a while, Woit knew.

"Did," Omar said, standing up. "Did for certain."

"Did not," Smolin said.

"Did too," Omar said.

"Omar," Woit said, interrupting the disagreement. "Please."

"We need your boss's name and number, or a contact for whoever owns this place," Smolin said.

"Why? I told you everything there is to know."

"Look, Omar," Woit said, "we can find out who the owner is on our own, if we have to, but how about you just tell us now and save us the trouble? In keeping with the spirit of cooperation we just agreed upon?"

Omar paused. He fidgeted in his seat.

"Omar," Woit continued, "this obviously has nothing to do with you."

"So why do you have to ask me all these questions for?"

"Because that's our job, Omar. We follow every road to the end, even if it's a dead one. Right now, this one narrow road leads to you. So, give us a name so we can confirm what you said about closing times—"

"Then he'll know I closed the place early!"

"And maybe ask him what the deal is with all the porn out back," Smolin interrupted.

"And then we'll leave. All right?" Woit said.

After a moment, Omar nodded his head.

"All right."

"So, let's start with the name and contact for the employee that missed their shift last night," Woit said.

Omar rose, and Woit followed him to the till. Taped to the counter was a list of employee and vendor contact numbers. Omar pointed out the appropriate one, and Woit recorded it. As Omar retook his seat, beside the till Woit notice a stack of pink matchbooks advertising The Pink Curtain strip club. She took one.

"See?" Smolin said. "Easy. Now the owner and his number."

"A number?"

"Yes, Omar, a phone number."

Omar pulled his phone out of his pocket, reluctantly.

He read Woit the number. She wrote it down in her notepad.

"And the name?"

Omar paused. He looked out the window as he spoke. "His name is Jack," he said. "Jack Struhl."

## 34

The redhead in the goalie mask had returned to check on Emma again. Despite her concussed state, Emma had made the effort to mentally record his name: Rowan.

Rowan had brought something for her to eat and a glass of water, but to prevent him from getting close enough to notice the loose binds on her arms and legs, Emma screamed in fear at the sight of him. It hadn't taken much acting ability.

When he went back upstairs, Emma heard the squeak of footsteps on the floor above her and the low muffled tones of distant voices. She sat in her chair, fidgeting with the duct tape on her wrists and ankles, waiting for her abductors to return to the basement and do their worst.

Now Emma realized she'd heard no sounds from above in . . . how long? How long ago had they last checked on her? Hours? She didn't think so. She guessed it was still morning, judging from the light coming through the sunken basement windows. One hour? She wasn't sure, but she knew they'd be back, and that upon close inspection the reapplied tape would fool no one.

She listened closely. A trickle of water through a pipe overhead, and the occasional tick of the water heater at the back of the room, but no creaks or other telltale signs of occupation from above.

Emma wriggled free from the tape, rose from her chair, and moved to the back of the room. Maybe the mechanic's tool box—red, with seven drawers and nearly the size of a small freezer—had some duct tape she could use to rebind her legs with. She could make a sort of cuff out of the tape and slip her hands into it to at least appear that she was still bound at the writs.

Maybe if she did a good enough job, they wouldn't know she had tried to escape.

She pulled open the top drawer and supressed a gasp. Laid on folded towels were a sawed-off shotgun with a short wooden grip, and a black submachine gun with a long, curved magazine.

Emma picked up the submachine gun. It was heavy, five to ten pounds, she guessed, curling the weapon like she would a gym weight for comparison. She set the heavy gun back in the drawer, slid it closed, and opened the next drawer. On more towels were three semiautomatic handguns and a snubnose revolver.

Emma listened for footsteps or voices from above.

She took up the revolver. She'd never held a gun before. She examined the weapon; it was black with a worn wood handle. The stubby barrel and cylinder were scratched and nicked, and a small area below the cylinder was filed smooth.

Emma looked at the gun in her hands. Could she shoot someone? If there was a time when it was possible, it was now.

Emma made her way across the room to the bottom of the stairs. She took three tentative and fearful steps up the wooden staircase, then paused, listening for voice or movement. She took a few more steps, still heard nothing, then completed the ascent to the landing at the top.

Emma put one hand against the peeled paint of the door. Save for the low humming of some large appliance, it was silent on the other side.

She opened the door fully and stepped into the living room. Two mutts lay clumped together in the middle of the floor in a deep sleep. Beyond the dogs, on the faded pine coffee table, was her phone.

She circled behind the couch and approached the coffee table from the other side, stepping slowly, trying not to wake the dogs.

As she reached for her phone, the head of a basset hound poked out from under the table.

Emma stopped.

The hound, tongue hanging long and limp from its mouth, crawled from beneath the table, sat before Emma, and gave one short and muffled but deep and throaty bark.

The pile's bottom-most mutt woke first, moving only its eyes around the room. When they finally came to rest on Emma, the rest of the animal's body followed, waking the bigger dog lying with one paw partially across the black fur of its wide, muscled back.

Emma backed away from the table, toward what she hoped was the front of the house, thumbing her phone on as she retreated. The dogs followed, stalking her to the hallway.

She pressed the icon on the bottom left corner of the screen.

The phone rang only once.

"Sammy?" her father answered.

"Dad!" Emma burst out, starting to cry.

"Where are you?"

"I'm here. They have me in a basement that stinks like weed, like a grow-op or something. One guy's name is Jack. He's skinny and white. Two other big guys, one is a redhead with a scar on his face, Rowan. The other's got a big Jesus tattoo on his shoulder. They want money. Fifty thousand dollars. They think Phil took money or their drugs or—"

The largest mutt gave three loud barks.

"Who's Phil?"

Behind Emma, in the hallway, a door opened. Emma turned to meet Rowan coming out of the bathroom, a magazine tucked under his arm.

Emma dropped her phone, raised the small revolver, pointed it at his chest and fired.

The trigger held resolutely in place.

"Samantha?" Eric Woodgrave said from the phone on the floor.

Rowan held a finger to his mouth, quieting Emma. He stepped toward her, took the gun out of her extended hand, and flicked the safety off with his thumb.

"Gun safety," he said. "Very important."

Eric's voice called out from the floor. Rowan bent over and picked up Emma's phone.

"Hello?" he said. "Who is this?"

"This is Eric Woodgrave."

"Your daughter's here. She's fine."

"You kidnapped her," Eric said. "Let her go."

"No kidnapping," Rowan said. He gestured Emma into the living room with his free hand, directing her to sit on the couch. "Bit of a misunderstanding, is all."

"Misunderstanding?" Eric Woodgrave said angrily. "Her car was towed from in front of some dump of a building. Who's Phil? Is this Phil?"

Rowan put a finger back to his mouth, shushing his captive audience.

"Yes! This is Phil," Rowan said. "We're having a bit of a, um, fight, is all, Eric. I'm sure you understand."

"Excuse me?"

"I said your daughter and I are fighting. You know how it is, right? Women!"

"What?"

"To work it out, we went on a little trip."

"What the hell are you talking about?"

Rowan paused, considering what to say next.

"We were away for the night," he continued. "Nothing to worry about. Samantha here is just a little upset."

The basset hound skittered over to Rowan's feet and collapsed in a pool of skin, ear, and fur.

"All right," Eric Woodgrave said. "What do you want?"

"I don't want anything. Samantha's fine. She was only calling to ask if she could have some money to get the car out of impound."

"Let me talk to her. How much do you want?"

Rowan looked at Emma blankly.

"Nothing at all. Everything's fine. We'll be in touch," Rowan said, and hung up. He twisted the phone until it snapped, then threw the pieces on the coffee table.

"He knows what's going on," Emma said. "He's not stupid. You screwed up. First, no one calls me Samantha but him and my mom, and second, I wouldn't have to ask him for money just to get a car out of impound."

"Yeah, well, I was thinking on my feet. I wasn't ready for that."

"Not your strong suit, apparently," Emma said. "Why didn't you ask him for money?"

"You're not exactly in the position to ask questions," Rowan said, waving the revolver at Emma. "Your old man's kind of a big shot, if you didn't know. We're trying to avoid becoming headline news."

"So why don't you just let me go?" Emma asked.

"Soon enough," Rowan said. "Turns out we found what we were looking for."

"Ransom money?"

"Nope. Your boyfriend took something of ours. Turns out his little friend has it."

"Ethan?"

"Sure. Looks like a ferret?" Rowan asked, recalling Wynne's description.

"A ferret?" Emma said. She thought about it. The description wasn't far off. "What is he supposed to have?"

"Money."

"If there's one thing I'm certain of, it's that Ethan doesn't have any money."

"Then that's going to be a problem for you," Rowan said. "And now that you've seen my face, the problem just got bigger."

## 35

Ethan was self-aware enough to realize he'd never been particularly ambitious, and so he was oddly grateful for the momentum recent events had provided his life. Gangsters were after him, his friend lay comatose somewhere, and he was basically homeless. But now he had purpose: to save Sam.

Ethan had no plan for this daring rescue—specifically with regards to where to get the fifty grand Sam's kidnapper had demanded—but for now the momentum was pushing him toward Hugo. Both Sam and the kidnapper had pointed in the hairy little tree creature's direction, and so that was the direction Ethan would go.

After hanging up with Sam's abductor, Ethan climbed to the front of the car, started the engine, and pulled out of the Thick Burger lot.

Phil's clanking Pontiac carried Ethan along Broadway, past hollow-eyed street people, past barred shops with handwritten signs in the windows, past the alley that once held Simon's body, and on through Ethan's own demoralized neighbourhood.

Despite living here, Ethan had never understood the appeal of the East Side. It was a mess of rundown houses, bedbug-infested apartment complexes, profuse homelessness, modern hippies, too many coffee shops. To Ethan, the young, thrift store–attired residents of the East Side were prisoners who'd come to accept the bars of their own cage—they weren't choosing a life of austerity; they were simply broke and unable to do any better.

If his last relationship hadn't dissolved into depression and jealousy, he never would have moved to BC in the first place. To escape the situation, Ethan had taken up with his old university roommate, Massoud Ebrahim, this time in Vancouver.

Ethan shook the reminiscence from his mind. He was nearing Hugo's apartment. It was just before nine AM. He parked a block from the building, turned off the ignition, then waited and watched for Hugo to depart for morning Mass.

Ethan flipped on the radio, then slouched down and waited for Hugo to leave.

The better part of two hours and an entire Premier League match later, Hugo sauntered out of the building and climbed into a dented green Honda Civic. It pleased Ethan that Hugo drove a car in worse shape than his. Or Phil's, technically.

The Civic rattled to life with a shudder and puff of grey exhaust, then pulled away from the curb. Seconds later, Ethan started up and followed.

The two cars pulled onto Broadway, Ethan trailing about a block behind. After a ten-minute drive and a few turns onto narrow side streets, Hugo steered into the parking lot of St. Mary's Cathedral, a shrunken Notre Dame replica resting in the oblong shadow of a neighbouring condo tower.

Ethan parked on the street opposite the church's south side. From his view of the parking lot, Ethan watched Hugo leave his car and enter the building.

Soon, vehicles began to stream into the lot, and people into the building at all its entrances.

When the flood had settled into a broken trickle, Ethan climbed the cement stairs of the church, passed through the tall wooden doors, and entered.

The pews—holding a few hundred people, Ethan figured— were already mostly full. He took a seat at the rear of the church and looked across the sea of repentant heads for Hugo, to no avail.

As the organ sounded its first hymn announcing the start of Mass, the last straggling parishioners entered the church and found the few remaining seats.

The choir joined in with the organ, and the doors to the lobby opened. A young boy in an altar server's white hassock, carrying a cross twice his size, began the procession, the cross threatening to strike a parishioner on the crown of their head at every pew. Two parishioners dressed in plain clothes followed: an old man in a grey suit with a beaming smile, and a woman holding a rosary and looking, Ethan thought, like she couldn't possibly exist anywhere outside of a church: an indestructible grey perm and a one-piece paisley printed dress the texture of 1960s living room curtains.

The ruins of an ancient priest brought up the rear. White eyebrows like bushy Maltese puppies perched over a set of round, thick-lensed glasses. Hunched, eyes cast to the ground, and moving incrementally with a black cane, it appeared to Ethan that the priest's whole being was focussed intently on basic respiratory functions and the difficult task of not falling over.

After the choir finished and restarted their hymn—the first pause marked by a short eruption of coughs from the congregation—the shepherd and his disciples completed their long journey to the altar. The man in the grey suit helped the priest into his chair.

Ethan listened to the next hymn with only half an ear as his eyes roamed the space: wall plaques depicting Jesus in his final days and hours, stained-glass saints in the window panes, a third-rate attempt at a baroque ceiling, a small boy sitting beside Ethan in the pew and playing a handheld videogame.

"What're you playing?" he whispered to the kid. The little blonde boy continued mashing buttons.

Ethan poked the kid in the arm with a hymnbook.

"What're you playing?" he asked again.

"*Danger Close 3: Forlorn Hope*," the kid said without looking up.

"Is it any good?"

"It's not as good as *2*."

"Which one was that?"

"*Theatre of War*," the kid said, looking up at Ethan for the first time. The child's face was so round and flawless, his eyes so disproportionately large and bright, even Ethan—no fan of children: too smelly—was taken in. The moonfaced boy looked like he'd landed from the pages of a Japanese comic book.

"Is that the one in New York?"

The kid shook his head.

"No," he said. "Halifax."

"Geez," Ethan said, slouching down on the bench to level himself with the child, "I must have missed that one."

An angry adult head peered down from the other side of the boy, assaulting Ethan with a sour look and a short, sharp shush.

The kid whispered, "This one is set in the future. Urban Winnipeg. The Mexican drug cartels are fully militarized: tanks, helicopters, whatever. Anyway, they've nailed down, like, a huge part of the States. Came up into Canada through Idaho—partnered up with some crazy racist guys. See?"

He tilted the screen toward Ethan. The barrel of a heavily modified assault rifle pointed at the cowering form of an injured and bleeding skinhead. The kid pressed a button, the gun fired, and the skinhead's head turned to shrapnel. Bits of digitized skull and brain painted abstract art on the wall behind him. The corpse fell to the ground and twitched epileptically.

The choir went on praising somebody or other.

"So, I'm like a CSOR guy," the kid explained. "I've gotta kill the Mexicans."

"CSOR?"

"Canadian Special Operations Regiment."

"How'd the Mexicans get tanks?"

"CIA, man," the kid said, shaking his head. "CIA is fucked."

The kid's mom slapped the back of his head.

Ethan stared up at the ceiling. He looked around and noticed quite a few other people doing the same thing. In the cracked and fading murals above him, angels and saints pointed and stood beatifically.

A voice echoed across the church.

"Good morning," it said.

Ethan looked over. The bent, ancient priest had made his way to the pulpit. Ethan had yet to register a word of the proceedings, including the just-finished gospel reading, but the small priest's deep voice had gained his attention.

"How're we all this morning?" the priest said.

"Good, Father Brutus," answered about a quarter of the church.

"How about the rest of you?"

Laughter rippled the surface of the congregation. A few more parishioners answered. Children cried. Someone sneezed.

"It's a beautiful day today, isn't it?" Father Brutus continued. "And what a beautiful reading to go along with it. Thank you, Beatrice." He raised his hand a few inches and attempted to turn his head to Beatrice, the polyester church lady seated behind him.

Father Brutus cleared his throat with a wet gurgle before beginning his homily.

"Yesterday," he said, "I presided over the celebration of two young people as they joined in the holy covenant of matrimony here in this very church."

The priest gestured to the front of the altar, where the couple in question had taken their vows.

"I told this young couple, as I tell each and every couple I enjoin—hundreds now—that the sacrament they were about to receive did not only bind their two souls into eternal union, but three."

Father Brutus paused and surveyed the room, allowing the congregation to consider the implication.

"That third soul, that universal soul, that fundamental soul, is of course the soul of God, whose directing presence is essential and omnipresent in all of our lives, and whose gracious and forgiving attendance is mandatory in a lasting, loving marriage."

Beside Ethan, the young boy continued his kill streak.

"The guiding hand of God in our lives is a force we, as Christians, implicitly accept, but of which we are not always wakefully aware. God's touch is dominant and governing, but subtle, and not always apparent."

Ethan agreed, thinking he had no clue who was steering his ship the vast majority of the time.

"Before marrying that young couple yesterday, I received a phone call from a man whose marriage I presided over more than a decade ago. His marriage was in disrepair, he said. He'd stopped going to church, he said, which I of course had already noticed. And when I asked why, he said it was because his wife didn't attend Mass anymore, so he had stopped attending himself.

"I didn't need to hear anything else," Father Brutus said, shaking his head. "I told this man that the problem was obvious: his marriage had lost its eternal bond, its guiding force. His marriage lacked God. He, and his wife, had chosen to push God from their lives, and, like many a delicate structure, the bond of marriage is more than the sum of its parts. Without God, it is nothing."

Ethan wondered where God's omnipresent guiding hand had gone.

He abandoned the priest's speech and resumed his search of the sea of heads for Hugo.

As Father Brutus continued, his words now visiting Ethan as empty static, Ethan considered what it was he should say once he found Hugo. He wondered if he should have brought the gun in from the car. He wondered if the sloth would have his bear spray at Mass. He hoped not.

Father Brutus struck his palm on the pulpit again, sending another loud clap through the speakers hanging along the sides of the church. The sound reclaimed Ethan's attention.

"The answer is yes," the priest said.

I guess that's settled, Ethan thought.

Father Brutus turned away from the pulpit and slowly hobbled back to his seat at the rear of the altar.

The Mass continued with more songs. Soon, a long line of parishioners formed to receive the body of Christ.

While the people received their daily bread, Ethan sat watching the little blonde boy mow through Mexicans and skinheads with what appeared to be a WWII-era flamethrower welded to a Gatling gun.

Pillars of atomic cloud stood apocalyptically over the desolate Winnipeg skyline. An American armoured tank, stuffed full of Los Zetas, rolled over the twitching digital corpses of Special Operations officers.

The Mass ended without Ethan or the young boy really noticing, both ensconced in the bloodshed occurring on the miniature video screen. It was only when the boy's exasperated mother tugged at his sleeve that either male realized Mass had ended: parishioners were streaming out of the church and into the cool, cloudy Vancouver day.

Ethan looked about the room. He caught the side of Hugo's squished head among a tableau of other faces exiting a side door.

Ethan followed, receiving sideways looks as he pushed his way through a throng of parishioners.

Outside, Ethan kept an eye on Hugo as he descended the stairs and began to walk across the parking lot. Ethan quickened his pace and caught up with Hugo as he reached his car and dug into a pocket for his keys. Hugo turned, displaying an unhappy grimace.

"What're you so pissed off about?" Ethan asked. "Father Brutus's sermon not up to par this week?"

"What?"

"You just came from church. Shouldn't you be awash in the glow of Christ's salvation?"

"Fuck you," Hugo said, pulling his keys out of his pocket.

"I don't remember that being one of the Holy Carpenter's teachings."

"I'm not up on my Bible studies," Hugo said, turning back to the car and slipping a key into the lock on the door. "Asshole."

Hugo got in the car and slammed the door. He turned the ignition and the engine sputtered to life.

Ethan banged on the window.

"Hey! Sam's been kidnapped, you tree beast! Open the god-damn window!"

A few parishioners still lingering in the parking lot turned their attention toward the profanity.

Hugo rolled down his window.

"Tree beast?" he said.

"I said Sam's been kidnapped!"

Hugo turned the car off.

"Fuck," he said. He took a book of matches and a bent cigarette from the car's dash, struck a match, and lit up.

Ethan circled to the passenger side, opened the door and climbed in.

"I just want to find out what this is all about, okay?" Ethan said.

"What do you think you can possibly do about it?" Hugo asked. A cloud of smoke billowed from his mouth and hung like a grey curtain against the windshield.

"Got a smoke?" Ethan asked.

Hugo pointed to the glove box. Ethan opened it and retrieved a nearly empty pack of Du Mauriers. He slipped one out of the pack, put the pack back in the glove box, then took a book of matches from the dash. The Pink Curtain, it said, the logo a silhouette of a woman peeking out from a curtain, one leg wrapped around a pole. The logo was also printed on the curtain in the picture, the first step in an infinite regress.

"Who took her?" Hugo asked.

"How should I know?" Ethan said. "I'm here to ask you."

"How should *I* know?" Hugo said, turning to face Ethan.

"You should know because you sent a walking slab of muscle to my place to fuck up me and my roommate!" Ethan said, taking a guess, one he didn't particularly believe in, but hopeful that it would at least get Hugo talking.

"What the hell are you talking about?"

"Wynne, you jackass!"

"Wynne was at your place?"

"Yes! Didn't Sam tell you?"

"Sam didn't tell me shit!" Hugo barked. A hunched and grey-haired couple getting into their Oldsmobile shot the two a crooked look. "Last I heard, she was hanging out with you, and she wasn't coming by anymore."

"Yeah, there's a reason for that, and it doesn't have much to do with me," Ethan said. "Wynne came by my place looking for money. He put my roommate in the hospital."

"Phil?"

Ethan nodded.

"I barely got out of there myself. When I got outside there was a car with a couple more thick meatheads in it. There's a hole or two in my car to prove it."

"A redheaded guy?"

"Didn't notice. I was too busy trying not to get shot."

Ethan explained the rest: finding Simon's corpse, a further rehash of Wynne's assault, and the phone call about Sam being kidnapped.

Hugo muttered something under his breath, then wilted into an even more puckered and sorrowful grimace.

"Simon was up to something," Hugo said.

"What?"

"To cut Wynne out, I think. To get more cash for something. Something to do with Wynne's boss, this guy named Jack. Not sure what, but they were hanging out."

"So, Wynne found out and shot him," Ethan said.

Hugo shook his head again. "Wouldn't explain why he came to you looking for the money. Plus, he wouldn't be so stupid as to leave him in an alley."

"Simon was getting a little big for his britches, I take it."

Hugo looked over. "What the fuck are britches?"

"Simon made a play he shouldn't have and got shot for it. The best idea Wynne's got of what happened to the money is that Phil and I took it, just because we happened to find Simon's body in the alley. Wynne's not somebody to fuck with, I take it."

"No, he's not," Hugo said. "But he's not a particularly big player, either. Bigger than Simon, obviously, but that's not saying much. Wynne's still just a foot soldier."

"What does that make you?"

"Not much," Hugo admitted. "Not much at all."

"So, you guys are all in the same gang?"

Hugo laughed. "I don't know anything about gangs, man. These guys, they buy together, operate a grow-op or whatever. Maybe sell some of it to some other guys, I don't know. But this week it's one guy and next week it's another. It's not like they're going around with name tags and membership cards."

"Not that free or Simon wouldn't be dead."

"That's true," Hugo agreed.

"You think they're still after me?"

Hugo shrugged. "Did you shoot him and take the money?"

"Fuck no. I've got nothing to do with this."

"How'd you know I know Simon?" Hugo said.

"Sam told me."

"I met Phil through Simon," Hugo said. "Simon was out one day, so he sent Phil to me. Did they say what they want?"

"They want the money. They say I give them the money, they let Sam go."

"Fifty thousand," Hugo muttered to himself.

"Fifty thousand?" Ethan repeated. His eyes lit up. "You've got the fucking money!"

"What?" Hugo said.

"You've got the money! You've got it," Ethan said. "You've got to give it back, man. They'll kill her. They're not fucking around!"

"I don't have any money. I don't know what you're talking about." Hugo started the car.

"You just said it! Fifty grand! How'd you know how much was missing? You've got it! You've got the goddamn money!"

"I don't have anything!" Hugo said. He reached across Ethan's body, popped the handle, and pushed open the door. "I know how much Simon had on him, or thereabouts, all right? That's it. Now get the fuck out of my car." Hugo shoved Ethan again. Ethan braced himself against the door frame.

"How?"

"I was his last pickup for the night. The night he got shot. He had the money with him. That's it."

Hugo pushed Ethan.

"Wait!" Ethan said. "What're you going to do about Sam?"

Hugo paused. "What can I do?"

"Give the money back, to start."

"I don't have the fucking money!"

They sat looking at each other. Ethan was sure there was something Hugo wasn't telling him, even if he didn't have the money.

"Where can I find Wynne?" Ethan asked.

"I thought you were trying to stay out of Wynne's way."

"If I wanted to find Wynne, where would I do it?"

Hugo pointed at The Pink Curtain matchbook on the dash. Ethan picked it up.

"That's one place," Hugo said. "The other is Corleone's, but I wouldn't expect him to show his face around there for the time being."

"Corleone's?" Ethan tried to place the name.

"A pizza place on Fifth, off Commercial."

The name registered with Ethan.

"Yeah, I know the place. That's where we found Simon's body. In the alley out back."

Hugo nodded. "I wouldn't go looking for Wynne, if I were you. Let the cops handle Sam. This is bigger than Wynne."

"They'll kill her."

Hugo shook his head. "She was in the wrong place at the wrong time. They won't hurt her. They'll try this angle then let her go."

Ethan opened the car door and put a foot out onto the pavement of the church parking lot.

"You seem to know quite a lot about this."

"Nope," Hugo said. "I don't know anything."

Ethan stepped fully out of the car. Before he could shut the door, Hugo stopped him.

"What're you going to do?"

"I'm going to save Sam."

Hugo laughed and shook his head.

## 36

Rowan grabbed Emma by the arm and pulled her from her seat, forcing her back to the basement.

Emma resisted and the two danced toward the front door. She brought a knee into his ribs, but he didn't flinch, giving her a single violent backhand as retribution, pitching her into a door in the hall. The door opened on impact, and Emma spilled awkwardly to the floor. Rowan followed her into the room, gave her a short kick to the hip, then slammed the door behind her.

Emma felt her face and came away with blood. She stood up, wincing at her bruised hip, and leaned against the wall.

Boxes of books and magazines were piled waist high along the walls of the small bedroom. A black typewriter holding a blank page sat on a short wooden desk. Emma stumbled forward and sat herself in the chair at the desk, trying to breathe away the pulse of pain in her hip.

To the left of the typewriter, an inch-high stack of pages—double spaced and numbered—were pinned face up beneath a

coffee mug. Emma made out the title at the top of the page—
*Bleak Reckoning*—before the door opened and Emma was
dragged out of the room by her arm.

Rowan pulled her into the living room and flung her onto
the couch. Emma sat herself up, then quietly watched her captor
make a series of unanswered phone calls.

The blind basset hound nosed its way to Emma and sniffed at
her leg: blood had dripped from her forehead onto her pants. The
two Rottweiler mutts circled, then lay beside her on the floor.

Finally, one of Rowan's calls was answered. Emma listened.

"It's Rowan," he said. "Yeah. No. I got a problem. No,
she's not dead."

Emma's eyes shot wide open.

"She got out. No, Jack, she's here. Right here, in front of
me. Yeah, she's fine. She's fine. No, the—hey, listen, don't talk
to me like that, all right?"

Emma watched as Rowan's face went red.

"No. I don't fucking know. I'm telling you because she got
a hold of her phone and called her old man. No. Enough, I figure. Well—no. No. Hold on," Rowan said. He cupped a hand
over the receiver. "What'd you tell him?"

Emma shook her head emphatically.

"Nothing," she said. "I didn't say anything."

"I fucking heard you. You said something. You're kidnapped and we want money. I heard that, so don't fucking lie
to me."

"Yeah, that's it. That's it. That's all I said."

"You tell him where you are?"

Emma shook her head again.

"No. Absolutely not. I don't have any idea where we are."

Rowan went back to the phone.

"No. Yes. No, it's not. She didn't get out of the house. I
know."

He looked down at Emma. Tears glistened on her cheeks.
Her hands shook.

"No," Rowan said. "Where are you? It's Sunday afternoon.
I'm coming there."

Rowan hung up.

"Come on."

Emma shook her head.

"Come on, now," Rowan said.

"No," Emma said, crying again.

Rowan stepped over the coffee table and grabbed Emma by the wrist. She screamed, fighting back and pushing her body into the couch. The dogs leapt and barked. Rowan took her other wrist, then held the two together in one of his massive hands. Emma screamed louder and kicked him in the stomach and legs, thrashing in his grip. Rowan reached back and threw a hard punch.

Emma stopped screaming.

She wheezed, then spat some blood onto the couch.

Rowan pulled her off the couch and dragged her back to the basement.

## 37

Eric Woodgrave had never been the type to panic.

At eleven years old, he'd broken his arm playing shinny on a Kitchener ice rink. The bone hadn't broken skin, but his hand and wrist had drooped unnaturally below the elbow. Other kids averted their eyes at its grotesque angle. One vomited a pale-yellow slick onto the ice. Eric skated off the rink, had a friend help him sling the arm, then walked the kilometre to the hospital, trying his best to stifle his prepubescent tears.

At forty-three, when his second wife had declared over breakfast that she was leaving him, Eric had simply nodded; he knew she'd be taking as much as the law and its expensive practitioners would allow. Eric calmly told her he understood, finished his coffee, then blew off his afternoon schedule to play a round of golf with an old friend and lament his latest failure. Panic and fits of uncontrolled anger were simply not in his nature.

So, when he hung up with his kidnapped daughter, though fear and violence pulsed low in his being, he did not panic.

Neither did he call the police. When he'd heard his daughter say "drugs" and "money," he thought of one man: Winston Carmello.

After hanging up with the kidnapper, Eric immediately scrolled to the entry for "Cello, W." and dialled, but received no answer. Next, he scrolled to "West End Health Club" and dialled the brothel on the twenty-third floor of the Gould Building.

At first the receptionist denied Winston Carmello's presence. But after some cajoling—a skill of Eric's that contributed to his great wealth—she changed her tune: yes, Winston was there, but he was occupied.

Probably with Tess, Eric thought. He liked that Winston gave the women—or encouraged them to give themselves—names outside of the expected, forbidding the most obvious Candy, Sandy, and Brandy monikers of less scrupulous establishments. Eric had once asked a perky young blonde named Lola—whom he visited regularly until noticing her resemblance to his youngest daughter, Charlotte—where she'd gotten her name, but she'd had no idea.

As Eric Woodgrave crossed the bridge from West Vancouver into downtown, he had no doubt that Winston would be waiting for him at the Gould Building. Eric had spent enough cash at the brothel over the years, and had recommended it to enough new clients, to warrant Carmello's occasional undivided attention. Beyond that, Eric did all the legal work on Carmello's various properties, including the papers he'd purchased for several units the yet to be built Nirvana tower. Carmello struck a hard bargain with the developers, Eric knew—sell me the units, and at a reduced price, or . . . or what?—but that's how these things went, and other, more ostensibly legitimate businessmen had caused him worse problems over the years, anyway.

Eric Woodgrave rolled his Jaguar into the garage beneath the Gould Building, parked it, then took the elevator to the twenty-third floor. He hadn't been to the "health club" in ages, but when he stepped off the elevator, the woman behind the receptionist's desk still greeted him by name—or rather, his alias,

Michael Riley—then apologized that his preferred girl, Darla, wasn't there any longer.

"That's fine," Eric said. "I'm not here for that. I'm here to see Winston, like I said on the phone. Did you tell him I was coming?"

"He's still in with a girl, Mr. Riley," the receptionist said. She was in her late thirties, slim, with glasses and her hair back in a ponytail. She wasn't the receptionist Eric remembered, but he recognized her from somewhere. Maybe she had retired from working the rooms.

"A few girls, actually," she continued. "I didn't want to interrupt him."

"Please interrupt him. It's very important."

"He'll probably be out shortly, Mr. Riley. Why don't I set you up in a room and have a girl come by to keep you company while you wait?"

"No, I need to see him immediately."

The woman looked seriously concerned. Maybe for her own welfare. No reasonable man wants to be interrupted mid-coital activities, and though Eric trusted Winston Carmello as a friend of sorts, it was reasonable to assume a man in his vocation was no stranger to violence.

Eric showed his teeth.

"Nothing to worry about, my dear," he said. "This is a matter of business Winston needs to hear about immediately. You tell him I'm here to see him, and that it's an emergency, and everything will be fine."

The receptionist nervously acquiesced, picking up the phone and dialling an extension. Her eyes went from the phone to Eric and back to the phone again.

"He's not answ—oh, Mr. Carmello. No. No. Yes, I'm sorry. I understand. But Mr. Riley is here to see you and he says it's an emergency. Yes. No. I don't know. Hold—hold on." She covered the receiver and looked up at Eric. "He wants to know what kind of emergency."

Eric reached out and nodded to the receptionist, gesturing for her to hand him the phone. He took it and spoke.

"Winston, I need to see you. No. Yes. No, it can't. It's about my daughter and I need help. Thank you."

Eric handed the phone back to the receptionist, nodded a thank you, then walked down the hall to Room 6, as Carmello had directed.

Standing beside the door to Room 6 was a giant. The behemoth's big white globe of a head escaped the high collar of a black leather trench coat, his scalp shining like the back of a glistening beluga breaching the surface for air. His jaw was hard and wide with a chin like a dented mound of granite. A vacancy to his eyes announced he should not be spoken to unless expressly directed.

The beast glared down at Eric and uncrossed his arms as if about to speak— when the door opened.

Winston Carmello, clammy with sweat, stood at the threshold wearing only his boxers, one hand resting on his expectant belly. White hair coated his chest and head save for some tufts of black in and around the ears. Black bags hung below his eyes. Behind him, a king-sized bed with silver sheets and pillows held two naked women: one smoking a glass pipe of weed—judging from the smell and smoke hanging in the air—and another sleeping, or passed out, behind her.

"Eric," Carmello said, smiling, "ready to party?"

Carmello dismissed the massive bodyguard and welcomed Eric into the room.

"Get them out of here, Winston," Eric said. "This is important."

Carmello smiled broadly, showing off a gold tooth toward the back of his mouth, his glazed eyes informed Eric that he was not to be trifled with, and that he was in no state to do any trifling.

"Now, Eric," he said, "how am I to take you walking into my place and trying to kick these lovely ladies out, hence spoiling my Sunday afternoon?"

The woman with the pipe crawled to the foot of the bed and offered it to Eric, who declined. Nonplussed, she handed the pipe to Carmello with one hand and stroked the grey hair on his round belly with the other. Beside her, a makeup mirror lay on the comforter, little lines of shovelled snow on its surface.

In the bathroom a toilet flushed, then a third woman, also fully nude, entered the room. She was a blonde with a little extra weight, or perfectly enough, covering most of her frame. She lifted an open can of Vanilla Coke and a prescription bottle from the nightstand, shook a few pills into her mouth, then washed them down with a swig. She turned to face the two men. She was without makeup and on the north side of thirty—a bit unusual for Carmello's roster, Eric noted—but a pretty woman nonetheless, despite, or because of, a short scar above her left eye.

"Oxy?" she asked.

Eric shook his head.

Carmello, in the middle of taking a long hit off the glass pipe, waved the blonde and her pill bottle closer.

"Yeah, yeah," he said, straining to speak through a lung full of smoke. "Hey, where the fuck did you find a Vanilla Coke?"

"They had them in the dressing room," the blonde said.

"They still make Vanilla Coke?" Carmello said. He tried handing the pipe back to the woman on the bed, but she was curled up and snoring on the corner of the mattress.

"I guess," the blonde shrugged. She picked up the remote from the bed stand, then sat herself in a taupe armchair and thumbed on the TV.

Carmello sat on the edge of the bed and shook a few Oxycontin from the bottle into his hand.

"Did you know they still make Vanilla Coke, Eric?" he said.

"Winston," Eric said, shaking his head.

"Huh?" Carmello said.

Eric held in some unkind words.

"Can we speak alone, Winston? Please?"

"Ah, it's fine, man," Carmello said, his eyes slowly drifting closed. "These girls got nothing to say about anything. Do you girls?"

None of the women answered.

"Winston," Eric said.

"Hmm?"

"Winston!"

Winston Carmello opened his eyes.

"Yes?" he said.

"My daughter's been kidnapped, Winston. I need help. Do you understand?"

"By who?" Carmello said, tuning in a little.

"Somebody looking for money," Eric said. He sat down in another of the armchairs beside the blonde woman, who was flicking through channels with the remote. On the TV screen in front of them, a Mountie in a red serge jacket and his white wolf followed a thief's trail through the back alleys of urban Toronto.

"What's this?" the blonde woman said.

"*Due South*," Carmello said.

"Canadian show about a Mountie?" the blonde woman asked.

"Yes," Eric said, wondering what flawed logic had driven him to come to Winston for help.

"That's Toronto," the blonde woman said, pointing at the screen. "I used to live on that street. Looks a lot different now. When is this, the '80s?"

"'90s," Carmello said.

"Wow," the blonde woman said, flipping the channel.

"Winston," Eric said, impatient, "listen to me. My daughter was kidnapped."

"Rough," said the blonde, flicking through the channels. She leaned over to Eric, apparently sympathetic to his problems.

"Sorry, Eric," Carmello said, getting up off the bed. "Mary, shut the fuck up, then get the fuck out of here. Ophelia?"

The curled woman on the bed was asleep. With a nudge from Carmello, she awoke. Carmello pointed to the door. Ophelia rubbed her head, swung her feet to the ground, then stumbled out of the room. The two other women followed.

Carmello sat on the edge of the bed and pulled a cigarette from a crumpled pack lying beside him. Before lighting his own, Carmello offered one to Eric, who refused.

"So, what's all this, then?"

"My daughter calls me in a panic. She says she's been kidnapped, and that the kidnappers think her boyfriend stole their drugs or money."

"So she escaped?" Carmello said. "I mean she called you, right? So she's out?"

Eric shook his head. "No, there was a guy there, he took the phone."

"How long has she been gone?"

"A night. She took off last night and didn't come back. I went to bed hoping she'd gone to a friend's. I got the call this morning."

"What else did she say?"

"She said it smelled like weed where she was. In a basement. And that one of the guy's name was Jack, a skinny white guy. She said there were two big guys: one redhead with a scar, one with a Jesus tattoo. I forget the redhead's name. Ronald. Rowan, I think."

Carmello's sexually sated, chemically dumbed eyes sparked back to life.

"What did the guy say?"

"He tried to pretend everything was normal. He said don't call the police."

"Or what?"

"Or nothing. He didn't say anything. He sounded like an idiot, frankly. Like he didn't know what he was doing and wasn't planning on calling me for ransom. But then he called back to tell me not to go to the police and demanded fifty thousand dollars."

Eric rose from the chair and began to pace nervously about the room.

"Winston, what do you know?"

"Well, I'm glad to say I believe I know who has your daughter, Eric," Carmello said. He picked up his cell phone. "I'll take care of this."

"You know these guys?"

"I do. But I won't for long," he said, dialling a number.

He looked up at Eric.

"Man, I'm really high."

## 38

After being accosted by Ethan in the church parking lot, Hugo called Sam to no answer, then picked up two double cheeseburgers from a Thick Burger and headed back to his apartment.

When he got there he found his neighbour, Quinten, shirtless and ensconced in a session of *Danger Close 3D: Privatized Terror*. At two AM the previous night, Quinten had parked himself in front of the big screen and, other than to use the bathroom or visit the fridge, hadn't moved since.

Hugo, being no fan of reality, particularly one which included a kidnapped Sam and enraged Wynne Duncan, joined Quinten on the couch.

He slipped on a bulky set of 3D glasses and packed an unusually large bowl. Despite the volume of weed in the apartment, burning enough of it to obscure his current predicament would be difficult. Hugo decided to give it his best shot, anyway.

In between bong rips and mouthfuls of Thick Burger, Hugo watched Quinten and his squad of soldiers battle extremist scum in the streets of Vancouver, 2025.

Hugo had to admit this one was a bit farfetched: radicalized Southern Baptists, ideologically armed by some obscure twelfth-century text, were invading Western Canada. Hugo didn't find the Lord's Righteous Emancipation Front to be a particularly believable terrorist organization. Neither did he find it plausible that all military operations had become privatized less than ten years into the future. But there was no denying that the graphics and game play were badass. And, finally, for the first time in war-themed FPS gaming history, there was realistic dismemberment. About bloody time, Hugo thought. Who gave a damn about plot, anyway?

Hugo boiled up another voluminous hit on the bong, drew in a zeppelin's worth of smoke, then let the force of his exhalation push him back into the couch.

His brain was a numb, buzzing sponge.

Some small stubborn piece of it, however, was refusing to concede to the miasma of THC and video games.

That small piece of brain reminded him that he liked Sam and that he missed her, in his own horny way.

It also reminded him that he was the last person to have seen Simon alive.

And, finally, it reminded him that Simon's money was missing, and that Wynne could be coming to him for it next.

Hugo took another pull on the bong.

Simon had visited the apartment the night before he'd been murdered. After talking to Ethan, Hugo's final conversation with Simon had acquired new significance.

They'd been smoking joints and playing a multiplayer round of *Danger Close: Pan-American Dream*. A black duffel bag stuffed with cash from Simon's pickups took up the seat on the couch between them. Simon had recently been given more responsibility, more cash and drugs to handle, and a long with it, more of his bizarre arrogance.

On the screen, soldiers navigated a snowy Albertan plain. Tanks rolled across the field, cannons firing. Rockets rose and burst in the air, glowing over the bloodstained battlefield.

"I built a quinzhee this winter," Simon said while buzzing around the screen, unleashing Canadian fury with a CSOR-issued rifle.

"What's a quincy?" Hugo asked.

"A snow hut. Like a . . . fucking snow tent," Simon said. He paused the game, swigged down the final gulp of his seventh can of Glacier's Best, then retrieved another joint from the coffee table.

"What the hell would you do that for?" Hugo said.

"Got to be prepared."

"For what?"

"Anything, man. The collapse of society."

"What are you talking about?"

"This is all just an illusion," Simon said, waving his hand, defining all that was in the world, in this case an enormous television, two unbefitting, upscale sofas, and the stale stink of lung-filtered smoke. "It's all built on a house of cards, as brought to you by the government. The financial collapse in the States? That was just the beginning. We're another government-perpetrated terrorist attack, or bird flu, or Wall Street meltdown away from chaos, Hugo. And when it happens, no one will be there to help."

"Zombie apocalypse?" Hugo said. He had just finished playing *Dead Electorate 2: Final Ballot* the night before.

Simon put his video game controller down and looked at Hugo.

"This is not a joke," he said. "I will be prepared. Jack's helping me."

"Jack?" Hugo said, surprised. "Wynne's Jack?" Hugo had never met him; he only knew that Wynne reported to Jack, or worked for him, or however you wanted to look at it. Hugo has seen Jack once, sitting in a booth at The Pink Curtain. He shared with Simon a sinewy, insectoid appearance.

"He knows a lot about this stuff," Simon said. "I'm learning."

Hugo took another haul off the joint. Simon resumed play on the video game.

"When can I get some more weed, anyway?" Hugo asked. He'd just handed over forty-five hundred dollars, Simon's last collection of the night.

"Soon," Simon said. "I have to talk to Jack. I got some meth and Oxys for you, too."

"I'm not moving any of that. Don't you go through Wynne?"

"Jack wants me to go through him. Supposed to meet up shortly. Thought I'd come by here and smoke a few on the way by, though."

"Good business this week?" At the time he'd thought it odd Simon was bringing the cash straight to Jack; all roads usually led to the beefy, ill-tempered Wynne.

"Fifty grand," Simon said, patting the black duffel bag. "And that's just what I have on me. But don't get any ideas." Simon leaned back on the couch and tugged up his shirt, revealing a matte-black handgun tucked into a brown leather holster.

"You like that?" Simon said. "It's a new Smith and Wesson. Jack got it for me."

If there were a list of people least suited to possessing lethal machinery, Hugo would put Simon at the top.

Proving Hugo's assessment, later that night Simon had wound up dead in an alley with two bullet holes in his face.

Part of Hugo—a large part, he admitted—wished that he'd taken the cash for himself.

"Hey," Quinten said, bringing Hugo back into the present. "You seeing this?"

Hugo was leaning into another bong hit. He vacuumed it in and felt his chest expand. He enjoyed the burn as long as he could, then sat up, blew out, and looked up.

A cinematic cutscene of the Vancouver skyline played out on the big screen. Bombs burst over the cityscape, illuminating the night-black mountains that backdropped the city. Lush swaths of city green space burned in napalm-blasted patches. Fire flickered in the windows of decapitated buildings, plumes of crushed concrete puffing from their open wounds. Rolling tanks tore up the streets. Choppers hovered in the canopy like fluttering dragonflies, showering soldiers and citizens alike in a deluge of hot lead. Women and children screamed. Soldiers begged for their mothers. Blood flowed like a spilled oil tanker, spurted like a freshly struck well.

"This is fucking awesome," Hugo said.

"Yeah, man," Quinten said. He sat up on the couch to take in the spectacle on the 73-inch screen. His generous belly rested between his thighs, gracing the seat of the couch, a clammy, sweaty, dangling appendage of congealed fast food, salty snacks, and carbonated beverages.

"What the hell is going on?" Hugo said.

"Turns out the LREF is just some bullshit US-fronted deal they sent in to provide an excuse for war."

"On Canada?"

"Yeah, man. The oil. It's all about the oil, man."

"So, the US is invading Canada?"

"Yeah, dude. Well, it's a coup, really. But still. Shit's heavy."

"They got their own oil though."

"What? Who cares dude, it's cool. There's a faction of the Canadian government that, like, wants us to become the fifty-first state. After this war settles down, that's what will happen. Should have happened a long time ago, if you ask me," Quinten said.

"Wow," Hugo said, and ripped another bong hit.

Hugo sunk back into the couch as the cutscene dissolved into more first person action: Quinten's squad of renegade CSOR operatives fighting back Americans, for the . . . uh, Canadian Dream? What the hell was that, Hugo thought? These games were getting too farfetched even for him.

The building's intercom buzzed. Some dope coming by to buy dope, probably. Sunday, midafternoon—maybe Kenneth. Do I ever not want to talk to Kenneth, Hugo thought, his bleary eyes wincing beneath the heavy 3D specs.

The buzzer went off again.

Hugo got out of his chair and walked to the cheap intercom-phone hanging from the wall in the kitchen.

He picked it up:

"Who's this?" Hugo said.

"Let me in."

"Kenneth?" Hugo said, now hoping it to be the case.

"It's Wynne."

"Wynne?"

"That's what I said."

"What're you doing here?"

"What's the difference?"

"You have your own key," Hugo said.

"I got thirty keys on this goddamn keychain," Wynne said. "Let me in."

Hugo pressed nine, buzzing the lobby door open for Wynne. A few moments later Wynne knocked on the apartment door. Hugo opened it.

"What happened to your face?" he said.

"Simon happened to my face," Wynne said, walking past Hugo through the kitchen and into the living room.

"Who's this guy?" Wynne demanded, pointing at Quinten.

"That's Quinten," Hugo said. "He lives next door."

"Hey Quinten," Wynne said.

Quinten, engrossed in the wholesale slaughter of phoney Southern Baptist revolutionaries, paid Wynne no heed.

"Quinten," Wynne said again, louder, knocking on the wall.

"Yeah," Quinten responded, his eyes still on the screen.

"Pause the fucking thing, would you?"

Quinten paused it.

"That the new *Danger Close*?" Wynne asked.

"Yeah," Quinten said.

"Any good?"

"Yeah, it's pretty awesome."

"What's that?" Wynne pointed at a bloody blotch in the corner of the screen.

"An arm."

Wynne squinted and cocked his head. "Realistic amputation?"

Quinten smiled and nodded. "Yeah, man."

"About time," Wynne said.

"Yeah."

"Listen," Wynne said, "I have to talk to Hugo. So you have to leave."

"I'm in the middle of a siege here."

"I didn't ask," Wynne said. "I told."

Quinten turned and took in Wynne's abundant frame. Thinking himself best suited to shortening the conversation, Quinten got up and left the apartment.

"Does that guy not own a shirt?" Wynne said as the door shut behind Quinten.

"He lives across the hall," Hugo explained.

"So?"

"Sometimes he's got a shirt."

Wynne pointed at the couch. Hugo took a seat, then Wynne sat down on the coffee table, facing him.

Hugo caught a glimpse of the smiling Jesus tattoo on Wynne's bowling ball of a shoulder. He'd been meaning to ask Wynne what it was about. What it symbolized.

Flat, hazy smoke paused in the air between the two men like a low-lying cloud. Wynne waved smoke from his face, then resumed staring at Hugo.

Hugo, ripped into oblivion, couldn't take the silence. He spoke:

"Man, I didn't have anything to do with the money, all right? Simon was fucking crazy, man. You know that. You know it. He was up to something with Jack, okay? Something about getting ready to live off the grid and building up money to do it."

Wynne raised an eyebrow, but said nothing. He waited.

Hugo continued. "Nothing to do with me, okay? You know Simon was crazy, and I've never met Jack, but you say he's crazy, too. Always going off about the government and whatever, right? And I don't know why you had to take Sam, you know? She doesn't have anything to do with it. And that Ethan guy and his buddy—I don't think they have anything to do with it either. They don't have the fifty grand, okay? Neither do I. I don't know what happened to Simon, but when he left here he was on his way to meet Jack. Simon had a semiautomatic he says he got from Jack too."

Wynne continued to stare.

Hugo leaned back into the couch and put his head in his hands.

"Are you going to say something or what?" Hugo said.

Wynne stood up.

He picked up the tall bong sitting on the coffee table and examined it. Comprised of thin molded ceramic, the base was shaped like a closed fist, the middle finger extending to form the tube and chamber. An opening at the finger's tip formed the mouthpiece. Wynne turned the bong around and looked in the shot glass–sized bowl that comprised the thumb; an acorn-sized clump of burnt weed filled the bowl.

It was Hugo's favourite bong. The length of the middle finger allowed for long pulls and provided thick, burly hits. The oversized glass bowl was a personal touch; he'd discarded the smaller wooden one that had come stock with the pipe. He'd just cleaned the bong thoroughly a few days ago, and it was really purring.

Hugo smiled.

"It's nice, eh? Want to roast a bowl?" he asked Wynne.

Wynne looked at Hugo incredulously.

"Aw, c'mon, man," Hugo said, wincing.

Wynne hurled the bong. The base struck Hugo square in the forehead and shattered, soaking him in stagnant bong water.

"No, I don't want to roast a bowl, you moron," Wynne said. "Who told you all that shit?"

"What?" Hugo said. A shard of ceramic stuck out from his forehead. A small stream of blood coursed its way between his eyes, around his nose and into his mouth, its metallic tinge mixing with the fetid bong water.

"Who told you all that, dipshit?" Wynne barked again.

"Simon! And that Ethan dude. He followed me to church this morning."

"You go to church?" Wynne asked.

"Yeah, man. Don't you? All the shit I do, best make sure I'm at least in halfway decent with the Big Man, you know? I mean, you're the one with the giant Jesus on his shoulder," Hugo said. He rubbed his head and felt the shard, then pulled it out, wincing. "What did you have to hit me for, man? I liked that bong."

"Jesus?"

Hugo pointed at Wynne's shoulder.

"That's my aunt, you stupid little asshole. What'd this Ethan ask you?" Wynne said.

"Same thing you're asking me! Where's the money? Where's Sam?"

"I've barely asked you anything yet, stupid. What'd Simon tell you, exactly?"

Hugo related what Simon had said about Jack helping him prepare for the coming apocalypse, and what Ethan had told him in the car in the morning.

Wynne sat back down on the coffee table and pondered the information. Hugo swept pieces of shattered bong from his chest and pants, then asked if he could go change out of his fouled clothes. He was rebuffed.

"The blonde girl was a mistake," Wynne said, contemplating his next course of action.

Hugo nodded.

"Hold on," he said, shaking his head. "Blonde girl?"

"Yeah, blonde girl. This Sam girl. Are you banging her too? Rowan said she's this Ethan guy's girl. Or the other one."

"No, man, Sam's a brunette. Dark skin, brown eyes."

"Blonde hair, blue eyes. Samantha Woodgrave."

"Who the fuck is Samantha Woodgrave?"

"The damn girl—" Wynne stopped himself, realizing the problem.

"The Sam I know isn't blonde, or a Woodgrave," Hugo said. "And, as far as I know, the Sam I know is the same one Ethan and Phil do."

"This Ethan thinks we have a different girl."

"Looks like," Hugo said.

"Where'd he say he was going to get the money?"

"He didn't. He doesn't have any."

"So, what'd he say he's going to do?"

"Says he was going to look for you."

"For me?"

"He didn't appreciate whatever you did to his roommate, I take it."

"I didn't appreciate what he did to my face. What else did he say?"

"That he was going to save Sam."

Wynne smiled.

Things were getting interesting.

## 39

A few weeks earlier, in a case of mistaken identity, a man had been stabbed in the side while relieving himself at a urinal in The Pink Curtain. The Pink Curtain, Woit also knew, was owned by Winston Carmello. Woit had gotten the case; she'd probably never solve it. The security cameras had conveniently not been working that night. No one could say anything about the attacker. Someone had been going after one of Carmello's men, and as much as that would upset Carmello, these weren't the type of people that wanted help from the police. They would want the attacker dead, not arrested. The injured man wasn't of their concern.

The stabbing was targeted at one of Carmello's men, an unexceptional stooge who seemed to have defected to a rival organization without bothering to give his two weeks' notice. Whatever sum of money the target had taken could not have possibly been worth his own life, Woit thought. Same went for the hitman: depending on who was used—a professional for a lot of money or a peon for very little—how was the cash worth the risk, first and foremost, to your own life, and second, of your almost certain time in jail?

No matter how often Woit investigated gang- or drug-relat-ed murders, she was always left with the same questions: How is this worth it? How can this be justified?

Coincidently enough, or more likely no coincidence at all, The Pink Curtain was Woit's next lead on the Simon Hough case. He'd worked there until just a few months before his death.

It was hard for Woit to believe people like Winston Carmello or Simon Hough could ever be anything other than criminals. For every impressionable youth lured into the life through peer pressure, greed, necessity, or bad luck of associa-tion—Woit thought of Omar from Corleone's—there were ten more born violent, immoral opportunists.

Corleone's was most likely a laundering outfit, Woit reason-ably presumed. She hadn't yet looked into its books, but she had discovered who owned the place: Vincent Struhl, born 1941, died 2001. Woit had identified the Jack Struhl whom Omar had mentioned as Vincent's nephew. If she'd found the right person, Jack Struhl had only one substantial line on his criminal record.

Photos from the incident in which he was charged, but not convicted, still occasionally surfaced in forwarded emails, intend-ed to provide laughs among the rank and file. A female mule, ostensibly Struhl's common-law partner at the time, had been caught at the border with a three-pound figurine made of pressed cocaine, painted and accessorized to crudely resemble Jesus Christ. The figurine did not make for a particularly flattering rendition of the Son of God: a face drooping on the left like a stroke victim, severe orbital dystopia, bleached blond hair, and skin sagging like a melting wax sculpture made for a Christ more like an aged Iggy Pop then a blessed saviour to billions.

From the stack of matchbooks Woit found at Corleone's, it was obvious someone was at least a fan of The Pink Curtain, if not an outright investor. The phone number for Struhl, obtained from Omar at Corleone's, went straight to a messaging service with no pre-recorded greeting. The phone itself was a pay-as-you-go device, commonly purchased at convenience stores. Struhl's current address was listed as a post office box in a UPS store at a strip mall. Struhl's rap sheet was clean save for the cocaine Jesus incident ten years earlier.

Sunday afternoon probably wasn't the best time to visit The Pink Curtain, but Woit thought it was worth a shot. She didn't bother calling Smolin: he'd only complain that there was no reason to be working on a Sunday, and really, he was right.

If she were lucky, Struhl, or even Carmello himself, would be taking in an afternoon show, and she could ask one of them. More likely, she could at the very least question some of their lackeys about what they knew about Corleone's, the dead body behind it, and why one of their goons had gone after a couple of deadbeat potheads in an unassuming apartment building on Maple Avenue.

## 40

E than had only fired a gun once in his life.

Four years ago he'd made a road trip to Las Vegas with his old roommate, Massoud. They'd driven Massoud's 1994 Mazda across the border and down Route 101, along the Washington, Oregon, and California coasts, then cut inland to Nevada.

In Las Vegas they'd gone to a gun range. Ethan had fired a Sig Sauer P226, a semiautomatic pistol manufactured in Germany and commonly used by law enforcement and military agencies. After missing with the first three shots, Ethan took careful aim at the hanging paper target and fired.

Now, having followed Hugo's tip as to where he might find Wynne, Ethan stood across the street from Corleone's, the stolen Glock tucked into the waistband of his pants.

He squinted at the sunlight struggling through a rare break in the tightly knit quilt of clouds. A stuttering trickle of cars staggered from traffic light to traffic light on the road in front of him.

He walked to the intersection at the end of the block and crossed with a handful of other pedestrians, pausing in front of a narrow convenience store next to Corleone's and watching a few hungry patrons enter. Ethan waited until the customers left, limp slices in hand, then approached the restaurant.

Ethan looked through the window, the shop's name arced in cursive red on the glass. Omar, the shopkeeper and pizza maker, stood with his back turned, sliding a pizza into the oven.

Ethan entered and let the door close behind him. He turned the sign hanging from a loop of string on the door from *Open* to *Closed*, then flipped the deadbolt.

At the click of the bolt, Omar turned to face his newest customer.

Ethan stood at the door, one hand under his jacket on the butt of his gun, his hair matted, nearly a week's growth on his cheeks, the T-shirt Sam had given him variously stained with condiments, and one leg of his pants discoloured by urine and blood.

"What the fuck happened to you?" Omar said.

"Lots," Ethan said. "Where's Wynne?"

"You know Wynne?"

"I do now."

Omar looked past Ethan to the door. Noticing that his business had been closed for the day, his face crumpled in dismay.

"Man, open the fuckin' door! I've got a business to run!"

"Where's Wynne?" Ethan repeated.

"How should I know?" Omar said. "I'm not his secretary. Can we open that door? There are people out there and I've got pizza to sell."

Ethan looked over his shoulder. A rotund customer stood out front, peering in through the window at the row of pizzas on the countertop.

Ethan tugged the pistol free from the front of his pants. He kept it in front of him, visible only to Omar.

Omar shot his hands in the air.

"Put your hands down, Omar, or this mozzarella ball behind me is going to think I'm robbing the place and call the cops."

"Aren't you?" Omar said, slowly bringing his hands to his side.

"No, I'm not robbing you. I need to find Wynne."

Ethan approached the counter and waved Omar to the back of the shop, poking him with the gun to urge him along. Omar yelped as the gun pressed into his ribs, sore from an earlier incident.

They entered a hall lined with shelves full of pizza boxes, cans of sauce, and jars of toppings. A tiny desk was crammed below a shelf of napkin bundles; beside it, the closed door to an employee-only bathroom.

Ethan motioned Omar to sit at the desk.

"Where's Wynne?" Ethan asked again.

"I told you, I don't know. Not here anymore, is all I care about."

Ethan kept the gun trained on Omar's chest.

"If you're not going to rob me, then what the hell is the gun for?" Omar said.

Ethan noticed a bruise on the side of Omar's face.

"What happened to your face and ribs?"

"Wynne happened to my goddamn face and ribs."

"When?"

"Like an hour ago."

"He thinks you took the money?"

Omar looked up in surprise.

"How do you know about the money?" he said.

"Is Sam okay?" Ethan said.

"Who?"

"Sam. Where do they have her?

"I don't know anything about a Sam."

Ethan rubbed his eyes with his free hand, then sat on the desk beside Omar. Ethan rested the gun on his lap, still holding it firmly.

"You don't know a damn thing, do you?" Ethan said.

"Hell no. I work in a pizza shop."

"This is no basic pizza shop. You launder money."

"I don't launder anything," Omar said.

"Not your clothes, certainly," Ethan said, and waved his gun at Omar's stained apron.

"I just cook pizzas, all right?" Omar said. "And do whatever other bullshit Wynne tells me to do. Anything else he does with the place has nothing to do with me."

"Who shot Simon?"

Omar shrugged.

Ethan poked him in the forehead with the gun.

"Who shot Simon?"

"I don't know who shot Simon, okay?" Omar said. Then his face seized in anger. "What are you, the fucking police? Why do you care who shot Simon?"

"This whole mess started with Simon," Ethan said, accentuating the nouns with pokes to Omar's forehead. "Me and Phil found his body behind this place one morning, next thing I know I've got this burly ape busting into my apartment and smacking me around with whatever's in reach."

"You don't want to get involved with Wynne."

"I didn't get involved with anybody. He came to my place looking for a bag of money that was supposed to be with Simon. They think I have it. They kidnapped my, uh, Sam, to try and get it back. I don't have the goddamn money, but maybe if I find out who shot Simon I can tell them who does and they'll let Sam go."

"Well I don't know who shot the guy, all right? Don't care either."

Ethan pushed the barrel of the gun into Omar's forehead a little harder, then flicked open the safety with his thumb.

"Simon was in here almost every day. I'm not buying what you're selling. Now spill anything else you know about him," Ethan said.

"He liked Hawaiian pizza with sausage instead of ham. How's that?"

"You told Wynne you saw us in that alley, didn't you?"

Omar swallowed.

"Didn't you?" Ethan said.

"Yeah, I saw your dumb stoned asses walking down the street. So I told Wynne. To get him off my goddamn back."

"What was he on your back about?"

"What do you think? The damn money!"

"Wynne mentioned the money?"

"Of course he mentioned the damn money!"

"I thought you said you didn't know what went on around here."

"I said I don't know much."

"Why was Simon coming here so late at night?" Ethan asked.

"No idea. Not my business to know what other people do with themselves."

"Where does Simon take the money?"

"Not my business to know that either."

Ethan drew the gun level with Omar's eye.

Inside the barrel, Omar found where Simon took the money.

Omar blinked twice.

"He used the safe," he said. He kicked something under the desk with his foot.

Ethan stepped away and looked down. A grey key-and-dial safe sat beneath the desk.

"Simon kept his cash in there?"

"Yeah," Omar said.

"How much?"

"I don't know. It varied."

Ethan pointed the gun at him again.

"Man, stop pointing that fucking gun at me," Omar shouted. "There's another box in there with its own key. Then he'd sit here and wait for Wynne to come pick it up."

"So that's why they dumped Simon out back. Somebody knew he kept the money in that safe, right?"

"Looks like."

"And Wynne doesn't think it was you?"

"It wasn't me."

"Doesn't matter if it was or not. Matters if Wynne thinks it was."

"He knows I'm not stupid enough to rob him, let alone show up for work the next day. Besides, I don't have a key for the box in that safe, and the box is still there as it should be."

"You could've shot Simon and taken the key."

"I could have. But I didn't."

"So what'd Wynne beat you for?" Ethan asked.

"Have to ask him," Omar said. "If I had to guess, I'd say it was just because he likes to beat people."

Ethan poked him in the head again.

"What'd Wynne beat you for?"

Omar shook his head in resignation.

"He found out the cops were here. I guess I told them something I wasn't supposed to."

"Like what?"

"I told them who owns the place."

"Wynne?"

"No, Wynne's boss, Jack Struhl."

Struhl, Ethan thought. Hugo had just mentioned the name.

"Guy I know says this Struhl character was in cahoots with Simon," Ethan said. "What do you know about that?"

"First I'd need to know what 'cahoots' means."

"They were, like, collaborating," Ethan said. "Partners."

"Why the fuck would Struhl partner up with a scumbag like Simon for?"

"Needed money for something. You know this guy?"

"Who?"

"Struhl."

"Not personally."

"He's some kind of nutbag survivalist," Ethan said. "He had Simon preparing for the collapse of society or something. They were stocking up on provisions, guns, whatever else you'd need for that." Ethan wondered what that might be. Bibles and toilet paper, possibly.

"That loser Simon was always going off about that kind of shit," Omar said. "I wouldn't pay much attention to it. Guys like Simon should be more worried about saving up to pay bail, not preparing for some apocalypse. Watch too many goddamn movies."

"What about Struhl?"

"What about him?"

"Maybe it was him that needed the money."

"You mean Simon's pickup? It was going to him anyway."

"Yeah, but from what I understand he's just a middleman, too. If Simon winds up dead, he would get the gross, not the net."

"What?"

"Struhl would get all the money."

"It was his!" Omar said again.

"The gross is before deductions, the—never mind," Ethan said.

Omar scowled.

"Man, you're thinking too goddamn much. This shit's not your problem."

Ethan rose from the desk and stepped away to the mouth of the kitchen. He looked out to the front of the shop and outside to the street, where a few more potential customers waited for the store to reopen.

Ethan turned back to Omar. Tacked to the wall above the desk was a *Girls of The Pink Curtain* wall calendar. The girl, Viva, was arced against her obligatory brass pole, wearing only a pink bikini bottom bearing The Pink Curtain's logo.

"Can you not point that thing at me anymore?" Omar said.

Ethan raised the gun.

"Oh, for fuck's sake," Omar said.

"Open that safe," Ethan said.

Omar's eyes went wide.

"You're going to rob me?" he said.

"Open it."

Omar moved slowly to the floor and spun the dial on the safe to the right, then left, then right again. He turned the handle and the safe opened.

"How much is in there?" Ethan said.

"Not much," Omar said from the floor. "Mostly money from the shop."

"How much?"

"Maybe four grand."

"Give it to me," Ethan said. "And give me Simon's box."

Omar grumbled something from beneath the desk.

"Give it!" Ethan shouted and kicked Omar in his bruised ribs.

Omar emerged from under the desk with a metal box and three short stacks of cash. He placed the cash on the desk, then shook the box to show Ethan that it was empty.

Ethan grabbed the bundles of cash. He took the box and shook it himself. It was empty.

"I said he doesn't leave no money in there," Omar said. "It's only in there until Wynne comes to pick it up."

Ethan shook the empty box again to be sure. It was empty. This was the best he could do.

"Call Wynne and tell him I'll meet him at The Pink Curtain," he said. "And tell him to bring Sam."

## 41

If Hugo survived the involuntary car ride he was presently enduring, he intended to serve notice to his employer. This nonsense wasn't worth the free rent.

He twice asked where they were going, to no reply. Wynne's hands remained firmly on the chrome and vinyl steering wheel, his eyes fixed on the road ahead. As the Charger rolled across the city, Wynne sat stoically in the driver's seat, wearing what Hugo thought was an odd little smile, considering the circumstances.

When he'd first started selling for Wynne, Hugo had grand ambitions for an illustrious career in organized crime. Cash and cars. Clothes and watches. A waterfront condo. An endless parade of women. Two years in and he was still living in the same dump, driving a one-wheel-in-the-junkyard Civic, wearing a Timex, and now, with the loss of Sam, completely womanless save for a slew of bookmarked pornography sites. Just after Wynne had demanded Hugo join him on a car ride of uncertain destination, and while brushing shards of ceramic bong from his clothes, Hugo had updated his goals: he would save as much cash as he possibly could, leave town, and become a mechanic. Hugo had always loved cars, and Wynne's gleaming '71 Charger was a prime example of his favourite type. Wynne had modernized the old Dodge more than Hugo would have, installing power steering, an automatic transmission, and modern safety features, but it was Wynne's car to do with as he pleased. Hugo would have chosen a '72, anyway. Now with circumstances escalating toward some unknown entropic oblivion, it was time to commit to the plan.

In due time, Hugo told himself, he'd open his own custom-collectible shop and build cars like this one. All I have to do, he thought, is still be alive at the end of this ride.

Finally, thankfully for Hugo, having feared a country road and a shallow grave, the Charger soon rolled into the lot behind The Pink Curtain.

A raccoon and its offspring skittered into the strip club parking lot then climbed into the green dumpster butted against the building's rear wall. At the backdoor, two girls in long coats smoked cigarettes, accompanied by a bald, seven-foot, four-hundred-pound bouncer, or bodyguard, or bipedal humpback, as far as Hugo could tell.

"Who's that guy?" Hugo asked, pointing at the pale beast.

"That is someone I did not expect to be here," Wynne said.

"Who is he?"

Hugo was deprived an answer by the ring of Wynne's cell phone.

Wynne answered. Hugo listened.

"Who is this?" Wynne said. "Omar? Slow down. Who? That's his last name? Blaze? Blasé? What kind of stupid name is that? Let me talk to him. No. When? What kind of information?"

Wynne looked at Hugo and smirked.

"Sure," Wynne said. "No problem. The girl will be here." He hung up.

"This day's getting better by the minute," he said.

## 42

Stephenson and the FBI goon were only in there an hour, thankfully. I waited ten minutes after their van disappeared into the distance, then prepared myself for another adventure.

It had been a long day and I was tired, ornery, and impatient—not the best combination of states to be making life-or-death decisions in. But I was still confident I could shoot the orc-ish bodyguard and the ratty butcher, then apprehend the proportionally challenged Jerome before any of the cretin's brains signalled to the rest of their bodies that something was wrong.

I was that good.

I still am.

I got my pistol ready, then pulled gently on the cold metal handle.

It was locked.

I rapped on the door, then moved to its other side.

Nobody came, so I banged harder.

A moment later I heard the lock turn. The door eased open. A giant foot in a black military boot stepped down from the building and onto the asphalt. I waited a second, guessing the goon would stick his big watermel-on of a head out—which he did—then kicked the door with all the force my tired frame could muster, trying to crush that big empty melon.

The goon grunted but didn't fall. I backed up a step and heaved into the door with my shoulder. Another grunt, but the goon was still standing.

I grabbed the door and flung it open. There stood Jerome's ugly monster, a torso the size of a vending machine, struggling at his waist for his gun.

I pistol-whipped the brute across his telephone book of a forehead, nearly jumping to make the reach. He only looked annoyed, like someone had bumped into him on the subway. But the second whip on the crown of his head stunned him and he stopped reaching for his gun. The third strike was accompanied by a sickly crunch, finally bringing him to the ground. For all the racket with the door and the pistol-whipping, I probably should have just shot him. So I did.

Now that he was motionless and I could get a good look at him, I recognized the beast, a walking ingrown muscle with a protruding lower lip like a Congo gorilla. He had at least ten grand in tattoos on his body, including a portrait of the Virgin Mary on his shoulder, scribbled there by either a blind man or some developmentally stunted child. I'd come across him before while working a job in Fraser: he'd been climb-ing the ladder of a delivery operation before being pushed aside for getting impolite with some rung or other on the way up. He was lucky he hadn't been killed. Until now, anyway.

Footfalls broke me from my inspection of Jerome's dead thug. Just as I looked up, the Mexican I'd watched enter the building earlier came running down the hall-way a sixteen-inch beef splitter in his hand, him and the cleaver all covered in blood.

I levelled and squeezed and caught him between the eyes. A final pink thought balloon erupted from the back of his head. He dropped like a punched-out boxer, his legs crumpling beneath him. The cleaver clattered to the ground.

I stepped over the two bodies and entered the building.

The door opened into a long, dark hallway. The smell irrefutably declared the place a slaughterhouse, and maybe not a particularly sanitary one.

A light was on overhead. Boxes and packaging supplies lined the walls. Pathetic, agonized groans came from somewhere down the hall. I walked slowly toward the sound, my pistol held out in front of me.

The corpulent figure of Jerome scuttled out of a room down the hall, fired a shot south—south being my general direction, which was as close as he got—and then turned and ran toward the depths of the slaughterhouse.

I took aim and fired, hitting him in the back of the knee. He pitched forward and spilled to the floor, the gun sliding out of his hand. I hopped over Jerome and retrieved the gun. He was cursing now and holding his knee with both hands. I stood over top of him.

"Rutherford—you're not supposed to be here yet," he screamed, and went on cursing.

I'd have to deal with that piece of information later. I gave him a sharp kick to the head, hard enough to stun him but not knock him out, then crouched and patted him down for other weapons. He was clean.

I stood up and moved deeper into the building. I flicked on the lights and checked the room Jerome was running toward, but the place was barren.

On the way back to Jerome I passed the walk-in cooler he and the little butcher had been working in. I've seen many violent horrors done to many men, deserving and otherwise, but the butcher, now lying dead in the hall, had fancied himself an artist, I could see, and no doubt took pleasure in his craft. His groaning canvas was strung to an IV, pawing hopelessly at his missing face with his missing hands. This was cartel work, intended to inflict terror on more than just one man: a tripod and camera were recording the message.

I put what was left of him out of his misery. Then it was time to deal with Jeffrey Jerome.


## 43

Ethan gave Omar a muzzle imprint in the center of his fore-head to remember him by, then stepped out into the alley behind Corleone's.

The stink of rotting food filled the alley. The boxes of porno and pulp were gone, but a few loose magazines and paperbacks still littered the ground. Ethan nervously checked both direc-tions, then walked to the mouth of the alley.

His new plan was to finger Jack Struhl as Simon's murderer in exchange for the release of Sam, but he wasn't willing to bet Sam's life on it. The only backup plan he could come up with was to gather as much of the fifty grand as he could in the next two short hours, and offer it, along with his theory about Struhl, as ransom.

Including the cash he'd taken from the safe—now stuffed into a Corleone's takeout box and tucked under his arm—he had another forty-six thousand dollars to collect.

He knew the plan to be poorly formed, but it was the best he had, and at least it was his—he was tired of being acted upon. And, he reasoned with himself, he had nothing to lose: no home, no job, no family. It was worth a shot.

Fueled by adrenaline and pointed vaguely in the direction of The Pink Curtain, Ethan left the alley with a purposeful stride, bumping into a passing pedestrian in a newsboy cap, slacks, and well-pressed shirt, and knocking the elderly man to ground. Ethan tumbled to the sidewalk, the takeout box slipping from beneath his arm and spilling cash onto the sidewalk, the gun slid-ing from his waistband and across the concrete.

He grabbed the gun and the cash and stuffed it back into the takeout box and fled. More pedestrians walked along the row of shops. A few sparse flecks of rain fell from the sky. He entered the first convenience store in his path, a narrow closet of a place clogged with snacks and drinks and other essentials, all priced with tiny red stickers.

A short, bony man in a faded blue polo was restocking cigarettes behind the counter, his back turned to the store.

"Hey," Ethan said.

The man placed a few more packets on the shelf from a torn open carton.

"Excuse me," Ethan said, louder this time.

The man turned.

"I need money," Ethan said.

The man chuckled, exposing queerly small and yellowed teeth.

"Me too," he said, shrugging and smiling.

"No, I mean give me your money," Ethan said. He opened his jacket, but not far enough for the cashier to make out the gun inside.

"No, no," the cashier said, and chuckled again.

Ethan took the gun out of his jacket and waved it at the cashier.

"The money," Ethan said. "Give it to me."

The cashier's face slackened.

## 44

A nude woman swaggered across The Pink Curtain's stage, a bright smile on her face, her fluid movements luring the scant Sunday afternoon audience to dig deeper into their pockets and hand over their bills.

Jack Struhl observed from a booth at the side of the room. A capitalist courtship ritual, he thought, examining the dancer. He'd use that line.

Nearly all of Thelonious R. Grave's characters were inspired by strippers or prostitutes (although Grave had turned to *Playboy* and *Good Sir* centerfold profiles for recent inspiration, including Verona Thunderly, the villainous female lead of the forthcoming *Bleak Reckoning*. Sales were slipping substantially, though. They'd never brought in a lot of money—no Rutherford novel had ever been optioned for the screen—but the last few books featuring Rutherford had completely tanked.)

Darla Carmine from *Cheap Thrills*, for example. Several women called Darla had worked at Winston Carmello's various establishments over the years, including the brothel in the Gould Building; the Darla who'd worked there until just recently had become one of Struhl's personal favourites.

The previous evening, while browsing fan groups devoted to Grave on the internet, Struhl had come across a few academic papers that discussed the role of women in crime and detective fiction. Grave's Rutherford series, and a few Grave standalone novels, were provided as examples. The papers were not complimentary.

Struhl dismissed the critiques as pointy-headed intellectualism, term papers written for a grade and an audience of institutionalized eggheads. Rutherford novels were entertainment, nothing more.

Struhl hadn't planned on visiting The Pink Curtain today, but he'd received calls from both Rowan and Wynne: the Simon situation was about to resolve itself unexpectedly. The deadbeat Ethan had told Omar, who in turn had told Wynne, that he had the cash and he'd be bringing it to The Pink Curtain. Struhl had no idea where this Ethan had found the money, but he wasn't about to complain. He'd take every dollar he could, regardless of source, to get his contractors off his back.

Additionally, Rowan had told Struhl that the Woodgrave girl had temporarily escaped her room and called her father. That was an imminent problem for which Struhl had no solution other than to drink his beer and hope for the best, the best at this point being a ransom paid by Woodgrave's father.

Struhl had settled into a booth at the side of the room and was trying to enjoy what might be his last visit to the club. At the edge of the stage, an old man, lonely thin strands of hair draped over a mostly bald head, lobes of fat dangling over his belt beneath his tucked-in blue T-shirt, held a beer in one hand, a bill in the other. He leered at the naked dancer onstage.

A group of four men in suits occupied a round table to the left of the stage. A few other pairs of males took up more tables, and the odd lone patron, accompanied by one of the few dancers, moved back and forth from the main room to the private booths.

Struhl sipped a Budweiser and spun his phone on the table. It had been ringing constantly: Wynne, Rowan, Wynne again, a variety of other gnarled idiot thugs pestering him for his time, and finally Winston Carmello, who had apparently returned from his East Coast trip. The voicemail from Winston had only instructed Jack to meet him at The Pink Curtain, immediately. Good thing Jack was already there.

The problem had been Simon. Getting involved with him had been a mistake, Struhl knew, but he'd thought Simon could be made useful: cutting Wynne out would save on payroll, and any more money Struhl gathered became more valuable with every passing week. Giving Simon the responsibility of handling more money and more drugs was supposed to be a short-term proposition, anyway, but it turned out to be an even shorter lived arrangement than he'd intended. The dead fool hadn't even even gotten as far as dealing with Wynne.

Struhl considered fleeing Vancouver with the hope the situation would sort itself out, but he'd never been the type to run. All of life's problems, he figured, needed to be resolved, one way or another, like loose threads of a plot. It seemed to Struhl that fate wanted it done at a strip club on a Sunday afternoon.

The waitress set another Budweiser on the table and collected the empty bottle. When—or if, at this point—Struhl moved to his new place up north, he'd stick to whiskey, he thought. He didn't intend to make the two-hour trip to Port McNeil from his cabin very often. But he'd enjoy the cold beer, here, while he could.

With the performance finished, the bank of speakers at each side of the stage briefly went silent. The dancer gathered her clothes against her chest and skittered off stage, her red high heels clicking against the shiny floor. Women circled the room and reposed themselves briefly on the laps of patrons. The fat old man at the lip of the stage laughed and draped a bloated arm around the waist of a girl perched on his knee.

Struhl turned his attention to the left of the stage. Two dancers emerged from the back, stopping at the announcer's booth to talk or joke or request songs for their upcoming sets. Behind the women a towering figure appeared, casting the small area through the door behind him into darkness. Two men emerged from behind the giant, through the gaggle of nearly naked women, and into the club.

Struhl didn't recognize the man in the lead, bald, soft around the middle, with a few days growth on his face, dressed in suit pants and a dress shirt. The second round and familiar form was that of Winston Carmello, dressed in black jeans and a black T-shirt.

Struhl reached into his jacket on the bench of the booth beside him and felt for his gun. He moved the jacket and gun onto his lap.

As Winston Carmello and the man crossed the front of the stage toward Struhl's booth, the speakers at the side of the stage crackled. The announcer, in a slick baritone that declared he'd been born for the job, broke the quiet and announced the next dancer.

The deep thump of a bass drum pulsed the air. Two young men sitting at a small table in the middle of the room cheered. As the jittery upstrokes of funk guitar joined the tune's heavy beat, a tall, thin girl, dressed scantly in white, eased out of the curtains at the back of the stage and strutted to the pole at its center. She took the pole in hand, tossed her long black hair behind her, and slid to the floor, as if struck by the three bursts of instrumental gunfire layered into the song's introduction. She lay crumpled fetal on the stage until the song's lyrics began, then pulled herself up the pole, wrapping a leg around it and arcing backward toward the small but enthusiastic audience.

Winston Carmello and his guest arrived at Struhl's table. They both bore down on Struhl with narrowed eyes.

"Where's his daughter, Jack?" Winston asked.

Struhl's face was still.

"Who is this?" Struhl asked, nodding at Carmello's companion.

"How many girls do you have stashed away that you need me to specify?"

"My daughter's name is Samantha," Eric Woodgrave said, looking at the table. "Samantha Emma."

"Never heard of her," Struhl said.

Carmello nodded. "So the guys I sent by your place aren't going to find anybody there?"

Struhl thought about it. They might find Rowan, and maybe kill him, which wasn't so terrible a thing.

"Not a soul," Struhl said.

Struhl's phone vibrated on the table in front of him. The screen showed Wynne as the caller.

"You want to answer that?" Winston asked. He turned to Eric Woodgrave. "How about you give me a minute here?"

Eric's eyes were wet and unfocussed. Carmello repeated himself:

"Go visit Clayton for a minute, Eric. This will all get sorted out here."

Eric Woodgrave looked to the back of the room. Winston's giant bodyguard, Clayton, stood by the bar closest to the stage. Eric joined him.

As Eric Woodgrave left, the server returned with another bottle of beer for Struhl. She asked Carmello what he wanted to drink. Carmello declined.

The girl teased Carmello that his back was to the stage.

"You're missing a good show," she said.

"I've seen enough shows," Carmello said, his eyes focussed on Struhl.

"Probably in the wrong place then," the girl said, and walked away.

Struhl left one hand on the gun in his lap and took a drink from the sweating bottle.

"You know who that is?" Carmello asked.

"Who?" Jack said. "The waitress? She's new, I guess."

"Not the waitress. Stop fucking around. How much did you ask him for?""

"I didn't ask him for a thing," Struhl said.

"But you've got the girl? I'm not chasing you anymore. Do you understand?"

Struhl understood. He was on his own.

Jack Struhl fingered the trigger on the gun in his lap. He looked about the room. A new patron entered the club.

"It was a mistake, Winston," Struhl said, watching the new patron cross the room. "But it's about to be rectified."

## 45

In the basement, Rowan sat the dazed Emma down in the lawn chair, then rooted through the toolbox at the back of the room in search of duct tape to rebind the girl's arms and legs.

If he'd had half a brain, Rowan thought, he would've defected to the Yoons six months ago when he'd had the chance. Struhl was an unpredictable weirdo, and Carmello allowed little upward mobility; he kept people in their place, or what he decided their place should be.

This operation had been a disaster from inception, but it was nearly done. He'd meet Struhl and the punk who claimed to have the money, collect his share, get out, and find some other crew to work with. Whatever happened with the girl and her father would happen after Rowan was gone.

The toolbox held no tape, but the bottom drawer contained a spool of speaker wire. Rowan took up the wire and returned to Emma, now lucid, a few tears running down her cheek.

"Put your arms along the armrests," Rowan ordered.

Emma did as instructed and Rowan began to wrap the wire around the white plastic armrest, tying Emma's arm in place at the wrist.

Before he could tie the knot, Rowan felt a wave of distorting pain ripple from his groin, followed by a roiling nausea.

## 46

He fell to one knee and Emma loosed her hands from the wire and took the scant moment to spring up and run for the stairs, half dragging the chair with her as the wire fell from her wrist.

She flung the door open at the top of the stairs and rushed into the living room. The basset hound lifted its head to address the new visitor. The other mutts barked in the yard.

On the coffee table was Emma's broken cell phone and its ejected battery. Next to them was the revolver. Emma ran to the table and picked up the gun. Rowan emerged from the basement. Emma raised the gun and pulled the trigger.

The bullet pierced the notch below Rowan's jugular, passed through his neck, and struck the doorframe behind him. He buckled, falling to his knees on the floor. His eyes were wide and he gasped for air through a throat full of blood. Emma pulled the trigger again. The bullet fired over his shoulder. Rowan held his throat with one hand. Dark blood sprayed through his fingers and poured down his shirt. With the other hand he dug into his pocket. Emma stepped forward and aimed the gun at his chest and pulled the trigger. He shuddered backward and fell to the floor, one hand still buried in his pocket, the other laying limp in a growing pool of blood at his side.

Emma, weak in the knees, sat on the coffee table and began to tremble, but stopped herself: there was no time for it.

She put the gun down and took up her phone and its ejected battery. She failed to put the two back together.

Emma left the broken phone and the revolver on the table and fled the house.

## 47

After getting no answer from Struhl or Rowan, Wynne got out of the car and stepped onto the wet lot. Broken glass and glossy business cards bearing seductive painted faces littered the pavement. Wynne crossed the lot to the rear door of the club, with Hugo following reluctantly.

Wynne pulled on the handle, found it locked, and knocked hard on the heavy metal door.

A moment later the door swung open to reveal the massive figure that had stood outside just moments before. The figure took up the whole frame, his bald white head like a full moon against his black coat and the black walls behind him.

With a furrowed brow the man bore down on the new visitors until he recognized Wynne, then ushered the two men into the back of the club.

"Clayton," Wynne said to the giant, "is Jack in here?"

The mammoth head nodded wordlessly.

"Winston too?"

Another nod.

Wynne walked through the back caverns of the club with Hugo in tow.

Seminude women lounged on black sofas and chairs, talking about weekend plans, bills, boyfriends, customers good and bad, new clothes and where to buy them. A woman in jeans, T-shirt, and ponytail, either done working for the day or not yet started, stood over one of the couches in the hall, holding court with two topless girls smoking cigarettes.

"He's like an animal," the one said. "And he treats us like animals. He never speaks, just always has this ugly smirk on his face, you know?"

The girls agreed.

"He won't say a goddamn thing and he won't let us talk neither. Just grunts and snorts like a fucking hog!"

The girls on the couch agreed.

"I keep telling Mitch the guy's a creepy motherfucker and to get him out of here, but Mitch doesn't care," the woman continued.

Wynne and Hugo walked past the girls and around the side of the stage. Clayton followed but stopped beside the announcer's booth, standing sentry over the club, keeping watch of Wynne and Hugo as they entered the room.

On stage, the dancer flicked her toe and cast her underwear to an excited fat man sitting at the rail.

Wynne surveyed the room. At a booth to the right of the stage sat Struhl and what looked, at least from the back, to be Winston Carmello. Struhl looked nervous, even from across the room.

Wynne grinned and approached the table.

## 48

One convenience store was just enough and one too many. Ethan was no robber and he knew it. He also knew, from his paltry haul, that he had no chance of amassing fifty grand in under two hours. The robbery had gone poorly; he could only assume robbing a bank would go much worse.

The dying Pontiac rattled along, smoke escaping from the hood in protest of Ethan's attempted spree. But the mission was in progress. An object in motion will remain in motion unless . . . something or other. Ethan couldn't remember the rest. The gist of it, he thought, gripping the wheel and heading west with a heavy foot and dissenting automobile, was that he wouldn't be stopped. He would meet Wynne and take it from there. He would save Sam.

He weaved in and out of a slow glut of Sunday drivers, passing dog walkers and aimless street people as they meandered the sidewalks on their way to nowhere.

Ethan turned onto Hope Street, then took the final corner onto First Avenue. Down a road lined with auto repair shops, car washes, sore-thumb homes surrounded by chain-link fences, and warehouses both full and empty, The Pink Curtain loomed ominously.

At a distance the brick one-story building, with its pointed roof, had the look of a family-run funeral home, a mistake encouraged by the presence of Montgomery & Sons three blocks down the road. When nearer, the lewd neon sign above The Pink Curtain's door cleared up any confusion.

Ethan pulled the Pontiac into the front lot. A steady trickle of black smoke escaped from under the hood and blew across the windshield.

He put the car in park and turned off the ignition. The engine shuddered an agonal breath.

Ethan paused. He leaned back in the seat and tucked the gun into the waist of his pants, then grabbed the takeout box of cash and stepped into the grey afternoon.

Ethan approached the front door. Made of weathered oak and arced at the top, it gave the entranceway the look of a giant wooden tombstone. A hip-hop tune thumped inside the club like a spectre intent upon release. Ethan recognized the song; it was the same Softwood Lumber track he used as his ringtone.

He pulled open the heavy door. Tremors of bass drum blustered through the handle.

A stout, unsmiling bouncer in a black polo—The Pink Curtain crest embroidered over the heart—stood behind a greeter's podium in the foyer. He was nodding his head to the beat, his bearish arms crossed over his chest, and puffy black crescents beneath each tired eye. He had the look of a man who had always assumed the world was out to get him. Ethan had read that line in *Cheap Thrills*. It fit the bouncer perfectly.

"The cover is thirteen dollars," the bouncer said, his head still nodding.

"I'm here to see Wynne," Ethan said.

"Still thirteen dollars."

"It's about business," Ethan said, urgently. He figured it would only be so long before sirens approached.

The stony-faced bouncer seemed to be in less of a hurry.

"If you're a businessman, you should have the thirteen dollars," he said.

Ethan pulled the takeout box from under his arm and opened it. He removed a twenty and handed it to the bouncer. The bouncer returned a five and two loonies. He stopped nodding and eyed the takeout box suspiciously.

"You keep your money in a chicken wing box?"

"This is the business I'm here to see Wynne about," Ethan said, tapping the box.

"You're here to see Wynne about where to buy a wallet?" the bouncer said.

Ethan said nothing. He made to move past the bouncer and enter the club.

The bouncer tapped a glass jar on his podium.

"No tip?" he said.

Ethan ignored him, opened the single black door and entered the club.

At the front of the room a woman strutted the stage in nothing but a pair of white stilettos. A few pairs of men sat at the dozen or so tables in the middle of the room, gawking and nursing their beers. On the left, a bald, middle-aged man in dress pants and a crisp white shirt, whom Ethan found passingly familiar, stood at the bar. The room smelled of stale beer and fog machine. A tacky gleaming planet hanging above the stage cast streams of blue, white, and red light across the otherwise dim club.

Ethan looked to the right of the club. Wynne and Hugo stood by one of the red-and-white booths that lined the walls. He crossed the room to the booth.

## 49

Woit pulled her unmarked Chevy Suburban into the back lot of The Pink Curtain. Of all the places she'd like to be on a Sunday afternoon, this was the last. The place oozed sleaze like a week-old garbage bag with a hole in it.

Woit parked between a silver Mercedes and a brown Ford hatchback. A black vintage Charger sat in the spot ahead of her. Woit got out of the Suburban, locked it, then circled the Charger.

When she was a kid, Woit's father had owned a fire engine–red '68 Mustang, endlessly in some state of tear down or rebuild on the lift in the garage. The car was a hobby that everyone in the house, save him, knew he had no time for. For himself, Herbert Woit gained nothing but frustration from the project. But at least the Mustang had instilled in his daughter a lifetime appreciation of American muscle cars of the '60s and early '70s.

The Charger in The Pink Curtain's lot was a '71 Rallye Hardtop, identifiable by the venting on the doors. Whoever owned the vehicle certainly loved it. It was flawless and shone even in the overcast light. If Woit ever had the money, she'd buy something similar. The '70 Chevelle SS was the prime aspiration of muscle car fanatics, and would be her first choice, but it would take a lottery win or an unexpected inheritance to bring that fantasy to life.

Woit peered through the Charger's tinted window. The interior was expertly done: soft new leather, a custom steering wheel, and a slew of personalized dashboard modifications. The owner's taste was not in tune with her own, but it was a finely detailed automobile nonetheless.

Too bad whoever owned it was ten to one a terrific waste of human life, Woit thought.

She scanned the rest of the vehicles in the lot, looking for the Jeep registered to Struhl, but saw nothing. If he was anything like a typical gangster, he drove several automobiles, most of them not registered to him.

Woit approached the rear of the building and hammered on the door. A hip-hop tune came from within. She tugged on the thin metal handle, but the door remained closed.

She abandoned the rear entrance and circled the block to the front of the building, on foot, passing the auto parts shop that occupied the corner lot of the block.

The strip club sat recessed from the street and was fronted by an ample parking lot currently holding another half-dozen cars, none of them Struhl's. A neon sign above the door marked the building as The Pink Curtain; nude silhouettes performed gymnastic feats on poles substituting for the *t*'s and *i*'s.

Below the sign, she watched the back of a man with a small box tucked under his arm enter the club.

Woit crossed the front lot and approached the main entrance. The thumping music from inside bled out of the building.

Woit couldn't stand rap music. She'd read somewhere that the steady metronome of the bass drum had a primal effect, established early in human evolutionary history; the drum imitated a heartbeat, the article had said. Or forewarned like the roll of a coming storm. Sounded like academic bullshit to Woit. Perhaps she hated the music because she associated it with the lechery of nightclubs and strip joints. She'd spent far too many hours in such places as a young constable and was now happy to avoid them as much as her new position would allow, which turned out to be nowhere near often enough.

Woit put her hand on the front door's long brass handle, expecting a stickiness that wasn't there, then opened the door and entered the foyer of the club.

The bouncer greeted her with a head-to-toe scan, a slight smirk, and a pronouncement that ladies didn't pay cover. Woit showed him her badge and the rock pile's mouth turned to a hard, straight line.

Woit chatted with the bouncer briefly, asking him how the day's business was and if he knew the people she was looking for, mostly for the sake of making him feel uncomfortable. The bouncer offered only monosyllables in reply.

Woit ended the conversation and entered the club.

## 50

Wynne stood at a booth at the side of the room, Hugo fidgeting nervously beside him. Winston Carmello and Jack Struhl sat in the booth, listening.

The room was bathed in a frantic light reflected from the disco ball hanging in the center of the room, beams of blue, white, and red washing over men enjoying the afternoon show.

A red-faced fat man sitting at the stage tilted his head back and laughed, waving a bill in the air. A nude dancer on the platform slunk toward him, bent at the waist, and plucked the bill from his pudgy little hand. Before tossing the bill toward the rest of her tips, gathered near the pole like raked leaves, she gave it a quick glance. An American single. Cheap bastard.

Softwood Lumber's The Bidness grunted in agreement from the speakers at the sides of the stage, a heavy beat trudging along behind him.

Wynne had just explained to Winston Carmello that a man was on his way with Simon's missing cash.

"I didn't know I was missing any," Carmello said.

Struhl peeled the label from his beer bottle.

Carmello's bodyguard, Clayton, stood watch by the stage.

Hugo stood by awkwardly, wishing he were somewhere else.

"Who is this?" Carmello said, pointing at Hugo.

Hugo said nothing, avoiding eye contact.

"This is Hugo," Wynne said. "He says Jack and Simon were in cahoots. Didn't you, Hugo?"

"Where's cahoots?" Hugo said.

"It's not a place, idiot. It means they were pulling something together," Carmello said. His eyes wrinkled in focus. He looked from Hugo to Struhl and back again. "Is that the case, Hugo?"

Hugo's eyes darted between the two men at the table. He felt Wynne's giant paw come to rest on the back of his neck.

Hugo nodded reluctantly.

"Simon told me he was hanging out with Jack. That Jack was teaching him things. And that he needed more money for something."

"And who the hell is Simon?" Carmello demanded.

"Simon is just a dead loser, Mr. Carmello," Wynne said, "but—"

"And who is this hobo?" Carmello said, pointing at a newly arrived visitor.

Ethan stood holding the takeout box of cash in both hands.

"I'm Ethan. I have money. And I think I know who killed Simon."

"What's he here for?" Carmello said. His brow furrowed in confused belligerence.

"He's here for the girl," Wynne said.

"I'm here to get Sam back," Ethan said. "Samantha Holley."

"Who's Samantha Holley?" Carmello said.

Struhl's face soured. He moved a hand beneath the table.

"First," Ethan said, "I didn't shoot Simon."

"Nobody said you did," Carmello said. "And who is this Simon everyone keeps talking about?" Carmello said.

"He was one of our street guys, Mr. Carmello," Wynne said. "He went missing last week. He had about 50K of our money on him."

"Fifty grand? Of my money?" Carmello said.

"Fifty-K gross, Mr. Carmello," Wynne said.

"Still," Carmello said. He turned to Struhl. "Are you behind again, Jack? Where's my thirty percent?"

Struhl grimaced. He tickled the trigger of the gun in his lap.

"I know who shot Simon and where the money went," Ethan said. "But you have to let Sam go."

"Sure," Carmello said, apathetically. "She's yours. What of it, then?"

"It was a guy named Struhl," Ethan said. "Jack Struhl. He shot Simon and took the money. And he took Sam."

They all faced Struhl.

Carmello leaned back in his seat.

"This is a whole lot to handle all at once here, Jack," Carmello said. "What have you got to say for yourself?"

"I made my mistake," Struhl mumbled.

"What's that?" Carmello said.

Then Struhl shot him in the gut.

## 51

Winston Carmello writhed back into his seat, clutching his stomach and cursing.

Struhl turned the gun, still held beneath the table, and fired two more shots. The first bullet struck the brass handrail of the bar across the room. The second hit Wynne in the leg.

Wynne yelped like an unseen dog underfoot and fell to the floor.

Woit pulled her gun, crouched for cover, and watched the scene unfold.

Ethan backed away from the table. He ducked into the neighbouring booth and crouched behind the long seatback. He slid his gun out of his pants and held it ready.

Carmello's bodyguard, Clayton, pulled his gun from his jacket. He levelled and fired into the booth, hitting Struhl in the shoulder. Another shot went clean through the cushion and into the booth where Ethan crouched, ripping a hole through his jacket.

Wynne fired into the booth from where he sat on the floor, but Struhl had slid beneath the table. The shot hit the empty red seat. A puff of foam stuffing leapt from the cushion. As Wynne scrambled backward on the floor he fired again, striking the wall above the booth.

Hugo froze where he was, hunched in fear, and put his hands over his head.

Struhl fired shots from beneath the table, hitting Hugo high in the leg, splintering shards of wood from the bar, and clipping a cowering waitress in the shin.

Winston Carmello, gut shot, kicked at Struhl beneath the table and spit blood across the glass tabletop.

Eric Woodgrave fell to the ground, crammed himself up against the bar and its brass foot rail, and covered his head with his hands. A bullet struck the bar above him. Splinters of wood fell across his back. He curled in on himself further, wishing for a better place to hide.

Hugo stumbled backward, clutching at his shot leg. His jeans grew darker with blood. It seeped through the denim and coated his hands in a warm, red slick. He tripped over a chair behind him and fell to the ground.

Ethan, thinking he was being fired upon, raised the gun over the back of the seat and fired three times, blindly. The first bullet rang off the brass pole in the center of the stage, now abandoned by the dancer. The second bullet broke the glass of the DJ booth, sending shards across the back of the man now crouched and hiding on the booth's floor. The third bullet struck Winston Carmello's bodyguard in the temple.

Clayton collapsed, an obsolete building demolished into free fall. The great whale's nearly four hundred pounds landed squarely on the profusely bleeding Hugo, who had no hope of moving him.

Struhl pushed to the back of the booth to avoid the gunfire and Carmello's flailing kicks. He raised the gun and fired, hitting Carmello in the ribs. Carmello stopped kicking. He slouched back into the booth, clutching his gut with one hand and his side with the other. Struhl pulled him under the table by the leg; Carmello slid to the floor and lay there, holding his wounds.

Wynne scrambled away from the table, pushing himself with his hands and one good leg. He raised his gun and shot into the booth and under the table where Winston Carmello now lay semi-fetal, a human blockade.

Shots hit Carmello along his bent back. He went limp.

A single bullet hit Struhl in the arm. Struhl dropped his gun and hid behind the body in front of him. Blood soaked into his clothes. Beer from a burst bottle dripped over the edge of the table.

Wynne slid further back along the floor and out of line with the booth.

There was no more gunfire.

## 52

Woit registered the first gunshot as part of the song shaking out of the speakers at either side of the stage. She knew the following shots were real when a steroid-enlarged gorilla of a man, clutching his leg, stumbled backward from a booth and fell to the ground.

Woit pulled her gun and readied it. She knelt behind the short counter of the coat check by the door and, over the course of the next nine seconds, followed the action with the sight of her gun—from the booth with the clutch of armed men in and around it, to the bald white behemoth crossing the room, then back across the room again. Club patrons ducked beneath tables.

The girls working the room dropped and screamed or fled to the back of the club. Gunshots popped like fireworks. A man stumbled away from the booth. A waitress dropped her tray, fell to the floor, held her shin and screamed. Three panicked men in suits ran out the front doors. The dancer on stage vanished behind the curtain at its rear. The bald behemoth's head snapped to the side; with nothing left to keep him standing, he collapsed, a victim of gravity.

The shooting stopped.

The song ended.

Woit surveyed the room.

The shot gorilla slid himself away from the locus of violence, his wounded leg painting a crimson brushstroke across the black floor. He stopped and leaned against the next booth over.

Nobody else moved.

Woit slipped her cell phone out of her pants, called in the events, then thumbed off the phone and slid it back into her pocket.

She announced herself and her authority to the room, quiet save for the sobbing of a frightened dancer and the moaning and baying of the shot waitress.

"I will fire if you move. I repeat, I will fire if anyone moves."

No one moved.

"Slide your weapons to the center of the room," she said. "One at a time. You over there: yours first."

The gorilla, leaning against a booth, cursed loudly. His eyes met Woit's, then her gun pointed squarely at him. He gave up his weapon.

"I'm shot," someone said.

The voice hung disembodied in the dim silence. Streams of light cascaded over the room.

"Who's that?" Woit said.

"Ethan," the voice said from the floor of a booth. He waved a hand up above the table. "Ethan Blaise."

Woit instructed him to slide his gun into the center of the room. He did.

"I'm shot too," Wynne said, leaning against another booth. "In the leg." He held his hands in the air. "I don't have any more weapons."

The behemoth lay face down on the floor with his belly smothering another man's face. Neither man moved. The two lay in a plot of blood.

"Who still has weapons?" Woit shouted. "More police are on the way. If you're holding weapons, this will not end well for you. If you're hurt, at least you're not dead. Or not yet. You have a choice."

"No guns," Wynne said. "No more guns."

"In the center booth there—weapons?" Woit said. Limp legs stuck out from beneath the table. Nothing.

"Jack," Wynne said, "give up your goddamn gun."

"I can't," Struhl said. "It's under Winston. I'm shot in the arm and I can't roll him off it."

"Winston who?" Woit said.

Nobody said anything.

"Winston who?" Woit said again.

"Carmello," Wynne said. "Winston Carmello."

"Carmello," Woit shouted, "give up your weapon."

"He's dead," Struhl said.

"What?" Woit said.

"Dead. He's dead, I guess," Struhl said, louder this time.

"Nothing here," Ethan said from beneath the neighbouring table. "Can I come out?"

"No," Woit said. "Stay put."

Ethan obeyed. He shifted to a more comfortable position on the floor of the booth.

"Why are you moving?" Woit said.

"I told you, I'm shot," Ethan said.

"Well, stay still," Woit said. "I don't believe any of you, but you stay there and shut up and we'll all get out of here without anybody else getting shot."

Woit then shouted across the room to the rest of the patrons and staff, telling them to abandon their weapons, if they had any, and then to stay put. No one else had weapons, or admitted as much.

"Over there by the bar? Weapons?" Woit said.

"No," said the bartender, crouched behind his bar.

"No," said a man crouched in front of the bar. "They've got my daughter. They've kidnapped my daughter."

"Who did?" Woit said.

"I don't know," he said. "The skinny one in the booth over there with Winston. They took my daughter. Samantha Emma Woodgrave. I'm Eric Woodgrave. I'm here to get my daughter."

"I'm here to get a girl, too," Ethan said. "Also Samantha. Samantha Holley."

"It's the same Samantha, moron," Wynne yelled.

"Mine's Samantha Holley," Ethan said.

"This box only has four grand in it," Struhl said from beneath the table.

"Everybody shut up," Woit yelled. "Where's this girl and which one is it?"

No one replied.

Outside, the urgent whirling cycle of police sirens approached.

Woit's phone had been vibrating steadily in her pocket. She answered and described the scene to a staff sergeant on the other end.

Moments later, with frenetic wails now surrounding the club, the police entered.

## 53

The injured were all taken to hospital in a small fleet of screaming ambulances, fleeing the scene like insects from a disturbed nest.

Before the lead car left the lot, Wynne Duncan, with Woit and another officer at his side, revealed where Emma Woodgrave was being kept, and who had brought her there. He offered one Rowan Durgham up for sacrifice.

Woit considered Duncan's testimony. She'd heard many men, and in far less incriminating circumstances, spit all variety of feeble nonsense in an attempt to free themselves. But during her brief encounter with Duncan on the floor of The Pink Curtain, as paramedics attended to his shattered leg, Woit thought she had glimpsed a buried seed of goodness in the thug, a moment of honest regret and genuine concern for the Woodgrave girl. Woit believed Duncan had truly wanted no part of the abduction.

Woit also knew, however, that regret was of little practical value, other than perhaps in lessons learned. And she'd long ago decided criminals were either innately incapable of such education or purposefully chose not to receive it.

Duncan's regret and concern notwithstanding, a heavily armed squad of police rushed to Struhl's bungalow, where they found Rowan Durgham dead in a wide spill of blood.

The girl was nowhere to be found.

It took about an hour for Woit to discover that Samantha Emma Woodgrave had been taken to Vancouver General Hospital, having been found screaming in the street by a neighbour.

When Eric Woodgrave, sitting in a squad car outside The Pink Curtain, received the news that his daughter was safe, he cried with joy.

In the hospital, after Woit interviewed Ethan, who insisted that a second Samantha actually did exist, Woit triggered a precautionary hunt. The search for Samantha No. 2, Samantha Holley, was a short one.

When two constables knocked on the front door of the Holley home, her father, who panicked at the thought of a missing child, made a flurry of calls. Sam, though not answering her cell, was soon located at the family's summer home on Barnette Island, exactly where she was supposed to be. A relieved neighbour found her napping in the living room, a book about Galapagos wildlife open in her lap, two friends preparing dinner in the kitchen.

Inside the club, police and paramedics dragged Jack Struhl out of a spill of blood, a contaminated bird from an oil-ruined beach. The first bullet had fractured the head of the humerus of Struhl's right arm. On his ride toward multiple surgeries, Struhl offered nothing, save for a grunted request for a lawyer.

Winston Carmello's giant bodyguard, Clayton Cete, in possession of a long and violent record, was dead. On his way out of this world, Cete had enacted one more piece of violence, smothering a young man named Hugo Gorvin to death, expediting what might have been a fatal gunshot wound to his upper thigh. Though it would take time to uncover the extent of Gorvin's involvement, or the portion of it that would be of use in whatever trial or trials that were to come of this mess, an initial check found no criminal record for him; Woit, without having time to give it much thought, figured Gorvin for an intern to the criminal life, his apprenticeship cut short.

If there was a windfall for Woit in the whole disaster, it was that Winston Carmello lay dead beneath a table in his own club. Carmello's death would have an impact on criminal activity in the city. How large it would be, and how long the vacuum it created would exist, was uncertain. Woit guessed not very, in both regards. Accounting for all the violence that accompanied Carmello's demise, Woit could hardly feel it was worth it.

By the time the injured were removed to hospital and the dead to the morgue, and The Pink Curtain was secured as a crime scene, the media herded to an appropriate distance, victims services informed and consulted, forensic analysis teams ushered onsite, witnesses interviewed, debriefings held, and endless reports written, Woit discovered it to be dawn on Monday morning, that she was still at her desk, and that she had not yet slept.

A new beam of sunlight fell on her arm as she typed and wrote, a gleam of warmth returning to the city like a visiting friend.

Finally, just after eight AM, she closed her files, shut down her computer, and left the office. With jumbo takeout coffee in hand, she returned to her small thirteenth-floor condo outside Vancouver proper and looking south over the suburbs toward the American border.

Thinking her still-busy mind would keep her from sleeping, she showered, then sat at her desk and reviewed the last chapter of her novel, conceived so long ago it felt as if it were written by another hand. Maybe now she would have time to finish it; and if she could ever find the time, she now had plenty of material to start a new one.

She wrote one sentence, then went to bed.

# 54

I dragged Jerome into a room off the back hall of The Smiling Bovine. Not the one with the desecrated corpse, but another one, used for butchering less dangerous animals.

Before sending him to his maker—if he had one: the man seemed more congealed of the earth's worst slime than constructed by any divine being—I extracted the rest of the plot from Jerome, with the help of a few nearby implements.

The 23rd. Darla had a specific date in mind for me to visit The Smiling Bovine, and it was for anything but my benefit. She'd first wanted me to focus my attention on Gainsborough, but once I had Jerome in my sights, she could resolve the loose end I had created for the Rossetti's instead: the loose end being me. She'd revised her plan and sent me on a goose chase that was supposed to finish with my own bird getting cooked.

Jerome was using the angry hillbilly supremacists as a dimwitted security force, kidnapping unit, and expendable assassin squad. In exchange he funded their hair-brained political campaigns and general hate-fuelled belligerence. The really creepy part was the FBI and Stephenson. Jerome wouldn't spit out what that was about. It was bigger than him, bigger than me, he said, and whatever I was about to do to him would pale in comparison to what they'd do to Jerome's family if he talked.

Whatever was going on between the Feds, Stephenson, Jerome, and Darla was beyond my pay grade, but I was definitely going to make knowing about it worth my while. I didn't like dealing with the bikers—hell, I don't like dealing with anybody—but Gainsborough would certainly be interested in what Darla had originally hired me to do. Darla would be giving me a significant pay increase, one that covered me knowing about her having her husband murdered to benefit herself, Jerome and, it seemed, perhaps two governments. I would have a very, very good retirement.

When my interview was finished, I drew my pistol and got on with the show, Jerome bleeding and pleading on the ground before me.

"Rutherford, you bastard!" he screamed. "This doesn't have anything to do with you! Forget you saw me or heard any of this and disappear! You'll be next, you know! This is bigger than you! I'll pay you double, you fuck! Triple, you worthless cunt! I'll have you—"

That was enough.

Goodbye, Jeffrey Jerome.

He died as if waking from a nightmare, yelping a short, sharp, guillotined scream, one hand clutching at the plastic butcher's wrap beneath him like a child at sweat-sodden bedsheets, the other hand held in front of his face, palm out in protest.

Darla would pay, and I would finally be done with this life.

You have to believe me, I don't enjoy it.

## Acknowledgements

Thank you to my parents, wife, and very loving family and friends for the tremendous support leading up to the publication of this book.